Advance Praise for *Devil's Bridge*

"Compulsively readable...Lilly has a knack for making you fall in love with his characters and turning the pages to find out what happens to them next."
~Rick R. Reed, author of *IM* and *In the Blood*

Praise for Greg's *Fingering the Family Jewels*

"Lilly leads the reader right smack into the thick of the plot and doesn't let up until the last page."
~Betty Conley, The Independent Gay Writer

"Lilly tells this story with grace and sensitivity. From start to finish, this reader was thoroughly engrossed—engrossed to the exclusion of all else, as this story moved inexorably to its conclusion."
~Rochelle Brener, Kudos Entertainment Weekly

"Author Greg Lilly hits a home-run with this intelligent, sensitive and highly engrossing masterpiece. Much recommended, definitely a full 5 stars out of 5!"
~Bob Lind, OURBOOKSHELF@Yahoo.com

Devil's Bridge

Greg Lilly

Regal Crest

Nederland, Texas

ISBN 978-1-932300-78-9

1-932300-78-3

First Printing 2007

9 8 7 6 5 4 3 2 1

Cover design by Donna Pawlowski

Published by:

Regal Crest Enterprises, LLC
4700 Highway 365, Suite A
PMB 210
Port Arthur, Texas 77642

Find us on the World Wide Web at
http://www.regalcrest.biz

Printed in the United States of America

Acknowledgments

Thanks to my fellow writers Viki Capaiuolo, Michelle Groce, Robert Herrin, Sharda Kumari Bose, and Diana Renfro for the feedback, laughs, support, and creativity. Some say never to critique while drinking, but that just made the advice easier to exchange. All of you taught me so much.

My family didn't think I was crazy when I decided to leave the corporate world, move west, and concentrate on writing—thanks Brad, Billie Jean, Jay, Kathy, Whitney, Justin, Courtney, and Forrest; and to the 'in-laws' Charlotte and Hank.

My first readers Angie McCoy, Tina Warholic, and Kayleen Fitzgerald-Rice encouraged me from the beginning and always believed I'd make the bookstore shelf.

Thank you to Regal Crest Enterprises's Cathy LeNoir, Lori L. Lake, and my editor, Jane Vollbrecht, for the direction and support.

Finally, thanks to Sedona, Arizona. The place is magical.

To Brad for helping me realize and live my dreams

Chapter One

MYRA'S HEAD ACHED as she pulled herself up onto the couch. Something warm like melted butter flowed into her right eye, but the stream stung, and her lid fluttered. With a tentative touch, she brushed her eyelid with her hand. Blood covered her fingers. Neither panic nor fear steered Myra's thoughts, only logic: *Damn, I should try to get my contact out.* She held the wall for support and staggered to the bathroom. The harsh, white light from the florescent bulb over the sink made her cringe and brought more pain to the bloody eye. She washed it with water and managed to remove the contact. The bleeding had almost stopped. It was just a slight cut from Gil's Timex. That was his way of being considerate—back-handing her with his left hand. He had never punched her with the full strength of his right arm, just a get-in-line slap with his left.

Her eye cooled with the little irritating piece of plastic finally out of it. She had gotten contact lenses back in college on the advice of Jennie, her sophomore-year roommate. Jennie had been a homely girl, but very popular with the boys. She helped Myra get more involved in social settings, and the first lesson was to lose the thick glasses that Myra had hidden behind since she was four years old. Now, she took the other contact out and opened the medicine chest to get her glasses. They magnified the redness in her eye as she stared into the mirror.

"Gil, why do you get so upset?" she asked her absent husband. "I try to make you happy, but maybe you deserve better." *You said it wouldn't happen again. You said you loved me, and I bring it on myself. How?* Tears rolled down her cheeks before she swiped them away with her sleeve.

The high-pitched ring of the telephone startled her, and for a moment, she wasn't sure what the harsh sound was. She found her way to the bedroom phone on the fourth ring, but the answering machine had already picked up.

"This is Gil Greer," Gil's voice boomed in the tiny room, "leave a message, and I'll call you back." Then, the nasty, shrill beep ricocheted from the machine and made Myra cover her ears.

"Hey, Myra—you too, Gil." She recognized the warm voice of Topher. "Myra, when you get in, call me. I want to come over and take you to the flea market. I'm looking for a present for Alex, and I need your help. Call me. Bye."

Myra hit the Erase button and sat on the bed, fighting the urge to call Topher back. He couldn't see her with the cut because he'd ask too many questions, come to the wrong conclusions, offer too much advice, and try to save her from herself. He'd confront Gil, maybe even accuse him of something horrible, and then everything would be worse. But despite all the reasons not to see Topher, she wanted to talk to him. She needed to talk to someone, and if, she reasoned, she phoned and told him not to come, he wouldn't see her eye, and they could still talk. He was her confidant, someone to talk to besides Gil, someone to talk with about Gil—and about her.

Her hand gripped the receiver of the phone.

She dialed Topher's number and waited. The machine answered, and she slammed the receiver back down. "Where did he go so quickly?" she asked the phone underneath her tapping fingers.

The morning sun streamed through the bedroom window, highlighting swirling dust in its beam, and cobwebs draped the corner behind the door like forgotten party streamers. The small apartment seemed to attract dirt and dust no matter how often she cleaned. On her mental ledger of what a good wife should embody, housekeeping was another of her deficits.

She picked up Gil's clothes and piled them into whites and colors for the wash. September in Charlotte, North Carolina, was a beautiful time of year when the dogwoods grabbed an early start on autumn color, bursting into bright crimson. The fragrant air drifted in the open bedroom window and reminded her of the crisp smell of a high school football field groomed for the first game of the season. Memories of the young boys on the field trying to be heroes in front of the giggling cheerleaders brought relief to her jittery, aching mind. She folded a pair of Gil's boxers and stared out the bedroom window to the apartment's parking lot. Her neighbor, Laurie, was leaving for work. Surely, Myra thought, she'd been a cheerleader in high school. She had on a white lab coat like a doctor, but in reality, was a cosmetics salesperson for Belk at Southpark Mall. Laurie had always told her that the right skin care regimen would do wonders for her looks. Myra didn't care much for the implication that her skin needed regimental attention, or that her looks needed that much of a boost. Although she knew deep down she wasn't the most beautiful woman, she was honest and tried to do good, and Topher said she was his best friend. She adored Topher, and if he liked her that much, she couldn't be too bad. After all, looks and good skin fade with age, but being a good person lasts a lifetime. She noticed Laurie's lab coat caught in the door of her midnight-blue Honda CR-V and watched the white material drag beneath the car until Laurie had driven out of sight.

Myra continued picking up shirts, jeans, and boxers, and piled them into neat mounds on the bed. She stopped and plopped down on the bedspread among piles of laundry as if a ton of clothes had just been dumped onto her shoulders. A swell of sadness hit her like her life had ended and no one mourned for the woman called Myra, long lost, maybe forgotten, then discovered dead. She started to cry. The grief welled up from a deep place in her that had been buried and ignored. She couldn't get her breath. Her stomach pushed the sobs and waves of tears up so hard it hurt. Sliding off the bed, she sat on the matted beige carpet and bawled.

THE DOORBELL RANG and Myra wiped her eyes and looked in the mirror. Her face was splotchy and her eyes red. The cut from Gil's slap still showed, so she pushed her glasses up and pulled her hair down to try to cover it. She looked through the peephole and saw Topher. She hesitated with her hand on the knob. Then he rang the bell again and knocked, so she inhaled, steadied a smile, and opened the door.

"I tried to call you back, but I got your machine," she said.

He kissed her on the cheek and walked to the kitchen for a glass of water—his usual routine.

"I hate the University area. It's so overgrown with shopping centers and bland, suburban restaurants. Traffic gets worse every time I come up here. Damn, it's almost as bad as when you lived down in Pineville. Why do you always end up in this urban sprawl?"

She just watched him move. They had known each other since high school and were comfortable in each other's presence. She knew Topher had something on his mind besides her and Gil's choice of neighborhoods by the way he'd breezed in and started talking nonstop. He had aged well, probably better than she had. At 36, they had now spent more than half their lives together, and she still couldn't take her eyes off his ass as he walked. It always pissed her off that his ass was smaller and so much firmer than hers. In a way, she realized, she was a little jealous of his looks. Yeah, he worked out and she didn't, but as long as she'd known him, Topher had always been tall and well-built. His looks had been what had drawn her to him in the first place. His hair, receding a little now, was black, thick, and full of body. His eyes were ice blue and quick, but still a little shy. She noticed when he was around new people, he had a habit of looking down every few seconds, as if he had a hard time holding their stare, or as if he didn't want them to comment on his eyes, as so many people did. Topher had large hands and feet, and Myra knew what that meant. In fact, she knew he was well endowed, not that she had ever had the pleasure, but she had talked to some girls from high school who had. Even though they had been platonic friends all these years, she still enjoyed looking at him and reveled in the envy of other women's glances when they were together.

"What are you thinking about?" Topher had his glass of water and stood in front of her, smiling.

Myra shook her head as if to clear the Etch-a-Sketch picture of her and Topher attending Laurie's Christmas party together. When she did, her tossed hair revealed the cut above her eye.

"What the hell happened to your eye?" He walked over, removed her glasses, and touched her forehead gently.

"I just ran into the door frame when I got up." She created the excuse as it came out of her mouth. "I didn't have my contacts in and my glasses were on the night stand, so I didn't see it." She held still in Topher's grip as he examined the cut.

"What *really* happened?" he asked turning her eyes to his.

"It's nothing... Really..." Myra couldn't turn her head because he still held firm, so she looked at the floor. "Just a little cut."

" 'Just a little cut,' my ass," he fumed, and let go of her. "Did that son-of-a-bitch do this to you? I'll beat the shit out of him. Where is he?"

"Calm down. It was my fault. I forgot to get eggs at the grocery store, so I didn't have any to make his breakfast this morning." She crossed the room and sat down on the couch. "That's all it was—a little slap, and his watch accidentally cut me."

He walked over to her and sat on the coffee table. He took both her hands and rubbed them with his. "Myra, look at me. This can't go on. If he loved you, he wouldn't do this. You're not safe here. Pack up your things and come to my house—if not for good, then for a couple of nights until you can sort things out."

"He loves me. I know he does." She thought of Gil, calm and enjoying life when they had traveled to Surfside Beach the past July. He fished off the pier while she sat in the sun. She remembered the salty breeze, the warm rough planks of the pier—where Gil carved their names as they waited for a fish to strike. The memory brought back a familiar comfort she had with her husband. "He does love me."

"Then why?" he pleaded. "Why does he treat you like this? Why do you take it?"

"You just don't understand. We love each other."

"That's a pile of shit, and you know it." He got up and walked across the room to the sliding glass door to the deck. He rested his head on the doorframe. "What do I have to do to save you?" he said in a weary voice.

"I'm fine. Really. Just let me have some time alone, and when Gil comes back he'll apologize, and things will be back to normal. I'll call you if I need you, but things are fine."

Topher turned to look at her, and she could see his blue eyes welling up with tears. His emotion filled the room. Myra glanced away to try to control herself, but she started crying again. He walked over to her and they held each other for a few minutes. She let go and pushed him away.

"Go on now. I'm okay."

He walked to the door, stopped, and said, "If he hits you again, I'll kill him."

Myra smiled and half laughed, "Thanks, Bubba."

She closed the door behind him, and then cried again.

TOPHER WALKED ACROSS the empty parking lot from Myra's apartment to his Chevy Trailblazer. He got in and sat in the warmth from the harvest sun, staring into space and thinking about what to do next. She had always been low on self-esteem.

Topher pictured a fifteen-year-old Myra ambling down the hall at John S. Battle High School. She'd had a bit of a weight problem then, and her thick glasses didn't help matters. They had first met in the beginning of their sophomore year when the autumn mountains reflected burnt orange, gold, auburn, jade, black, and maroon on the school windows. That had inspired Topher to do an abstract painting in art class full of the pain and loneliness he felt since his father had left, and he and his mother had moved back to Bristol. Walking down the empty hall in the middle of third period, Topher carried his covered canvas to class.

"Chris," Myra's voice squeaked.

Topher stopped and turned to see pudgy Myra. Her stringy brown hair clung to her round face, and its only hint of body came from where her horn-rimmed glasses held it out of her eyes like little "wings" on either side of her head. It reminded him of blinders on the horses in Central Park.

"I go by Topher, not Chris." He looked at her lime green painter's pants and yellow sweater. Green and gold were the school colors, and there was a pep rally for the football team that day. *Damn, she can't even get the school colors right.* "What do you want?"

She hesitated a little and then smiled shyly and said, "I just wondered what you painted today."

Topher didn't know what to say. No stranger had ever taken an interest in his paintings—even his family and friends hardly noticed them. Stunned by the question, he just stared back at her.

"Have you been painting long? Gina Rankin..." She rambled. "Do you know Gina? You see, Gina paints some, and I really like what she does. She paints mostly landscapes and a few portraits. She did one of Mr. Bledsoe, the French teacher, and it really kinda looked like him—if you squint—but she was afraid to show it to him because he might be offended or something."

Topher couldn't help but grin at her uneasiness. "Gina's an idiot," he said and rested the canvas on the toe of his left oxford shoe.

"Well, sometimes." She laughed. "So, what did you paint?"

He hoisted the canvas up on his knee, pulled back the cover, and watched as her brown eyes scanned the painting. Within the dark, swirling colors of the autumn, Topher had painted a faint outline of two people embracing, not in a loving manner, but in an effort to support each other.

Myra stepped back and straightened her glasses. Her face lost what little color it had.

"It's called 'Dependency.' I painted it for my mom." He waited for her response.

"She'll treasure it, for sure." She started to laugh a little, even though he could tell she tried not to. Topher smiled, trying to repress a laugh too.

BUT HUMOR WASN'T what his mother expressed when she saw 'Dependency.'

"Why are you always trying to imply something with these paintings?" Maggie Langston stood in Topher's grandmother's kitchen eating cold fried chicken and mashed potatoes over the sink. Topher watched his mother's face as she surveyed his painting. "Why don't you paint a picture of your grandmother or a bowl of fruit?"

"You just don't understand. I want to show emotion, hurt, pain—something people can relate to."

His grandmother, who had been sitting at the table smoking a cigarette, offered, "Hell, do like your mama said and paint my picture. I can show you pain. I just think about the time your mama ran off with that good-for-nothing father of yours. He took her to New York, and then runs off with an I-talian gal half his age. Now, that's pain."

"Exactly." Topher moved the painting to face her. "Can't you see that pain in this? I'm trying to convey that same story with these images."

"Christopher," his grandmother shook her head, "try to learn a trade."

Maggie sat down next to Grandma, lit a cigarette, and didn't comment. Topher realized mother and daughter were becoming one. Lost was the encouragement Maggie had given him in New York. *Could your spouse's desertion make you so empty*? Why had their lives fallen apart just because a man, who was never at home in the first place, left them for good? Why had that crumpled his mother?

Topher went to his room and lit a joint in the dark.

"I COULD USE a joint now." Topher started his Trailblazer and drove out of Myra's parking lot. The vehicle bounced a little as he pulled onto the main road. Soon, he inched down Highway 49 toward downtown Charlotte. He decided to forget the flea market and instead go see Alex because he wanted to talk with someone about Myra—someone who would understand him, someone who could offer compassion, someone he trusted and loved.

Alex lived in Fourth Ward in downtown Charlotte in a small, three-story townhouse. One thing Topher noticed was space: space between people talking, cars in traffic, furniture in rooms, graphics in an ad. The Fourth Ward spaces were very vertical and tight. Alex's townhouse had maybe two rooms on each floor, which meant a lot of space wasted on stairs. The bottom floor was a bedroom and bath, the middle floor was the main entrance, with dining room, kitchen, and small den, and the top floor had another bedroom and bath. This space reminded him of a castle tower where fair maidens were imprisoned for being too beautiful or too loved. But this castle tower had a view. The front looked out to the city skyline, and the back looked over Fourth Ward Park. Topher had to admit, he liked to lie in Alex's bed and see the lights of the Bank of America building looming over him. It gave him a feeling of New York in his childhood.

The city lights were good for a short stay, but he would always crave getting back to his own house, a house he had bought on the west side of town, in the woods where he could paint and sit on his deck to listen to the wind and the geese flying south. No traffic, no sirens, no noise from neighbors on the other side of a shared wall—just a place of silence, calm, and contentment.

Topher pulled in next to Alex's BMW and bounded up the steps to the door. He hated to drop in without calling.

"Hey, come in." Alex greeted him and held the door open. "I thought you were going to Myra's."

Topher smiled at what a handsome man Alex was. He stood in front of him in a Hugo Boss shirt and Brooks Brother's khakis with Kenneth Cole loafers—no socks. If there was ever a man who could wear a name brand, it was Alex. His hair was a perfect light brown wave to his right, and his wire-rimmed glasses made him look like a prep school boy. He had the same build as Topher, which worked out well because if they moved in together, they would each double their wardrobe options. But their styles were so different that neither ever attempted to borrow any clothes from the other.

"Myra wasn't having a good day."

"What happened? Did her girdle break?" Alex laughed.

"Not funny." He knew Alex was a little jealous of the time he spent with Myra. "Gil slapped her and left a cut over her eye."

"Oh, I'm sorry. Is she okay?"

"Yeah, but I just want to kick that redneck's ass all the way back to Darlington."

"It is Saturday and time for the breeders to get frisky." Alex's joke was lost on Topher as they went back to the den and sat down.

"It just pisses me off that she stands for abuse like that. Of course, she doesn't see it as abuse, just a little argument, like all couples have. If you ever hit me, this relationship would be over, and I know you feel the same way."

"Don't worry. Let them calm down and work this out. As long as Myra knows you're on her side and support her, she'll be okay." He reached over and rubbed the back of Topher's neck.

"My Aunt Martha, back in Rocky Mount," Alex said, "went through the same thing. Her husband would get mad and storm around the house until he blew off steam, and then everything was fine. A lot of families work that way. We talked about this before. You do the same thing. You always keep things that bother you inside until you blow up over something little. You're getting better at letting me know when you're mad, but you should understand how Gil feels. He's acting like men are brought up to act: don't show emotions, don't get mad over little things, don't communicate. Then it all comes out in a big fight over nothing." He closed his explanation with, "I do it, and so do you."

Topher considered it. "But, the difference is we have an argument that never results in violence. Why does Gil feel the need to slap her?"

"He's proving his dominance over her." Alex stood up and paced as if he was making a crucial point in court. "With two men, a physical fight is too even for one to always be dominant. Dominance is determined by intellectual, emotional, sexual, or maybe economical comparisons, or sometimes dominance shifts depending on the situation—like with us. But with a man and woman, the man will always get the upper hand by resorting to the physical. We know that Myra can out-think Gil. Slapping her is his way to show he's the leader in the relationship."

"You should have been a psychologist instead of a lawyer."

"Attorneys have to be psychologists sometimes. Now, I have to finish some paperwork at the office. I was just on my way out. What time do you want to come over tonight? I thought we'd walk to Alexander Michael's for dinner and maybe rent a movie."

"Okay, okay, I know when I'm being thrown out." Topher walked back toward the door with Alex following him.

"We can talk more about this tonight. Don't worry. Myra will be okay."

"Thanks...I really love you." Topher waited for his response.

"Thanks. Now go, and I'll see you tonight." Alex closed the door.

After nine months of dating, Alex had never said what Topher wanted to hear. The first time Topher had taken the risk of telling his feelings, Alex had said he was not quite ready to say he loved him too, but he was "very close." Now, all Alex would do was smile or say thanks. Topher's tires squealed as he tore out of the parking lot—partly from anger and partly from sadness.

Why can't he love me? Topher drove toward home, fighting tears. The questions fired through his mind: *What am I not doing? What more does he need? Am I not successful enough? Attractive enough? Smart enough?* He fished a pack of Marlboro Lights from his glove compartment and clinched a cigarette between his teeth, forgetting to light it. *Why can't two people be in love at the same time?*

How many times had he settled for someone just because they were crazy about him and he felt indifferent? Names and faces came running back to him—girls in high school and college, guys that were so handsome he felt lucky they had chosen him. But he had felt nothing for them. Myra had had a crush on him through high school and he knew it, but they worked it into a close friendship, although she would still make comments that made him wonder if she thought she could change him and make him a suburban husband. His thoughts flowed back to Alex. Was that how Alex thought of him? Someone to date until the true prince rode up to the Fourth Ward castle tower to rescue him from boredom and settling for lovers that mark time?

Emptiness gnawed at him. He threw the unlit, but chewed, cigarette out the window. Thoughts of a loving Alex and the good times they had helped to calm him down. As he drove, he pictured Alex with him in the woods, gathering firewood for the coming winter, knowing and loving each other to such a depth that no words needed to be exchanged; glances and gestures conveyed more meaning than any spoken statement could.

Jets, seemingly in slow motion, hovered across the highway as they lined up with the airport runway. There had been a time when Topher wished he was on one, flying away from Charlotte, but he could never decide where to go. But now, his life felt right—almost. By the time he returned home, he had resolved the conflict in his mind. Alex cared about him, but wasn't yet in love. All he had to do was love and support him and Alex's love would eventually come.

Chapter Two

"YOU'RE GOING AS lesbians?" Myra asked. The brisk, fall breeze drifted across the patio of the Mimosa Grill. The oppressive humidity of summer had left with September, and with the cooler days, the city came alive again. She watched the downtown business people rushing around during their lunch hour.

"Sure, everyone assumes gay men dress in drag for Halloween, so Alex and I decided to take the easy way out. No makeup, no heels, no big hair, no tight dresses. It's great. We're wearing jeans, flannel shirts, and work boots." Topher took another bite of his burger.

"That's mean," she teased. "You know how *you* hate to be stereotyped."

"It's just for fun. We can make fun of each other and get away with it. If a straight person did it, it'd be offensive." A sly grin slid across his face.

Silence settled over their table.

"I'm sorry I didn't call you back last week, but I got really busy with work and things." She poked at her grilled chicken salad.

"I've been thinking about you. I'm glad things are better with Gil." He reached over and held her hand for a moment.

Topher had called her to meet him for lunch. Myra's office in the Wachovia building and his job as a graphics artist in a small advertising firm just a few blocks away made meeting for lunch a common occurrence. Although this time, she knew by the low gaze of his pale eyes he wanted to talk about something serious.

She started. "Something's wrong. What's going on?"

"It's you and Gil. And it's me and Alex. It's a little bit of everything. How can you stay with someone who treats you that way? You said he apologized, and he didn't realize he had cut your eye, but that just doesn't make sense to me. One time should be all it takes, apology or not."

"What's going on with you and Alex?" she asked.

"Don't try and change the subject."

"Okay, we're getting along fine, now. He was just having a bad day and lost his temper. The scratch over my eye was an unfortunate accident." She stopped for a moment and looked directly at him.

"Since then, he has been so loving and attentive—I couldn't ask for anyone better."

"Better or not, how do you know he won't do it again?" Topher pushed his plate away, leaving more than half of his burger. "I just can't understand how you can stay with someone who hit you."

"It's very simple: I love him." Myra moved in close to him. "I know, I know. That's what all those women on daytime talk shows say, and everyone in the audience groans, but I understand what they mean. He loves me. He just has a hard time expressing it." A thought streaked across her mind like a flash of lightning, sizzling a path to the deepest part of her soul. *Am I trying to convince myself?* Just as suddenly as it had appeared, she dismissed it.

Topher sighed and shook his head.

She continued with a little more force. "When he gets in one of his moods and it turns violent, he apologizes and says how much he loves me." She paused, and then looked into Topher's eyes. "I love him more than when we got married. At work, I think about him, and I'm so happy my eyes mist, and I can't help but smile—that's the way love is supposed to be, and that's the way my love is for Gil."

"But, he hit you," Topher said.

"The first time it happened—"

"The first time?" The words shot out of him.

"Let me finish. The first time it happened, I wanted to leave."

"Damn, Myra, I'll kill him. How many times—"

"Hold on. Please let me finish. I wanted to leave. I thought 'That jerk will never get the chance to do it again.' After I cooled off, I weighed my options. If I left, where would I go and what would I do? There's no one else I want to be with—it's only Gil. I would love for him to be always thinking of me, calling me in the middle of the day just to say 'hi.'" She took a sip of tea. "It would be great if he put my feelings, wants, and needs before his, and acted like we're dating and treated me to dinner on the weekend, but the world wasn't put here to run the way I want it to run. That's just facing reality.

"If I can't have him the way I want," she straightened up a little, "then I'll take him the way he is. I can't change him. I'm smart enough to know that. I either accept him as he is and love him for it, or leave him. I won't leave the best thing that's ever happened to me." She searched his expression for understanding. Topher's eyes had a slight glimmer of perception, but he remained silent.

"I'm learning to deal with his mood swings," she said. "Usually I can tell when they're about to hit, so I stay out of his way. I just give him his space, and he's fine."

"Is that really how you want to live—walking on eggshells, afraid to say what's on your mind?" He spoke in a low voice, almost to himself.

"I have analyzed this a lot since that Saturday. My problem is I judge Gil and compare him to other relationships. That's not fair. This is a different person and a different relationship. What happened with me and Kevin can't be used to gauge Gil."

"Kevin never hit you."

"True. Kevin was sweet and brought me flowers and never got angry, but he screwed around on me constantly. I couldn't trust Kevin. That's what happens when men act so sweet, they're trying to hide something. At least I know what Gil's bad habits are. With men like Kevin, you never know."

"Not all men who are good to you are cheating."

"You're good to me, and you're cheating on me with Alex," Myra kidded.

"You really sound like you have it figured out."

"I love him. That's all that matters to me."

"You matter to me, and I want you to be happy. Are you happy?"

The waiter interrupted. "More water? How was everything?" He spoke to Topher as if Myra didn't exist.

"Fine," they said in unison and waited for him to leave.

"I always get such good service when I lunch with you. That waiter has stopped by more than he ever does when Tina and I eat here."

"You didn't answer my question: Are you happy?"

"The definition of 'happy' changes throughout our lives. At this point, yes, I'm happy. I have a job I love, a wonderful best friend who watches over me," she rubbed his hand across the table, "and a husband I'm crazy about. Maybe, someday, we will have children. What more could I want?" She sat back and smiled. "So, Toph, what about you? Are you happy with Mister Pretentious?"

"He's not that bad. He's an attorney," Topher said.

"Well, then, that gives him the right to be arrogant and condescending." She laughed, knowing he would take up for Alex even though everything she said was true.

"Cut it out. I'm very happy with Alex. He's taught me a lot about myself. He wants me to buy a place up on North Davidson as a studio. I could live in the back of the building and open the studio as a gallery to sell my paintings."

"I can see the two of you, especially Alex, living in an old storefront with all those canvases and wet paint. His Armani suits would be ruined."

"He didn't say anything about joining me there." He looked at the table and fiddled with a sugar packet.

Myra tried to take Alex's point of view. "Now, how long have you two been dating? Six months, seven?"

"Ten months, next week." He continued flipping the sugar packet over and over.

"You have to give it at least a year before talking about moving in together." She knew how much he wanted a stable relationship. He'd always gotten his heart broken, but Alex had been different. The look in their eyes when they were together was the same look her grandparents had for one another—respect, friendship, loyalty, trust, passion, and excitement just to be near each other. Sure, she thought Alex could be pretentious at times—especially for someone who grew up in Rocky Mount, North Carolina—but, she believed they were right for each other. "Don't worry about how he feels about you. You know how hard it is to express those feelings. You took years to say how much I meant to you."

"Yeah, I probably didn't express it very well...I wasn't sure about myself, and I didn't want to get either one of us into a premature marriage."

MARRIAGE. MYRA'S MIND went back to the year they graduated from college—he from Virginia Tech and she from Radford University. While he had looked for a graphic arts position, Topher worked as a bellboy at the Martha Washington Inn. Myra had put her teaching degree to use as a third grade teacher at a local elementary school.

"Hey Myra, I'm working late tonight. Want to meet me at the Pub after my shift?" Topher's voice over the phone had brightened her dismal Friday afternoon—Halloween weekend, and no party, no date.

"That would be wonderful. I had planned to grade papers, but drinking with you is so much better. I hope that waitress who's hot for you will leave me alone. I feel like she wants to smack me every time we're together."

"Melissa? Forget about her. There's nothing going on. Besides, she's dating a Marine, and I'm not about to get my ass kicked over some flirty waitress. Oh, we might go up to Room 403 after a few drinks to visit Beth."

"That's just creepy."

"Come on up. If you don't want to go, you don't have to."

At the Inn, a private Halloween party flowed over into the maze of old hallways and dark corners. The main house had been updated several times since its original construction in the 1830s, yet it still retained a noble expression of the past it had survived. Wicker rocking chairs greeted guests on the long front porch, white pillars supported massive gables, and rich, hunter green carpets complemented deep burgundy walls. The party-goers from the county government and local hospital were the society of old Colonial Abingdon and dressed in the traditional vampire and witch costumes, with a few historical figures thrown in for the benefit of the party's location. They hovered around the porch, lobby, and hallways, drinking and laughing as Myra squeezed through them. The management of the MaWa, what the locals called the Martha Washington Inn, had required the staff to dress for the Halloween weekend. Myra made her way through the crowded, dark halls and downstairs to the Pub. She recognized Topher immediately. He was sitting at the bar talking to Kendall, the bartender, while Melissa, dressed in a French maid costume, rubbed his back. Myra walked up and nudged Melissa away by putting her arm around Topher's shoulder.

"Myra! I'm glad you made it." He turned, and she saw he was dressed in a Confederate uniform with fake blood smeared over his chest and a bloody bandage wrapped around his head, covering one eye.

"What are you supposed to be?"

"Why, I'm John Stoves, Beth's beloved. Hopefully, she's waiting for me upstairs." He laughed.

"Myra?" Kendall, dressed as Sebastian from *Suddenly Last Summer*, interrupted. "Are you going with us to find Beth tonight? The MaWa has kept that room unoccupied this weekend, and there's a tour going on. But as soon as the clock strikes one and we close the Pub, we'll find her for real."

"Kendall, you're such a flake. Go away." She waved him off and turned to Topher. "This is morbid. The story of Beth and John is a beautiful love story, and all anyone can talk about is her ghost."

"It is Halloween. Come on, let's take the tour. The last one's in ten minutes, then we'll wait until Kendall and Melissa finish up, and we'll go back to scare up Beth."

A man dressed in black led a group of ten up a carpeted hallway lit only by flickering candles to Room 403. No one spoke. The guide stopped at the door, and everyone gathered around. Topher and Myra stood near him as he began his tale.

"This is where our tour begins and ends. During the Civil War, the Inn was the Martha Washington College for Girls. You might have noticed initials scratched into some of the glass in the lobby windows from the diamond rings of the 'Martha Girls.' In the mid-1800s, a girl had to come from a wealthy family to attend college, and these girls were from the best families in Southwest Virginia. The classes in courtesy, grace, fashion, and etiquette were interrupted by the war. In early 1863, a young girl named Beth was a student here, and part of the college had been turned into a hospital for wounded soldiers."

The guide opened the door and escorted the group into a candlelit room. A canopied bed sat in the middle of the room with small tables on each side. One table had a washbasin containing rolled bandages, a Confederate hat sat next to it. Beside the table and in front of the curtained window was a violin lying in a rocking chair. Myra noticed the man's reverence for the room—how carefully he touched items, and the way he looked over the room: like a priest surveying his chapel.

"This is the room where John Stoves was brought after being shot up in a local battle. No one expected him to live, so they just tried to make him comfortable." The guide walked to the rocking chair and rested his hand on the back. "Assigned to change his bandages and comfort John, Beth soon fell in love with the handsome young man. When he found out she could play the violin, he asked her to play for him to help ease his pain. He lived longer than anyone expected, and many said it was because of Beth's attention and her music."

Myra leaned against Topher, and he put his arm around her shoulder.

"One night, John was in terrible pain, and he called for Beth. He asked her to play for him. In the warm sound of her loving music, John passed on.

"A few weeks later, Beth died, too. Some say it was typhoid fever, but others say it was a broken heart.

"Ever since then, there has been a presence here. Maids have reported seeing a young woman with flowing, dark hair sitting in this chair. A security guard reported speaking to a young woman in the hallway who did not reply, but floated up the stairs and through the door to this room. Still other reports come in late at night of the sounds of a sorrow-filled violin coming from here." He patted the chair.

Myra felt a chill, as if the existence of Beth's spirit could be a possibility. She wanted to believe in a love that pure and lasting, a love that she wanted for her own.

Later, after the Pub had closed for the night, Topher, Myra, Kendall, and Melissa slipped back into Room 403. Kendall left the light switch off and lit a candle. Myra glanced at the dancing shadows made by the lone flame. Melissa kept looking at Topher, and then back to Kendall. She ran her hand over the low-cut neckline of her maid's costume, pulling it open more to reveal her exaggerated cleavage.

Kendall plopped down into the rocking chair. His hand rested on his crotch. "Okay, girls," he began, "it's time for the pagan dance to the spirits of John and Beth. Melissa, shall we begin?"

He stood up, and he and Melissa began dancing silently in slow erotic motions, their hands caressing each other. As she rubbed her short skirt into his growing erection, Kendall started to unzip her costume.

Myra looked to Topher for an explanation. He just stared back with his mouth open.

Melissa's dress was on the floor. Kendall began kissing her below her push-up bra. He made his way down her stomach to her panties; his hands quickly pulled them down and buried his face in her soft flesh. Melissa winked at Topher, unhooked her bra, and tossed it to him.

"Myra, let's go." Topher grabbed Myra's hand and pulled her out the door.

"Come back!" Melissa came running after them, her bare breasts bouncing. "We're just playing around."

MYRA STOOD NEXT to her Honda Civic while Topher apologized. "I'm so sorry. They're such jerks. I didn't know they wanted to have sex. I guess when people know you've slept with both women and men, they think you'll sleep with anyone, anytime. They had joked around with me, but I guess it wasn't a joke. People can be such assholes." He calmed down and apologized again, "Sorry. I'd never put you through that. You're too special to me."

"That's okay. In a way, it was kinda funny. At first it was scary, but now it's funny."

"Yeah, you were right about the John and Beth story being romantic. I wish Kendall and Melissa had a little respect for it." Topher kicked a piece of gravel across the asphalt. "You know, I can see me and you as John and Beth."

Her heart sped up, and her throat felt as dry as a desert. "I hope we don't end up like that."

"No, what I mean is if I felt I needed to get married today, it would be you. You're the only girl I care anything about."

The parking lot seemed to spin. Myra managed a smile. "Thanks. You're the only one I could see myself with too."

"Goodnight." He kissed her quickly on the cheek. "I'll talk to you tomorrow." He walked away.

Myra trembled for a moment, watching him disappear into the darkness.

A COOL WIND blew across their table bringing Myra back to the present. "Would you have ever married?" she asked.

"I'd marry Alex in a minute, if it were legal in North Carolina—or anywhere." Topher put the sugar packet down.

"What I meant was a woman," she said.

"Oh. Maybe. But it would have been a huge mistake, and I would have ruined the life and dreams of some sweet woman. I know a lot of guys who did that. I'm just glad I overcame all the negative images that were driven into all of us and learned to accept myself."

"I'm glad, too," she said, without meaning it completely. The questions she had struggled with for years came to mind. Could the right woman make a difference? Could she have made a difference if she had acted on her feelings years ago? *Is he really happy?*

"I'm glad you accepted me so easily. You're a true friend."

She smiled. *Am I really? I try, but I'm not so sure.*

Chapter Three

"LOOKS LIKE SQUIRRELS in your attic." Gil watched the old woman's wrinkled brow tense.

"Can you get them out?"

He glanced back into the dark hole of the pull-down stairs he had just descended and then again at the gray-haired widow wringing her hands. This house was like most of the houses in the Sedgefield and Dilworth neighborhoods—close to, if not over, a hundred years old, and full of insects. Of course, the old trees and shrubs brought a lot of pests into the houses, and the owners couldn't do much except contract with Bugg Off to spray the house and grounds monthly. "Here's how it is, ma'am. We're not supposed to get into anything but bugs, but I can put some rat poison up there that will get rid of them. There's no smell if they die up there—they dry up into little brown husks."

She wiped her hands on her housedress and asked, "Isn't there a nicer way to do it? Couldn't we run them out and patch up the hole they came in?"

"If you want to spend the money to get a man in here who specializes in critter removal, he can walk them out of here on a leash. But, I was just trying to save you some time and money." He bent his huge frame over and began gathering his sprayer and clipboard.

She looked around the hallway of the old house and then back up into the attic. Watching out of the corner of his eye as he fumbled with the hose on the sprayer, Gil waited.

"Okay, go ahead and exterminate. I can't have them running through the attic and in the walls." She turned and walked to the kitchen.

Gil went to his truck to get the pellets he'd bought at the grocery store for two bucks a box. "I can put these pellets down in the attic and that should do it for you, Mrs. Weaver," he called into the kitchen as he walked by.

In the attic, Gil opened two pellet boxes and set them in opposite corners. He looked around at the items Mrs. Weaver had stored in the attic. Working in an attic in November beat the hell out of July, so he took his time before going back downstairs. Of course, the more time he killed, the harder the old lady would think he'd worked. Deciding to inspect the attic for spiders, he prowled around the dust-covered boxes and old furniture. He noticed a worn cardboard box with "Albert's pipes" scrawled on the side. The other boxes on top of it held bedspreads, drapes, men's clothes. He made sure he remembered the stacking order of those boxes. Opening "Albert's pipes," Gil found a collection of tobacco pipes individually shrouded in bubble wrap. They were mostly hand-carved, and some in ivory. He estimated the value of the whole set. His thoughts popped up as he handled the expensive pipes. *Why does she hold on to this? Bet she doesn't even know it's up here.* He returned the boxes to their original position and climbed back down the stairs. He found her sitting in the front room.

"It's all taken care of. After a few days, you won't hear those squirrels anymore." Gil stood next to her chair making her lean back to look up at him.

"What do I owe you?"

"The regular monthly fee for the insect treatment. The squirrel treatment is on me." He smiled down at her.

"No, no. I'm going to pay you for that." She pulled herself up from the chair and reached for her pocketbook on the coffee table. "You saved me from having to call someone else out. What do I owe you?"

"Just put that money away, Mrs. Weaver. I been spraying your house for five years. You're like my own mother. I can't charge you for that work." Gil put his beefy arm around her thin shoulders.

"Now, I want to give you something for your trouble—especially since you've helped me for so long."

"I tell you what," he began, his mind spinning a web to pull the old woman into his plan. "My uncle used to smoke pipes and had quite a big collection."

Her face brightened.

Gil continued. "When he died, he left it to me, and I took an interest in them. I know that the late Mr. Weaver was a pipe smoker too, so I thought if you had any of his old pipes lying around, maybe you'd let me have one." Innocence dripped off him like honey.

Mrs. Weaver patted him on the arm. "Come with me, Gil." She led him back to the pull-down stairs. "Go back up in the attic. There should be a box of Albert's pipes up there. You can have every one of them."

"You are a jewel. Bless your heart. Thank you." Gil hugged her and pulled the stairs back down.

SITTING IN HIS truck in the back corner of the Atlantis Restaurant parking lot on South Boulevard, Gil wedged a tooth pick between molars fishing for a stringy piece of beef caught as he'd inhaled his lunch before his next appointment. He picked up his cell phone and dialed Myra's office.

"Human Resource Development, Myra Greer." She answered the phone with perk.

"Hey," grunted Gil, still digging at his teeth.

"Hey back at you. How's my man doing? Have you had lunch?"

He sighed and patted his belly. "Yeah, just finished. Best food in town is at the Atlantis."

"Don't you mean second best?"

"Nope, Mama's in Darlington, not Charlotte." He laughed, knowing Myra's reaction.

"I can out cook your mother any day of the week, and you know it. Besides, I give better dessert." He thought he heard a smile in her voice.

He leaned down in the truck and rubbed his crotch. "Baby, you give the best desserts I ever had. Can you talk?"

Her voice quivered. "Maybe... Well, okay." She dropped to a whisper and began the script he had taught her. "I have been thinking about you."

"And..."

She hesitated.

Gil urged her on. "And..."

"And I imagine you and me walking through the woods. We come to a clearing with the sun streaming through the trees making shadows on the soft pine needle covered ground. I begin to rub your shoulders as you lean against me. My hands run up and down your back and then around to your chest..."

He looked to see if anyone was nearby, then closed his eyes, and unzipped his fly. Myra's voice caressed his mind as he drifted into her story. Within minutes, he came into a paper napkin and tossed it out the window into the parking lot.

"Damn," he cooed back into the receiver, "that was good—nothing like a nooner over the phone. Thanks, baby. I'll see you tonight."

"I'm glad you liked it." Her voice faltered, then she said, "Gil, I...I love you."

"Yeah, me too. Bye." He snapped the phone shut and drove off.

GIL MANEUVERED HIS truck through Dilworth to his next client's house. As he pulled up to the house on Mount Vernon, he surveyed the two-story Victorian. The lawn was in perfect condition, with a winding walk flanked with monkey grass. More than ten bags of leaves lined the street, and the carpet-trimmed lawn seemed to refuse any others. *Damn, faggots must chase every leaf out of the yard as they start to fall.* He pulled himself out of the truck, grabbed his sprayer, and lumbered up to the front door. An autumn wreath welcomed him as he rang the doorbell. *Wonder if the little woman's home today?*

"Good afternoon, Gil," a small middle-aged man greeted. "Come on in. We have had a terrifying time lately with pill bugs. George says they're getting in from the mulch, but I think they're coming from the crawl space." His thin frame wobbled even with the assistance of a cane as he led Gil into the house.

Without thinking, Gil held his breath as Jamie turned and spoke. "I'm glad you made it today. George and I are having friends over for Thanksgiving, and I'd die if a bug crawled across the table in the middle of dinner." Jamie turned back and slowly led the way to the kitchen.

Gil let out his breath. *You'll probably die soon anyway—bugs or not.*

"There. Right there." Jamie pointed his cane at the baseboard next to the stove. "That's where I saw those little bastards coming in."

Gil sprayed the corner. "That will take care of them. I'm going to go ahead and get the rest of the house."

"That's fine. I need to rest. If you need me, I'll be in the sun room." Jamie hobbled off.

Gil worked his way through the first floor of the house and then climbed the stairs to treat the second floor. As he sprayed the baseboards of the bedroom, he opened the closet door. The walk-in closet held two rows of suits, trousers and shirts, and the floor was lined with expensive-looking leather shoes. *These guys have more clothes than Myra. I hate working in this faggot house*. Standing in the middle, Gil sprayed the baseboards, shoes, and the bottom row of clothes in one swift motion.

He heard a faint cough from downstairs, but continued spraying the other second-floor rooms. The hallway was lined with framed Broadway show posters, and the other bedrooms looked like no one had ever stepped foot in them except to dust. The bathroom had matching towels labeled "His" and "His."

I'll never get used to this. Gil looked at a framed tropical vacation photo of George and Jamie. *Guys acting like they're married. Wonder which one's the wife? Hell, I know who—Jamie's got the virus. He's the one taking it up the ass. Fucking disgusting. Spending time with Topher and Alex is Myra's way to "educate" me, but I still can't stomach fags. All I can think of when I'm around them is what perverted things they do when they get alone—sucking and fucking, sticking their dicks where they don't belong. Topher can talk NASCAR all he wants, but that won't make him a man.*

Again, he heard a cough from downstairs, but this time louder and harsher.

"Gil..." a weak voice called.

He stood at the top of the stairs and waited.

A long, hacking, strangling cough filled the house.

Gil waited.

Choking groans and a thud ushered in silence.

Gil listened for more—nothing but a car driving by.

He slipped down the stairs and to the front room. Jamie lay in a heap at the foot of a rocker, blood flowing out of his mouth, his eyes barely open. Gil didn't move.

Jamie's arm moved a little and he coughed up more blood. The Persian rug soaked up the dark puddle as it formed.

Gil backed out of the room and quietly left through the front door. Standing on the porch, he looked for any neighbors who might be in their yards. No one was out. Cold sweat rolled down his forehead and down his chest. He lost his breath. From where he stood, he could see through the window to Jamie's body lying on the floor. He wasn't certain if the body moved again.

With turtle speed, he inched himself off the porch and down the walk to his truck. In his sheltering cab, he began to breathe normally, and his thoughts began to flow again. *What in the hell am I supposed to do? I could get something if I touch him. I hate going into that house, anyway. Hope no one saw me*. Just as he put his key in the ignition, a white minivan pulled up, and a young woman got out and headed toward the house he had just abandoned.

Gil jumped out of his truck with his equipment and caught up with the woman on the walk. "How's it going today?"

"Fine," she answered. "Are you here to spray Jamie's house?"

"Yep. Just got here and was filling out the paperwork when I saw you drive up. I'm going to start out here first. Tell Mr. Campbell I'll be right in to do the inside." He walked around the side and waited for her scream.

Chapter
Four

"SO," HE DREW out the word as he thought up conversation, "how was work today?" Topher looked across the table at Alex. He set his glass of merlot back down and waited for Alex's reply.

"Fine."

"That case you're working on, did you find the information to support your client's claims? I know you were having a hard time getting with the doctor."

"Yeah, I got to talk to him this morning."

Topher paused before saying anything more, hoping Alex would pick up the conversation, but he just let it drop. Glancing around the restaurant for something to talk about, Topher noticed an older gay couple laughing and talking. He watched them for a little while, then looked back at Alex.

His stare seemed vacant. He sipped his wine, not really looking at Topher, but not actually looking at anything else, either.

"I was thinking of starting a new painting," Topher said.

"Oh?"

"Yes, I'm trying to decide how to show the process of collaboration, but I'm not sure in what context. Music has been done to death, what about in problem-solving?"

"Hmm."

Topher held out for more, but Alex just stared.

He decided to try again. "What are you thinking about?" He hated the question as soon as he heard himself say it.

"What? Oh, nothing."

Talk to me. What is going on in that mind of yours? Frustration boiled in Topher.

Alex smiled at him. "I'm so glad we can just sit here in silence and be comfortable with each other."

Comfortable? He sighed. *Guess he doesn't want to talk.* Topher took another sip of his wine and looked for the waiter and their dinner. This wasn't the kind of silent communication Topher had dreamed of. He wanted a shared language of intimacy. Could Alex be there, in that state of oneness, and Topher not be attuned? *Alex works hard all day talking to people, I guess he needs some time to collect his thoughts*. He fixed his eyes on the back of the wine bottle and read the label.

TOPHER FELT THE bed shift as Alex got up and went to the bathroom. He glanced at the clock on the dresser—6:49 a.m. glared back in red. The sun was slowly reclaiming the sky. Warmth and sleepiness kept him from getting out of bed, too.

Alex ran back and jumped into bed. "Oh, it's cold." He snuggled next to Topher and kissed him hard on the mouth.

"You brushed your teeth. Does that mean what I think it means?" Topher was wide awake.

"Maybe, maybe not."

He grabbed Alex's bathrobe and hurried to the bathroom. After peeing, he looked in the mirror and had to laugh at his image. His hair was sticking up all on one side of his head. The corners of his eyes housed white stuff he had never learned a name for, and his face was covered with a full day's beard growth. *Why does Alex like sex in the morning?* After brushing down his hair and running a cold washcloth over his face, he brushed his teeth and headed back to the bed.

Yawning, Alex stretched the full length of the bed. Topher crawled up next to him and rubbed his hand across Alex's firm stomach. A kiss was the response, and then his hand was guided lower, following the stream of hair that Myra had always called a man's goody trail. The strength and power of Alex's flesh combined with the thick, soft hair covering him had always intrigued Topher. He stroked his partner's thigh lightly, running soft fingertips up his leg to his stomach and chest, then back down the other side. One of most beautiful things Topher could remember seeing in his life was the first vacation they had taken together.

He thought back to the morning after they arrived in Miami. Alex had gotten up from bed to look out the curtains at the sun rising from the blue ocean. His silhouette created by the darkened room and the rising sun had made Topher think of Apollo ushering in the morning and had led to a painting he completed and framed for him called "Apollo's Sunrise."

That painting now hung over the bed, and Topher thought of Alex as the incarnation of the Greek God. *Apollo – beautiful, and always on the run.*

His finger traced the line of Alex's pectoral muscle from his shoulder to the middle of his chest and then back down to his navel. He lingered there, swirling the hair with his finger. Alex shifted his position so Topher's touch would get closer to the final destination. He felt Alex's excitement and rolled over on top of him. His look of longing stirred Topher into wanting to say the three magic words again, but he knew it would ruin the moment for both of them. He dropped his head to Alex's shoulder and mouthed the words into his skin, then pretended he heard them back in the responding sighs and moans.

AS THE SUN drove higher in the sky, Topher read the Sunday paper and Alex cooked Mexican omelets with peppers, onions, and salsa.

"Says here," Topher straightened the paper, "that it's going to be a great ski season this year. Last year, you promised to teach me. Now it's November, and we're still together—"

"You'll love skiing, but I don't want to try to teach you. You could probably get in a class. Besides, I don't get to go very often, and I love spending time on the slopes. Maybe Dustin and Erik can go with us. That way, I can ski with Dustin while Erik teaches you. It's more fun if I have someone to ski with."

"But, babe, the reason I wanted to go skiing was to be with you." Topher walked into the kitchen knowing this would start a serious discussion.

"I know, but I don't like to ski alone, and I'm not a good teacher. It'd be best for you to have Erik or a professional trainer and not get fouled up by me." Alex flipped the omelet.

"Thanks for the concern," Topher shot back. "I only wanted to spend time with you, but if the main reason you want to go to the mountains is to ski, then maybe you should go without me."

"Don't get upset. Erik is a good teacher. He can show you better than I could. And, yes, I want to ski while I'm there. We can be together here in town, but when we're in the mountains, we can be together some and ski some. We shouldn't have to be stuck side by side all the time."

"Stuck?" Topher yelled. "Do you feel stuck with me?"

"Calm down," Alex soothed. "Come eat your omelet." He slid the eggs off the pan and onto plates.

"We're not going to ignore this. How do you feel about me? Are you feeling stuck?"

"Topher, I'm crazy about you, and I'm crazy about skiing." He set the plates on the kitchen table. "I want time to pursue both those interests. Will you give me that?"

Topher couldn't decide if he'd given an acceptable answer. It certainly wasn't the answer he wanted to hear, but at least he made the list as one of Alex's top interests. "Okay. It's just that I'm a little insecure about us. I know I love you, and I know you're not quite sure how you feel, and that makes me uneasy."

Alex walked over to him and hugged him. "Don't feel insecure. There's no one else in my life but you. Just give it some time, and we'll be fine."

"YOU NEED TO get your ass out and have some fun." Daryl threw a beanbag pumpkin over the tall, gray cubicle wall at Topher.

Topher picked the pumpkin up and threw it back, hitting Daryl in the head. "No thanks."

"You dented my 'fro."

He stood up and looked over the wall at Daryl surrounded by layouts, magazine clippings, and a poster of Lenny Kravitz in all his shirtless glory. "You call that one-inch growth a 'fro? Don't you remember the seventies?"

"Old man, I was born after disco. My mama had a 'fro, and she looked beautiful."

"You'll never look as good as your mama."

"Honey, I already look better." Daryl laughed and threw the pumpkin back at Topher. He walked around to Topher's cube. "Seriously, go out to the bars with us this weekend. It's a lot of fun, and I bet you meet someone."

"I haven't been to a bar in years."

"Great. You will be new meat. Every tired ol' queen there will be all over you." Daryl laughed and pulled out a pick to fluff up his hair.

"I don't want to meet anyone. I've met the one I want. Besides, I've seen some of the bar trash you kick out on Sunday mornings."

"I never kick a trick out. At least I sling a Pop Tart on a plate for his breakfast before telling him I got things to do—alone."

"That's nice. Is that Emily Post etiquette or Miss Manner's?"

"Stop raggin' me. I got someone in mind for you: six foot two, blond and blue-eyed and—" Daryl picked up a ruler from Topher's desk and held it up.

Topher laughed and kicked Daryl's thick-soled boots. "Okay, but can he talk? I've had enough Ken dolls to last me a lifetime."

"Talk? Talk? Who cares?"

"I do. Now leave me alone. I have to finish this layout before lunch."

Daryl stopped at the doorway and turned to conclude, "If I was as picky as you, I'd make my mama proud. She's been waiting for me to bring home a nice doctor or lawyer son-in-law. Bet your mama wet her panties when you told her about Alex—Attorney at Law."

Not quite. Topher's mind went back to the night he told his mother he was gay.

"NO YOU'RE NOT. You're just confused. No son of mine would turn out to be queer. Your father—that's where you're getting these weird sexual feelings—you inherited them from him." Maggie had stood in the kitchen glaring down at him.

Why wasn't this going as he had planned? In his mind he had played out the scene: she accepted him, and they became closer. *This can't be happening. I didn't want her to freak out. It's still me.* Tears filled his eyes. "Mom, I tried. I really tried to date girls, but I know it's not me. I feel like I'm lying to them and to myself."

"Have you had sex with another boy?" She turned her back and busied herself with the plates in the sink.

He dropped his head and whispered, "Yes." The silence filled the room pushing all the air out, and Topher couldn't breathe. He'd said what he had dreaded telling her for years, and she couldn't accept him as he really was.

"You're nineteen. You're experimenting. Don't commit to something that is just a phase. Haven't you seen the papers? Gay men are dying, and no one knows why." She began to cry. "I don't want to lose you because of silly, childish experimentation. I can't lose you, too. You're all I have."

He knew he had to be strong, to be the man he had grown to be. Topher walked up behind her and put his arms around her waist, hugging her hard. "Mom, I know you're scared. I am, too. But this is who I am. I've struggled with it for as long as I can remember. The papers say—and I've read everything I can—that this disease is spread by bodily fluids, and I've done nothing that would put me at high risk."

His grandmother shuffled into the kitchen. "Christopher, what's wrong with your mama now? If that woman ain't weeping over one thing, it's another." She plopped down onto a chair at the table and stared at them both. "Hell, boy, you're crying too. Did I die and not know it?"

"No, Granny." Topher sniffed. "We're just practicing for when you do."

She laughed. "You little shit."

Maggie turned and glared at her mother. "Mom, leave us alone for a little while, we have things to discuss."

"Fine, fine." She pushed herself out of the chair and hobbled out of the room, waving one hand. "I know when I'm not wanted. You'll be calling me back when it's time for me to fix your supper."

After allowing time for her to be out of earshot, Maggie continued. "You have to give normal sex another try. I know you care for Myra. Why don't you sleep with her? I know, she's not the prettiest girl, but she followed you to college. I know she loves you. Give it another try."

"Who said straight sex is normal? I'm following what is normal for me."

"Myra, try Myra," she urged.

Topher dropped a heavy sigh. "I don't think of her that way. I know I couldn't do it. We know each other too well for me to act out a lie with her. And, besides, I'm tired of living a lie."

Maggie lost her temper. "Who? Who are you sleeping with to put all these crazy ideas in your head? Is it Richard? The two of you are way too close for normal college boys. I should have known he was a faggot, and he's trying to turn you into one, too."

"That's it." Fury snapped his tension like scissors clipping a tight rope. "I'm going back to school tonight. I can't talk to you when you're upset. You need time to deal with this. It took me years, and I can't expect you to understand in a few minutes." He headed for the door and stopped. Turning to meet his mother's hard eyes, he said in a calm voice, "I'm not sleeping with Richard or anyone. I'm still the same person I was when I came home last night. You just know me a little better. After you've calmed down, we'll talk more. I love you, Mom."

"Don't say anything about this to anyone else. It would kill your grandmother."

Topher went upstairs, packed, and left without another word.

Numbness held him during his drive back to Blacksburg. The feeling of relief wasn't there; in fact, no feelings settled on him. Telling parents was supposed to lift the burden of lies to them and to yourself, but it only left him in limbo—between two worlds where he didn't fit completely in either one.

At Bogen's over a couple of pitchers of beer, Topher had tried to explain his loss to Richard.

"The Topher she knew died today. That was her worst fear...and mine. Everything we both had thought—spoken or not—changed. She'll never have grandchildren. I'll never have a wedding. I'll never be able to hold the hand of the person I love in public or kiss them good-bye at the airport." He looked at Richard for him to contradict him.

"You're right. We're outcasts." He shifted his tall frame in the dark booth and ran his fingers through his hair. "But the alternative is to lie to yourself and try to make believe you're something you're not. It would be like asking your mother to be a lesbian because it's what everyone expected of her. Could she do it? Would she do it? No."

"No, she wouldn't." Topher exhaled the breath he didn't realize he had held. "I can't hide who I am. I'm still shaking from telling her." He rubbed his hands on the wooden tabletop. "I feel stronger in a way. I'm just not sure what to do now, I mean, this was a goal, to be open and honest, but now what?" He sipped his beer without tasting it. "Have I lost the only family I have?"

"She still loves you." Richard poured more beer into Topher's glass. "Give her time and she'll see you're just Topher doing what is right for you," he said. "Your family needs time to adjust. When you told Myra, she accepted you right away. That was a good start. Your mom, on the other hand, might need a little more time."

DARYL'S LAUGH IN the next cube brought him back. *Am I doing what's right for me? Is being with Alex what's right or is it just what I think I should do?* He picked up the phone and dialed Myra's number.

"YOU'RE THE ONLY one who knows what's right for you." Myra shifted the phone to her other ear. "I like Alex. He's good to you, and you love him, but if you aren't happy, maybe the two of you need to put a little distance between yourselves." She knew his loving and caring personality made him vulnerable to rejection—not everyone he encountered had the same intensions for settling down that he did, although many a woman would have loved to find a man with his qualities. "Try being Topher for a while, not Topher and Alex, or Topher and Jim, or Topher and whoever." She waited for his response, hoping she hadn't said the wrong thing.

After a seemingly-long pause he answered, "I think you have a point."

She sighed, relieved that he understood what she meant.

"Sometimes," he said, "I feel like I've lost part of myself. Not that Alex is overbearing or tries to influence my decisions, but I try too hard to make it work. I know I do. It's just that I know he's the one, and I want everything to work out. I'll stay away from him this weekend, and get my head together. Then Wednesday, I'm driving to Bristol for Thanksgiving, so that will give us more than a week apart. That will help."

Myra twisted the phone cord around her index finger. "Stop calculating. Just do what you need to do and what's right for you. There aren't any rules." She knew the analytical side of him would come out; when the intuitive side didn't seem to work, he would switch to logic. "If you find you want to see him or talk to him, do it. Don't put these time limits on yourself and think it will be solved in a week's span."

"Okay, okay. I'll play it by ear. You know that's hard for me to do, but I'll try. Have a good weekend, and I'll talk to you before I leave Wednesday. And thanks. I really love you."

"I love you, too. If you need me, call."

She hung up the phone and looked out her office window. The sun had set, and a steady stream of taillights snaked out of the uptown district toward the distant night. The business world of Charlotte transformed to the family world where soccer moms and dads took ruddy-faced children to practice, dance classes, school functions. Thanksgiving and Christmas loomed ahead, and those families would be gearing up for large gatherings of relatives. She remembered Christmases of the past when her parents, grandmother, and sister had all been together, laughing, enjoying, and sharing the intimacy of their lives. Family now consisted of her and Gil.

By the time she arrived home, Gil was entrenched in his easy chair, drinking beer and watching the six o'clock news. The television station enticed its viewers with a "Watch and Win" contest where Gil had to match the number on the screen with the number on a flyer he had received in the mail.

"Damn it to hell," he muttered when his number didn't match.

She bent over the recliner and kissed the top of his head. "We aren't millionaires yet, but one of these days..."

"Baby, I wish I could give you everything you want. But, I think we do okay."

She smiled and ran her fingers through his thick hair. "I have everything I need and want. Just you and me—our own little family—getting by. In fact, we have enough in savings to think about getting that house we talked about. I can get a good rate on a home loan through work."

"Yeah," Gil agreed, "we should start looking around. I'd like to have room for a dog."

"A dog? I was thinking of more room for children." She laughed a little.

"Kids?" His voice sounded slightly irritated. "What's for dinner?"

"I thought we could go out. It's Friday night, and we'll be eating leftover turkey next Friday, so let's live a little." She shook off her coat and sat her briefcase by the door. "So?" she asked and sat on the arm of his recliner, kicking off her shoes.

"Myra," he turned to face her, "I have to eat out every day for lunch. I want a home-cooked meal once in a while."

"I can fix you a roast and potatoes tomorrow night. It's just so late now, and I had a long day of standing in front of a classroom full of bankers trying to get them to act like they genuinely hate to turn down people who are bad loan risks. I'm just simply worn out."

Gil stood up quickly, almost knocking her off the arm of the chair. "And you think I just play around all day? I work my ass off crawling around under houses and in attics spraying God knows what kind of chemical, and I want to relax in my home at night instead of hauling off to some loud, crowded restaurant. I don't *stand in front of a classroom full of bankers* all day," he mocked. "I work hard. Is it too much to ask for you to get your fat ass in that kitchen and fix me supper?"

She backed away from him. "Gil, I'm sorry, but I didn't plan on cooking. I might be able to find something to fix..."

"Don't put yourself out on my account. I guess I ain't worth a home-cooked meal. Maybe I can find a woman who wants to cook for me."

"She's in Darlington." She felt a little braver, so she said, "Like you reminded me the other day before I had to sit in my office and get you off over the phone. Do you know how degraded that made me feel?"

"You're so stupid," he yelled. "So you'd rather have me go find sex with another woman than give me that one little favor?"

"No, but don't you ever think I'd like you to come home and share your sex life with me—in person?"

He moved toward her and she backed into a corner. Gil lifted his hand and she flinched. Gently touching her cheek, he whispered, "Baby, you know men have a higher sex drive than women, and sometimes I need that release."

A cold chill ran through her body. The thought of his hands touching her caused an icy sweat to break out on her forehead as if a copperhead had slithered across her foot then turned to decide if it would strike.

Gil continued, "I don't want to have to go looking for someone else to satisfy me when you're not around. I want you. I love you. You know I love you, don't you?"

Not moving, she looked him in the eye. "Yes, Gil," her voice squeaked.

He stroked her cheek some more and said, "I just want us to be happy. Let me do things my way, and everything works out. I never cheated on you, and I never will, as long as you allow me these little pleasures. And besides, you're so good at phone sex. I really like it, almost as much as screwing. So, what's the harm in you doing what you're good at and letting me enjoy it? Okay?"

"Okay, Gil." Her body trembled like a string stretched across a cello, and he had begun to play her.

"Now," he backed away a little, "what about ordering a pizza. You can go pick it up, and we can eat here at home."

She inched her way along the wall toward the kitchen. "I'll call the order in."

"Good girl." He sat back down in the recliner and kicked back with his feet up. "While you're out, stop and get some more beer. This is the way I like it. We both get to relax after a long day."

In the kitchen, Myra began to breathe normally again. The tension drained out of her body so quickly she had to lean on the countertop. She tried to regain her composure, reason out his temper—a bad mood from a long hard week.

As she drove to the pizza parlor, her hands quivered on the steering wheel. Her head began to ache from the stress of the evening. She rubbed her temple, trying to get the dull pain to disappear, but it continued its relentless hold on her forehead like a rubber band tightened by Gil's words and only released by the snapping of his temper. That relief hadn't come, but she knew it was building. The rubber band would not loosen until a big fight. The oncoming headlights hurt her eyes, and once she had picked up the pizza, the smell of tomatoes and cheese caused her stomach to churn. At the grocery store, she bought Gil's beer and a bottle of aspirin for herself.

"THIS SHIT IS cold!" Gil yelled and slung the slice of pizza back into the box. "Heat it up. Did it ever occur to you to get the beer first and then get the pizza? How fucking stupid are you?"

"Gil," Myra said in a slow calm voice, "I'm not stupid. I'll heat it up." The rubber band tightened.

He ignored her and tromped back to the den.

She warmed part of the pizza in the microwave and then carried it out to him with a beer. Without looking at her, he took the plate and the beer. Back in the kitchen, she opened the bottle of aspirin and took three.

"Damn it, it's too hot now," he yelled. "You are a stupid bitch."

She heard the plate hit the floor and him storming toward the kitchen. The only way out was the hallway to the bathroom. She hurried down the hall. With the bathroom door slammed shut and locked, she braced herself for his attack.

"Get the fuck out of there." Gil pounded the door with his fist. "Clean this mess up. I'm going out."

The sound of the front door slamming brought a sigh of relief. She waited for any other sounds, but the apartment lay silent. The storm had passed. Slowly, Myra opened the door and peeked out. A force from the other side of the door knocked her back so hard she fell through the shower curtain and into the tub. Gil stood over her. His face drained of all color.

"Why do you try to piss me off?" he yelled. "Do you enjoy this?"

Myra pulled the ripped shower curtain around her for protection. "Please, Gil, don't." She could see the rage in his eyes, the pure hate, almost like he didn't recognize her. She tried to reason with him. "Gil, please calm down. I'll clean everything up. Just go to the bedroom to lie down and rest. I'll take care of everything—"

"Shut the hell up!" His shouts drowned out her voice.

She pulled the shower curtain around her body.

Gil's eyes flashed. "You do what I say, and you do it right. Stop being so stupid. How did you ever take care of yourself before me?"

Tears slipped down her face.

"Get up and clean the den, then get my dinner on the table." He turned and stood outside the doorway, waiting.

The rubber band around her head was so tight that Myra shook uncontrollably. Pulling herself out of the tub, she dragged the torn shower curtain behind her, not realizing she still held onto it.

As soon as she cleared the bathroom door, the bottom of Gil's shoe connected with the small of her back and kicked her down the hall. He had pushed so hard she fell forward on her face. She hoped he was finished. She stayed down, not moving.

"You disgust me." Gil stepped over her and walked out the front door.

She sat up, leaning against the wall. *I disgust him?* Her body ached, then she felt it. A cramp stabbed at her like she was being ripped apart, and then she noticed a slight wetness between her legs.

She pulled herself up and went back to the bathroom. She had begun to bleed. "Oh, God," she cried, "what have I done?"

Immediately, she called her gynecologist. The answering service said they would page him. "God, help me," she prayed. She had been counting the weeks, and even taken a home test, hoping the baby was there —the beginning of her family. Her appointment was for next week.

Pain jerked her again.

Tears stained her face. "Who? Who can I call?" Her mother was dead, her father hadn't been in contact with her in fifteen years, and her only sister had dropped out of her life after a fight several years ago. *Alone and dying*, she closed her eyes. "Gil," she whispered, "I need you, come back." Reaching for the phone again, she dialed Topher's number, but hung up, wondering if the doctor might be trying to call her at that very moment.

She lay on the bed, her mind taking comfort in the images she had built in her head of the baby. Gil would be so different, gentle, playing with the baby and loving both of them. After the first—a boy, she hoped—they would have a little girl. Myra pictured the house on Sedgefield Road that she wanted, brick and sturdy, like the family in her mind.

She stared at the clock, then at the phone, willing it to ring. Retreating again to her fantasy, she rocked herself back and forth.

"I can't lose this. I'm okay, I'm okay," she reassured herself. The pain had dulled, but she could still feel the blood. She cautiously walked back to the bathroom.

When the phone finally rang, the doctor's voice was drowned out by the sound of people talking and laughing.

She tried to explain about the bleeding, but realized she wasn't doing a very good job.

"You could just be late," he said. "Stress could cause irregular menstruation. If it's heavier than normal, or if you feel anything out of the ordinary, call me and I'll meet you at the hospital."

"I have sharp pains..."

"What brought this on?"

"Nothing," she said. "I did stumble and fall..."

"Better get to the hospital. I'll meet you there in twenty minutes."

Gil came back home just as she hung up the phone and curled up on the bed again to soothe the latest round of stabbing pain. "Myra?" His voice was full of apology.

She pulled the covers up over her head as she heard him walking toward the bedroom.

"Baby, I'm so sorry. I had such a hard day, and I know you deserve better than me." He patted the bedspread covering her head.

The cramping continued to knot her over, and she cried from the short sharp pains.

Gil gently pulled the spread back and kissed her forehead. "Don't cry. I can do better, and to show you how sorry I am and how much I love you, we can go out tomorrow night to any place you want to go. Hell," he chuckled, "if you want, I'll even cook supper for you."

"I need to go to the hospital. I think I had a miscarriage."

"Miscarriage?" he whispered. "You're..." Tears welled up in his eyes. "Let's go. Oh, Myra, I'm so sorry. It's my fault. I shouldn't argue with you."

"Let's just go."

Chapter Five

"I'M GOING TO have a Christmas party in a couple of weeks. I don't know where to begin." Myra sat in Tina's office after a short meeting. Tina had been her boss for five years, and they had formed a quick friendship. After last Friday night, Myra wanted to talk to someone. Topher was in Bristol with his mother, and Tina seemed like the only one who might possibly understand.

"Oh, come on, you had parties before." Tina sat behind her desk in front of a window that looked over downtown Charlotte. Growing up in Bristol, Myra had never thought one of her best friends would be a black woman twelve years older than she. Not that she had been raised to be prejudiced, but all through school, she had never been around black people. All she knew about them had been from television. Living in Charlotte had exposed her to wonderful, warm people of all races.

Myra blushed a bit. "Actually, no. This will be my first party." The statement even surprised her. "Wow, I never thought that much about it, but even when Gil and I got married, the ceremony was in a clerk's office. No rehearsal dinners or bridal showers, we just decided to do it. Sometimes I wish we'd married in a church with a religious ceremony. But with my grandmother in Tennessee and my sister who knew where, there didn't seem to be any reason."

"Lady, I had both my weddings in a church with crowds of people, and neither marriage lasted. I wish I'd found a man who adores me the way Gil adores you." She smiled a brilliant smile, and Myra stared out the window without expression.

"Myra." Tina tapped the desk to get her attention and looked her square in the eye. "I thought you had Thanksgiving plans. I had you scheduled to be off today. What's going on?"

"I needed to get out of the house." She took a deep breath. "Gil went to work this morning, so I was all alone, and I felt like getting out."

"Problems? Did you two have a fight?" Tina asked.

"You wouldn't believe it." Myra paused for a second. "You know how men get about their turkey and football."

"No, I don't believe I do."

"It's just..." She hooked her hair behind her ear. "Gil is...I mean... Honestly, Gil and I are having some problems. I don't attend to his needs as well as I should, and that usually leads to arguments. In fact, these arguments have been getting worse."

"Getting worse? How bad?" Tina leaned forward, propping her breasts on the desk.

"Oh, not too bad." Myra's eyes scanned Tina's desktop and settled on a memo. "Although," she turned the memo around acting like she was more interested in it than what she was saying, "he did lose his temper and slap me."

"What? When did this happen?"

"It was nothing, really, and it's been months." The guilt of lying constricted her throat. She coughed.

"So this is why you came to work today? Did anything happen yesterday?"

"No, Gil and I had a nice quiet Thanksgiving dinner, and he watched football."

"You aren't telling me everything."

Myra felt sweat break out on her upper lip. She wiped it away and felt the familiar tension building in her head. The tension told her she was treading on the line of revealing too much. "That's all there is to tell."

"Um, um, um," Tina shook her head as if she knew more than Myra. "If you need to talk, please don't hesitate to come to me."

"Thanks, but I'm okay. I was a little sick last weekend, and it's put me on edge. Since I was out on Monday seeing the doctor, I just felt I needed to get caught up on some work. That's why I'm in today," she concluded, with a little too much decisiveness in her voice. She knew it sounded as if she had just come up with it.

Myra looked at the family photographs on Tina's desk: her two sons' school pictures; a family picture of Tina, her mother, and the two boys; a snapshot from last summer's vacation in Williamsburg.

After her own mother died and her sister left, all she had was Gil. Then last weekend, she lost a chance at having a child. The prospect of a loving family, the family she never had, the family she yearned for had been lost. One bright spot was Gil's absolute affection for her since the fight. No arguments, no raising of his voice—the miscarriage had turned him around. He said they would try for a baby as soon as the doctor said Myra was up to it. Maybe the possibility wasn't drifting away after all.

Tina stood up and glanced out the window to the clear, blue skies. "Let's take a long lunch and do a little shopping at the Party Warehouse for your Christmas affair. No one's going to miss us. That is, if you got caught up on all that work you wanted to do."

Myra smiled. "That sounds great. You can help me pick out some things."

Driving down South Boulevard in Tina's Mercedes, Myra pointed out the Atlantis restaurant. "That's where Gil usually has lunch. I don't see his truck. He must be running late today."

"So, tell me about this party. How many people? Dressy or casual? What kind of food? What are you serving to drink?" Tina prompted her.

Myra's mind settled on the party, and her excitement grew. "I didn't realize there would be so many decisions. This is going to take some planning. I want it to be really..." She saw something familiar and lost her thought. "Could you turn around and go back by that pawn shop?"

"Good idea. Sometimes you can find nice crystal punch bowls and things in pawn shops."

"No, I think that's Gil's truck parked there. I wonder what he's doing. Park around the side."

Tina pulled the car around the side of the gray cinderblock building. Myra could see just enough around the corner to glimpse the back end of Gil's pickup truck. "Would you do me a favor? Go in and see what Gil's up to."

"Sure, but why the Nancy Drew adventure?"

"Why? I'm not sure, but I'm a little concerned Gil might have money problems he isn't telling me about. He doesn't communicate very well, and something is making him edgy. Wear your sunglasses so he won't recognize you."

"No offense, but I get the feeling Gil thinks we all look alike."

Myra laughed. "That isn't true."

Tina went inside. Myra waited and watched for Gil's truck to leave. She slid down in the seat and peered out a corner of the window. What could he be selling? *It had better not be my grandmother's silver. Maybe he's buying something? Something to make up for the miscarriage. I know he feels bad. Maybe a diamond bracelet.* She kept watching the corner of the building for Tina's return or Gil's truck to move—neither happened.

She glanced at her watch. Only ten minutes. It seemed like an hour. A Jeep Cherokee pulled into the lot and parked at the corner of the building, obstructing her view. "Damn it. I'm going in." She crept to the Cherokee and peeked at Gil's truck. Empty. He was still inside the pawn shop. *What if this sets him off? He might think I'm spying on him. Well, I am. He's been so sweet and kind lately, I should just go. Damn, Tina's in there. Come on, Tina. Let's go.* She headed toward the car, but she heard the squeak of the truck door opening. Crouching behind the Cherokee, she caught sight of Gil climbing in his truck with a small, crumpled paper bag. After he drove away, Myra went through the iron-barred glass doors and found Tina in the musical instrument section looking at a trumpet. Myra whispered, "What did he do?"

"I'm thinking about getting this trumpet for Justin's Christmas. He wants to be in a jazz band when he grows up."

She shook Tina's arm to get her attention, "No, what did Gil do?"

"Oh, Gil. You know he didn't even show a glimmer of recognition. I knew he thought we all looked alike," she said as she sighed.

"Tina, what did he buy?"

"A gun. A good-sized pistol. Just like a white boy from South Carolina. Can't have enough guns."

A cold chill ran through Myra. "We agreed not to have guns in the house. He said he would never have one." Fear filled her memories of the last fight, only in this version, the gun kicked the door open, and laid her on the floor. "He said he hated guns."

"He seemed to like the one he bought. He was waving that thing around, testing the weight in his hands. And they say women have penis envy and treat objects as phallic symbols. They never saw a man holding a new gun." Tina laughed, then looked at Myra. "Don't worry about that gun. Men get those things to show other men. Just make sure he locks it away."

THAT NIGHT, AS Myra set the table for dinner, Gil watched the news. She had searched the closet and the dresser drawers for the gun as soon as she got home, but it was nowhere.

"Gil, dinner's ready. What can I get you to drink?"

"Sweet iced tea. Sweet as you." He walked into the kitchen and put his arms around her.

She smiled and gently broke loose from his embrace. "Go ahead and sit down." He left the kitchen, and she tried to think of other places he could have put the gun. If she knew where it was, she'd feel safer. It was like a snake in the house. If she knew it was there, but didn't know where, she'd never sleep, but if it was confined in a place she knew, she would feel safer.

"I didn't think you had to work today. Why'd you go in?" Gil asked as she set down his tea.

"I just needed to get caught up on some things. And this way I can save that vacation day for the day of our Christmas party. The party's still on, isn't it?"

Gil grinned at her. "Sure. But I reserve the right to lock myself in the bedroom if I get bored."

"That's okay. I won't let anyone stay too late. Is there anything we need to put away before the party? Like good crystal? Uh, no, I know that's not a problem. What about anything that might be dangerous? Like your sprayer and chemicals or knives?" *Or guns?* "Or heavy blunt objects that might be tempting to a drunk." She laughed and knew it sounded fake.

"No," Gil said between bites of turkey and gravy. "Keep my tools in the truck, and the only heavy blunt object in the place is me." He chuckled.

Gil had told her he would never own a gun—an incident from his past had scared him off them. So, why buy one now? Her head reeled. *It's in the truck. That's good. No grabbing it in a fit of rage—by him or me. But things have been so good lately. Maybe he bought it for his brother's Christmas present.* That thought brightened her face.

"You don't think people will get that drunk, do you?" he asked with a mouthful of turkey dressing.

"Oh no, I was just making a little joke. Everyone invited will behave. Who do you want to invite?" Myra asked.

"If they have to behave, then I don't know of anyone. Nah, really, I wouldn't want to invite anyone from work. None of them clean up that good. Besides, I don't think they would mix well with your friends. Who do you have in mind?"

Myra composed the list. "Topher and Alex—"

Gil rolled his eyes.

"Come on, you like them."

"I don't think Topher has ever liked me. I think he's got something going with you," Gil winked at her. "Of course, I can't imagine what. Hey, how does a queer rape a woman?"

Myra snapped, "Gil! Don't use that word—"

"He holds her down and redoes her hair and makeup."

"That's not funny. That's like using the n-word to talk about a black person." She waited for his sheepish grin of an apology, then she continued, "Tina, Jenny, Bill, Allen, and John from work and their spouses."

"Wait. How many nig...blacks does it take—"

She interrupted him and continued with the list. "Laurie and her new boyfriend. She met him at the mall. She was filling in at the men's fragrance counter during lunch, and he bought two hundred dollars' worth of cologne, shaving cream, body wash, all that kind of stuff. Then as he was paying, he asked her out. He's a banker, but not with my bank. He works for First Catawba. He's one of the top loan officers in the city."

"Sounds like a fruit to me."

She shot him another look.

He laughed and changed the subject. "Did you tell them not to bring kids? I can't stand a bunch of kids at a party—" He stopped and looked at Myra with regretful eyes.

She felt tears well up and swallowed some tea to wash down the hurt. "There won't be any children."

"I'm sorry." Gil reached across the table and held her hand. "I didn't mean it like I didn't like kids. I'd love to have kids. Our kids would be well behaved, and everyone would love them as much as us."

"I know. I know you mean well. That's what keeps me going." She leaned over and kissed him. He was back to the Gil she'd married. With her arms around him, she heard his stomach growl, reminding her of a distant thunderstorm whose flashes of lightning and rumbles of thunder would lull her into a deep secure sleep.

Chapter Six

TOPHER STRUNG WHITE lights across the artificial spruce. His mother had put one of her Christmas albums on the stereo, and he had forgotten how scratchy an LP sounded. This particular album was one she bought after the divorce, a disco version of traditional Christmas carols. The little drummer boy had given up his single snare drum for a synthesizer that rattled the old speakers. His mother walked into the living room and sprayed a can of pine-scented air freshener. Her calico cat ran for cover under the couch.

Topher coughed. "Damn, Mom, are you trying to choke me with that stuff?"

"Just getting into the Christmas spirit." Maggie smiled and patted his butt. "Don't just sling those lights on—place them evenly. I want everything to look nice when you bring Alex here."

"I told you, we haven't decided what's happening for Christmas. In fact, it might be better if he goes to his family's gathering and I come back here." He straightened the lights a little. "I can't predict what mood he'll be in. Sometimes he's all up for coming, and other times he acts like it would be such a chore."

"You tell him to get his act together. He doesn't know how lucky he is to have you." She started handing him ornaments. They were all new ornaments—none he had ever seen before. Apparently noticing his stare, Maggie confessed. "Yes, I bought new decorations at the after-Christmas sales last year. Those old ones were worn and scratched."

"But some of those were from 86th Street. Didn't you keep any from when I was little?"

"Don't panic. Anything that wasn't broken or chewed up by rats is in a box in the basement. I thought you might want them." She handed him crystal icicles.

"Is everything you bought clear or white?" He shuddered at the thought of an icy tree with packages wrapped in cold white paper.

"Yes. Isn't it a great idea—so formal and elegant?"

"Don't you want a cozy tree with reds, greens, and blues?"

"No, I had that mismatch for years. This year, the tree will look like it came out of a magazine." Maggie smiled with pride and pointed to a stack of magazines on the coffee table fanned out into a perfect arc.

Since his grandmother had died, the house and his mother had taken on a new personality. The look of clutter had left the house, and in its place came a stark, clean, cosmopolitan air. It didn't feel like home anymore—nowhere felt like home.

"Try to get Alex to come here for Christmas. When we first met, everything was so hurried, and I haven't been back to Charlotte since." His mother rearranged the lights.

His mother's first meeting with Alex had not been something he had strategically planned, but more of a natural occurrence. She had been on her way to Myrtle Beach and stopped to spend the night with Topher.

"Mrs. Langston." Alex stood and nodded when Topher and Maggie arrived at the restaurant for dinner.

She reached out to shake his hand. But instead of a handshake, Alex lifted her hand to his lips. She giggled.

He's got her now. Topher made all the introductions, and they followed the maître d' to the linen-covered table in the corner. The restaurant occupied the entire top floor of a downtown office tower and provided floor-to-ceiling views of the city skyline lights.

"I heard the most wonderful things about you," Alex said to Maggie.

"And I hear about you all the time. In fact, my son gushes on and on about 'Alex did this' or 'Alex said that.' You, dear boy," she leaned in toward him, "have captured my son's heart."

"Mom," Topher pleaded. "I feel like I'm eight years old and you're talking to my teacher."

"It was the funniest thing," she continued to address Alex, "he had a crush on his third grade teacher. She looked like Mary Tyler-Moore, and it was so precious I had to tell her about it."

"Funny," Alex raised an eyebrow at Topher, "I would have guessed the teacher would have looked more like Bjorn Borg or John Travolta."

Great, he's driving the gay point home.

Topher's mother laughed. "That boy—"

"I'm sitting right here, Mom."

"I know, dear," she said and patted his hand. "It's true, Topher always seemed to have a hero worship thing going on with the men on television. And who wouldn't? Look at you, Alex. You are perfect." She reached over to touch Alex's cheek.

On their drive back to Topher's house, his mother kept going on about how wonderful Alex was. "The man is an attorney, he's well-read, he is definitely handsome—all said, I say he's a keeper."

In the reflected light from the dashboard, he could see Maggie's smile. "Thanks, Mom. I was a bit worried you wouldn't like him."

"If you're happy, that's all that matters."

Happy? Topher handed his mother another string of Christmas lights for her tree. *Is that all that matters?*

THE NEXT DAY, Topher drove south on I-77. The traffic thickened as he traveled through Statesville and on into Charlotte. *My life had such purpose, a direction: I wanted to paint.* Designing ads and brochures for corporate clients didn't fit his goals. The images of his dreams floated through his mind like clouds, puffy and scattered.

I haven't painted since this summer. I'm not sure if art means that much anymore. The dreams in his mind turned wispy and thin.

Topher noticed the sky had darkened, and rain dripped across his windshield. Once home, he dropped his bags by the door and checked his answering machine. There was one new message. He hit the Play button and waited.

"Hey, Toph, Alex here. Guess you went to your mother's for Thanksgiving. Hope you had a good time. I went to Dustin and Erik's. We had a great time. They asked about you. Dustin said you had left town for Thanksgiving. I wasn't sure what to tell them. I just said you went to Bristol. I hadn't heard from you in a week. I wasn't sure.

"Is that the way I'm supposed to know where you are? Hear it from someone else? Why didn't you tell me? Wait, I'm sorry. But, if you want this relationship to work, you have to have a little respect for my feelings."

"Asshole," Topher commented, and reached for the phone to call Alex back, but stopped as the message continued.

"I know things haven't been the way you want them to be. I do care about you, or I wouldn't be babbling on this damn machine. Call me when you get in. Please."

Topher sat down on his bed and replayed the message. Did he want to talk to Alex now? The house was still gray and cold. He hadn't switched on any lights or turned up the heat. He lay on the bed staring at the ceiling, thinking.

He opened his eyes, and the setting November sun had left the bedroom black, except for the bright red display on his alarm clock that read 6:32. Topher couldn't determine if it was morning or night. As he pushed himself off the bed, the phone rang loud and intrusive, shaking him fully awake. He answered the ring.

"Hello?"

"Are you asleep? Are you alone? Let me talk to him, whoever he is." Dustin's voice chided Topher. "Where have you been? Erik asked Alex for both of you to come for Thanksgiving, but to our surprise, Alex was solo. He didn't seem to have his facts straight on your whereabouts. Have you found another cowboy?"

"Oh, shit. Have the rumor mills started, or did you just come up with that one?"

"That's one I just thought of. Is it true?" Dustin asked.

"Is what true?" Erik's voice joined from their other extension.

Dustin answered his partner. "Topher has a new cowboy."

"Really? Who?" Erik replied. "Anyone we know?"

"Don't know. I have seen him check out a few guys at the gym."

"Can I just hang up and let the two of you talk to each other?" Topher pushed into the excited conversation. "No, there is no one else. I went to Bristol to my mother's. I didn't tell Alex because I wanted to see if he would even notice I was gone."

"Well, well, well. This is even better than another man," Erik cooed. "What are you doing for dinner?"

"Yes, come over, and we'll go to dinner and talk," urged Dustin.

"Dinner? Is it dinnertime? I thought it might be morning. No, thanks, I want to unpack and call Alex."

"Okay, what about tomorrow night, or at least lunch on Monday?" Dustin asked.

"Lunch Monday. Dusty, I'll see you at work, and we'll meet Erik downtown for lunch. Okay? Thanks for calling."

Glad to be off the phone, he sat there for a moment. Saturday night, and he didn't want to be alone. Erik and Dustin were too much of a happy, longtime couple—more married than any straight couple he'd met, and he just couldn't face a Saturday night as the third wheel. He needed to talk things over with Alex. He dialed his number.

"Hey, it's Topher."

"How are you? I'm sorry about that message I left. How's your mom?" Alex avoided following the tracks of his emotional message.

"Mom's fine. I want to talk about us. Let's go have dinner."

"I'm really tired, and I'd like to just stay in tonight."

"Can I come over?" Topher almost pleaded.

"Not tonight, maybe tomorrow."

"Fine." Topher slammed down the phone. *How does he manage to do that*? His thoughts made him angry. *How does he turn every situation around so that it's me asking for permission to see him?* Then the answer hit him. *He knows I'm in love, and I won't break up. I'll show him. Maybe it's time he didn't feel so secure about me.*

He turned on the bedroom lights and looked for clean clothes. On his bed, he laid out black Levi's, boots he'd bought in Dallas, and a black T-shirt, and then headed for a long hot shower to plan his evening.

His mood shift neared its destination. He felt the weight of Alex and his noncommittal attitude fall with his jeans and sweatshirt as he undressed and stepped into the steaming shower. The lyrics of Diana Ross drowned out the noisy water flow. She sang about a lover not treating her right. His muscles ached after the long drive and the conversation with Alex, but the water soothed them as it ran over his face and shoulders and down his back. Pushing his hair back out of his eyes, he squinted at the harsh overhead light. He reached out of the shower and flipped the light off. Total darkness enveloped him with the warmth of the surging water striking his body. He leaned back so the spray hit him full force in the face. His eyes closed against the strike of the water, he imagined a mysterious lover, handsome, loving, available. The caressing hot streams felt like hands tracing down his neck, across his chest and stomach. Lower and lower his own hands went. The slickness of his skin, the sensation of fingertips and hot water tracing the length of his cock, the stirring of his sexual desire created a more detailed image of his phantom lover. In his mind, the mystery man's face began to appear. It was Alex. Topher's eyes sprang open, and the fantasy was gone.

Wrapped in a towel, Topher called Daryl to see what time he was going to the bar. He knew there was no need to ask "if," just "when." They made plans to meet at 10:30 at a popular bar on Freedom Drive. Never being much into the "bar scene," he felt nervous, but excited about doing something different.

At 10:15, Topher dressed and was halfway down the stairs when he turned and went back to the bedroom. Just as he stuffed two condoms in his wallet, the phone rang. He almost answered it thinking it might be Daryl, but then if it was Alex, he wanted him to think he was out—which he would be in two minutes.

"Topher. It's Alex. Just calling to say goodnight. No need to call back. I'm heading to bed in a few minutes. I have to take a rain check on tomorrow too. We can get together early in the week. Bye."

"That's it. You don't have time for me, and I don't have time for you." Topher erased the message and left.

WALKING INTO THE dark smoky bar, Topher looked for Daryl. He didn't see him, so he went to the bar and ordered a beer. *This is so weird. Everyone is either in their twenties or close to fifty. Where are all the guys my age? Home with their partners.* His thoughts were interrupted by a man who had just walked up and spoken to him.

"Hi, my name's Jerry. I haven't seen you here before, but, you look familiar."

Fresh meat—Daryl's prediction came back to Topher. He looked at Jerry to decide if he should brush him off or talk to him until Daryl showed up. He wasn't a bad looking guy, blond (but he never cared much for blonds), only one visible piercing (his left ear), probably in his late twenties, too much jewelry, but his eyes drew Topher's attention. He wasn't surveying the crowd for his next target or scanning Topher's body. He was looking directly into his eyes. Finally, he answered, "Topher, nice to meet you."

As they tried to talk over the loud music, Daryl appeared with a man in tow. "Glad you made it." He did the Hollywood kiss—into the air by each cheek. "This is my love of the night. Wait, don't tell me...Steve?"

The man corrected him. "Simon."

Topher turned to Jerry and laughed.

"And who do we have here?" Daryl asked.

"Daryl, this is Jerry. Jerry, Daryl and Simon," he said.

"Well, baby. It looks like you do fine without me. I'm going to heaven tonight with Steve here—"

"Simon," Topher corrected.

"Whoever. If this doesn't work out, I'll be back." He looked Jerry up and down then whispered into Topher's ear, "I'd do him."

"Thanks for your approval." Topher waved good-bye as Daryl led Simon through the crowd and out the door.

He turned to Jerry. "You know, you look familiar, too."

"Oh?"

"Yeah, I know. You work at Halstead Lumber."

Jerry smiled nervously. "Yeah, have we met before?"

"Just briefly. I came in there with my friends, Erik and Dusty, to help them get cabinets for the kitchen they're remodeling."

"Oh, good." He relaxed. "I thought I might have met you in a bar and been rude. That would have been a terrible start. My grandparents own Halstead. I work there, and I do some real estate on the side. What do you do?"

"Graphic artist. I work with Daryl and my friend Dusty, who was with me at the lumber yard."

Jerry moved in closer. "Are you seeing anyone?"

"That's hard to explain."

Jerry moved back a little.

Topher laughed. "No, don't worry. It's nothing weird. I dated the same guy for almost a year. I was more committed to the relationship than he was. So, I decided I needed to make a break." He mentally punched himself—*Damn, did I have to slice open a vein and tell everything to the first person who walks up?*

"Sorry to hear it. Been there, too. I dated the same guy for four years, and we broke up a year ago. It would be nice if we could get a guarantee on relationships."

Wow, he's actually listening to me. A distraction came from the front door. People were yelling and running out. "What's going on?" Topher went toward the door, and Jerry followed.

A woman looking out at the parking lot said, "Someone just got beat up. Some of the guys chased them down the street, but they got away."

Topher's heart raced. He was never around this and had forgotten how cruel and dangerous some people were. A group of people rushed into the parking lot with cell phones beeping and calling for help.

Topher and Jerry tried to see what had happened. Pushing through the crowd, Topher saw Daryl lying on the gravel, bloodied and holding his side. Simon, also bruised and bleeding, held Daryl's head in his lap. Everyone else stood back waiting for the ambulance. Topher crashed through the circle of onlookers. He sat down beside Daryl and held his hand. "Are you all right?"

"I'll live. They hit me in the face. I might not be as pretty as you for the next couple of weeks, but I'll regain my title." He chuckled, but grabbed his side in pain. A deep gash bled across his cheekbone, and his split lower lip slurred his speech. "Look at them, all afraid to help me because I'm bleeding. I'm not positive. I'm safe to touch."

Topher started to cry. "I know. Everyone's just scared. Don't blame them. Did you see who did it?"

"White guys. Can you believe it? On Freedom Drive? I thought if I ever got attacked on Freedom Drive, it would be brothers trying to rob me." He coughed and held his side. "These assholes didn't want money. They just wanted to beat up a queer, and to make it better for them, they found a black queer."

"Hold still. The ambulance will be here soon." Topher looked up at Simon. "Are you all right?"

"Yeah, I'm okay. They jumped us as we opened the car door. Daryl kicked one of them in the balls, so they all went for him, and only turned on me when I tried to stop them."

Jerry shook Topher's shoulder. "I hear the ambulance."

"Jerry, I'm going to the hospital with Daryl and Steve—uh, Simon."

"I'll come too," he said.

"No, let me do it. I'll call you at the lumber yard next week, if that's okay, and let you know how they are."

"That would be fine. If you need me, I'm in the book. Jerry Halstead."

"Thanks." He turned his attention to Daryl and Simon, then back to Jerry. "Why would someone do this?"

"I don't know," he said. "I get mad every time I hear about stuff like this. Bigoted county commissioners, hell, remember Jesse Helms—the bastard kept getting elected. Hate, it's everywhere. In North Carolina, nothing a bunch of rednecks do should surprise you."

"But it does. What have we done to fill them with so much hate?" Topher wiped his eyes.

The crowd began to separate as the ambulance arrived. Topher followed it to the hospital, and they allowed him to stay with Daryl all night.

ALEX SAT ON the couch in his townhouse facing Topher. "I'm glad Daryl is okay, nothing but a cracked rib and a couple of stitches.

No leads on the guys who did it."

"You talked to the police?" Topher asked.

"Yeah. All they know is that it was two young, white guys—"

"I wish I had been there when Daryl bashed them in the balls." Topher stood up and paced in front of the couch. "God, this pisses me off."

"Sit down. Getting mad won't accomplish anything." Alex grabbed his hand and pulled him back to the couch.

"You know," Topher sighed, "this really opened my eyes to what goes on here. You and I are lucky to be where being gay isn't an issue. Our friends, gay and straight, don't have a problem with us. We don't push it on anyone. We're just trying to live in peace—like everyone. I just don't get it. But to realize we wouldn't be safe in a bar parking lot is disturbing." Topher folded his arms across his chest.

Alex rubbed his shoulder. "If a gay basher wants to be sure of finding a gay man, that's the first place to look. By the way, I didn't think you liked going to bars."

Topher's mind left Daryl and focused on Alex. "I was tired of being alone." He shifted on the couch to face Alex. "I want someone who wants to be with me, and I feel like you don't want to. No, sometimes I know you do, but I want someone who's there with as much enthusiasm and happiness as I have. I know I don't make you happy."

Alex was silent for a minute. "You're right. You don't make me happy. You can't make me anything. I'm responsible for my own happiness and you for yours."

Topher waited for more. Finally, he realized that was all Alex had to say, so he said it. "What does this mean? Are we breaking up?"

"I don't want you out of my life." Alex studied the floor, then looked directly into Topher's eyes. "Let's take some time off and rethink what we want and need."

This is it. All the time and effort put into this relationship and it's over. Tears began to well up in his eyes. "Why did it take this long to realize? I should have known you would never love me. I just kept hoping...eventually..."

"And I might love you one day," Alex offered. "It's just not the time, yet."

"I'm not waiting anymore, Alex. If you cared anything about me, at any time, you wouldn't string me along like this. I won't let you. It's over. I still love you, I can't just turn that off, but I won't continue this farce with me playing the fool." He stood to leave.

"Topher, I care about you, and I want you to be happy. It hurts to know I put you through this. You do what you need to do. Hate me, date other people, or whatever, just remember, I'm here for you. I'm your friend, and I don't want to lose you completely." His voice cracked. "I'm not walking away from you. I'll be here. There's no one else in my life. I just need to clear things in my own head before we go further."

Topher crossed the room. Before closing the door behind him, he turned and said, "We've gone as far as we can. I love you, Alex. Goodbye."

Chapter Seven

"OKAY, TELL ME, what's going on?" Dustin yelled over the roar of the whirlpool. "You canceled lunch on us, and I'm just now catching up with you."

Topher pointed to his ear and shook his head, trying to indicate to Dustin he couldn't hear him, but that just made Dustin more determined to communicate. Although they were the only two men in the whirlpool, Dusty moved within inches of Topher.

"Can you hear me now?" Dustin yelled, the sound bouncing off the tile walls.

"Get back. If someone should walk by, this would look funny."

"What? It would look like we're talking."

"No, it would look like we're cruising each other."

"I've been married so long, I forgot how to cruise. Am I doing it right?" Dustin laughed. "So, tell me about Alex. What's happening?"

After recounting the story about their breakup, and the 'Daryl bashing' as Daryl had started referring to it, Topher concluded, "That's where we are. Same as always. I'm not sure it's completely over. He's a little more vocal about his feelings now than he was before, but he's still not ready to commit emotionally. I decided not to wait. I'm going on with my life, and I have a date with the cabinet man from Halstead Lumber this Friday night."

"Get outta here." Dustin reached for his towel. "You don't wait around."

Topher noticed Dustin's towel was on the "E" hook. "E for Easton," Topher commented.

Dusty smiled. "Nope, E for Erik."

"How sweet, and I thought you chose that hook for your last name. If that's the method, my towel will be constantly moving up and down the alphabet," he joked. A relationship like Dusty and Erik's, solid and loving, that was the sort of thing that inspired him, not the bar life of Daryl where he would have to seek and cultivate a wide range of friends and lovers.

He wished he could be more outgoing, and keep up friendships with a lot of people, but he fumbled in small talk. "What am I going to talk to the cabinet man about?" he asked Dustin.

"Don't worry. Go to a movie or a concert. You can discuss that." He opened his locker, and started to pull on his Brooks Brothers boxers. "Why don't Erik and I go to dinner with you? No, you should have a first date alone. If it makes it to a second, we can all go to dinner."

Wait, Erik and Alex have been friends for years. Is this going to fly? Who gets the friends in a divorce? Topher decided to keep them out of the mess. "Thanks for the offer, but let me go this alone. I want him to like me for me, not for my wonderful friends."

Dustin grinned while buttoning his shirt. "Okay, we'll try to stay out of any budding romances, but when you start picking out china patterns, call me—you haven't got a clue." He laughed. "You didn't even know what a charger was."

"I never needed one. If I can't eat off it, I don't want it on the table," Topher said. He already missed the comfortable weekends with Alex. Prospects of a first date made their relationship seem better than it was. "Have you two seen Alex lately?" He asked the question hoping they hadn't. *Let him be sitting at home alone poring over legal briefs, and missing me.*

"Get dressed and call the cabinet man." Dustin propped his shoe on the bench to tie it. "Don't wait around for Alex. If he thinks you still care for him, nothing will change, and you'll get strung along like a calf to slaughter just waiting for him to get bored and the ax to fall. You don't want to end up as veal parmesan, do you?"

"You're starting to use food analogies. It must be your dinner time." Topher began dressing. "It's so hard not to think about him, or want to see him. I don't know about Jerry—"

"Who?" Dustin asked.

"The cabinet man. Anyway, I'm too tired to try a new relationship."

"Wait. It's not a new relationship. It's a date. No one expects you to fall in love. Just go out and have a nice dinner. Get to know him, and then decide if you click." Dustin looked so imposing in his suit that Topher pulled on his pants and stood up to be eye to eye.

"Advice, advice, all I get is advice. I understand what you're saying, and sometimes I jump ahead in my thinking, but..." A heavy sigh escaped his lips. "I know you're right. One date is nothing. We might end up being really good friends."

"Right, that's one advantage of being gay. We get to date our best friends." Dustin slapped him on the back, and walked toward the door of the locker room with a John Wayne swagger. He tossed his towel in the bin and yelled back, "Take a chance. Don't end up veal."

THE LOW ROAR of conversation drowned out the soft music of the restaurant on East Boulevard where Topher told Jerry they'd meet.

The restaurant was in an old house named after its address, 300 East, and its customers were as diverse as the neighborhoods surrounding it. Gay, straight, and interracial couples mingled comfortably together. Everyone was relaxed—except for Topher. He sat at the bar waiting, worrying, checking the door. He felt a bead of sweat roll down from under his arm, and rubbed his elbow against his side hoping the perspiration wouldn't show through this light blue shirt. He took another drink of beer, and smiled at the bartender, Brenda. She winked and finished making drinks for one of the waiters.

"Toph, you look as nervous as a whore in church. It's just a date." Brenda emptied his ashtray.

He had known Brenda and her lover, Jennifer, for several years. Jennifer had recently left town to pursue a career in Arizona as a Reiki therapist, and Brenda had stayed in Charlotte.

"I'm just out of practice with dating. How about you? You dating much?" he asked.

"As a matter of fact, no. Jennifer and I have talked a lot on the phone, and I might just pull up stakes and go to Sedona to be with her. The only problem is my father. He's not doing too well after this last stroke, and I can't bear to think of him here alone."

Topher lit another cigarette. "What about your brother? Can't he help out?"

"Excuse me a minute." She poured another beer for a man at the end of the bar and collected his money. After gathering up a few empty glasses, she came back. "Ted and his wife are busy with their two kids in Wilmington. I'm the one with 'no family,' so it falls on me to take care of Dad. I don't mind. He will always come first in my life, but I feel like I lost Jennifer."

"That's tough. I'm glad my mother is in good health. Yeah, it seems the unmarried kids end up taking care of the elderly parents."

Brenda wiped the bar with a towel as she talked. "It's very subtle, but it's just another way our relationships aren't seen to be as important as opposite-sex ones. I'm not blaming Ted or his wife, but I have a life too. They could help out."

His date walked up to Topher and patted him on the back. "Hello." Jerry sat down on the stool next to him.

"Hey, Jerry. Thanks for meeting me here." Topher smiled, although he felt like every eye in the place watched him because he was with someone other than Alex.

Brenda took Jerry's drink order and gave them some privacy.

"I'm glad we could get together for dinner. How's your friend?" Jerry leaned toward Topher; his breath smelled like coffee.

Backing away a little, Topher's mind raced: *Friend? Does he mean Alex? No, he doesn't know Alex.* "Oh, Daryl. He's doing much better. He'll be back at the bars by next weekend. He's afraid everyone will forget him if he stays away too long."

"Any news on who did it?"

"No, and I don't think the police care. Just another fag-bashing, in their view. This town makes me sick sometimes. To be such a 'progressive' city, it's about as backward as any hick town in the eastern part of the state." He caught himself jumping onto a hot issue even before they had had their first drink. "Sorry, I'm just a little pissed about the whole thing."

Jerry smiled. "I've lived here all my life, and you wouldn't believe the changes in the past fifteen to twenty years—not just economically, but socially. There was a time when you would never hear anything about gays. Now, the newspaper and television stations do stories portraying us realistically, not just stories about the fringe—drag queens, leather men, and all the other stuff that scares the family-values folks." He took another drink of his beer.

"That's true, although the radio stations still air morning personalities who make fag jokes." Topher snuffed out what remained of his cigarette. "I'm glad we have a liberal newspaper. If it weren't for the *Charlotte Observer*, I'd have bailed out years ago. It's good to see acceptance when you get surrounded by conservative politicians spouting hate and Bible verses."

"Wow, you get right to the point. I was worried about making small talk, and here you are getting political." Jerry laughed, and put his hand on Topher's shoulder.

That's a little too friendly. He flashed Brenda a distressed grin, almost a grimace.

Brenda dropped a bowl of pretzels in front of them. "Eat up, boys. I just put your name on the list for dinner. It should be about thirty minutes. Sorry."

"Oh, that's all right," Jerry replied with a toothy smile.

She looked at Topher, and winked. "I'll see if I can bump you up the list."

"Thanks, Brenda." Topher turned back toward Jerry. He wasn't that bad of a guy. Kind of cute, a bit younger than Topher liked, an extrovert—not bad at all, but bottom line: he wasn't Alex. He couldn't say exactly why he craved Alex's company, or why he was so indifferent toward Jerry. Alex seemed to know him; they had history together. The thought of establishing a new relationship overwhelmed him.

Over dinner, they talked about work, Topher's dream of painting for a living, and Jerry's volunteer activities at a hospice. After dinner, Jerry suggested going for coffee, but Topher turned him down. Then, he asked Topher, "Your paintings sound intriguing. Could I see some of your work?"

"That would be nice, but not tonight, I have an early day tomorrow." They stood in the parking lot as the cold wind blew gunmetal gray clouds quickly across the night sky. Topher longed to ride one of the clouds away. He noticed Jerry watching him watching the clouds. *What am I waiting for? I don't want to kiss him goodnight out here. I'm not sure I even want to kiss him.* "I had a nice time, Jerry. Goodnight." He held out his hand.

Jerry's smile faded as he looked at Topher's outstretched hand. He shook it, and said, "Thanks, I had a great time. Do you think we might get together again?"

Topher's body tensed. Should he, when he would really rather stay home? But then, what's holding him back? This was just one date, and Alex had only popped into his head about 32 times during the two-hour date. "Why not?"

"SO, WHO ARE you bringing to my party?" Myra asked.

Topher looked at the gleaming, crowned Bank of America building towering above them as they walked to lunch. He flashed back to the same view from Alex's bedroom window. He smiled. "I don't know yet. I would have more fun with Alex—maybe. Jerry and I are so new to each other. It might not be a good idea to throw him into a room full of strangers."

"Keep talking. You're convincing yourself to bring Alex." Myra steered him into Founders Hall. "I want you to bring the one you'll have the most fun with. No one is holding a gun to your head saying, 'Date someone new.' You can even come alone. You'll know almost everyone there. In fact, no—well, maybe..." her voice trailed off.

"What?"

"I'm inviting this guy I work with—"

"No. No fix-ups," he said.

She countered, "But he would be great with you. His name is Michael, and he's very nice—"

"Didn't you just say, 'No one is holding a gun to your head,' or did I imagine it?"

"Okay, I just want you to be happy." Myra stopped, and stared into his eyes. "Bring Alex, or bring Jerry, or come alone. Whatever you're comfortable with. You'll be among friends."

"Thanks. I just feel so overwhelmed lately." They stood in the frescoed lobby with the lunchtime crowd hurrying around them. "On one hand, I want to stay with Alex where it's cozy and known, but on the other, I'd like to get to know myself again, without Alex or anyone else. Do you know what I mean?" He noticed Myra's expression: almost blank, but with a tinge of recognition.

"Yeah, I think so. Of course, I've been with Gil for so long, we've almost become the same person."

"God, I hope not."

"He's been great. Just wait till the party, you'll see."

He grinned for her benefit, hoping it was true.

Chapter Eight

GIL WANTED TO make love to Myra. The yellow haze from a streetlight outside their bedroom window granted a shadowy image of her sleeping next to him. Before the miscarriage, he wouldn't have thought twice about rolling her over and waking her up with a little midnight mischief, but now, she seemed so fragile and unreachable. Her breathing raised and lowered her side in slight movements. She wore a flannel nightgown that most men would have found unappealing, but Gil loved the feeling of it against his skin and would leave it between them, grinding the soft material up and down her with his hips until he pulled the gown up and entered her. He couldn't take the thoughts any longer.

"Myra, you awake?" He nudged her shoulder with his finger. "Myra?"

She slept.

"Myra, baby, I was thinking about you," he whispered into her ear. "I miss being with you. You look so sexy tonight."

Slow, steady breathing.

He sighed, and lay back down. *Did she really have a miscarriage, or is this something to get attention?* His thoughts began to fade. *How will I know when she's ready again?* Slowly, he fell into a light sleep.

GIL WATCHED MYRA set his breakfast in front of him: scrambled eggs, bacon, sausage, biscuits with gravy, and grits. Already dressed for work, she stood in the doorway of the kitchen eating a bowl of cereal.

"Come over here, and eat with me." Gil motioned to the chair across the table.

"I'm in a hurry. If I don't leave in five minutes, I'll get caught in the peak of rush hour and be late. Oh, Topher wants me to go to the gym with him one day this week. He says it will give me more energy."

Good. You need it.

"And, with Christmas coming, exercising will help keep my weight down. I'm really kind of excited about it. I'm going to take an aerobics class at lunch tomorrow, and maybe meet Topher after work on Wednesday. Is that okay if I come in late Wednesday night?"

He considered it. "What time would you be home?"

"Not too late, maybe 7:00?"

"That would be okay. If I get hungry before you get home, I can start dinner."

Myra stared at him with her mouth open. "You are going to start dinner? Well, thank you."

He laughed. "Sure, I made dinner before."

She walked over and hugged him. "That's wonderful. Thanks."

After she left, Gil piled his dishes in the sink, and dressed for work. *Why is she on this exercise kick? The doctor did tell her she needed more physical activity—I take that to mean having more sex, not going to an aerobics class.* He winked at himself in the bathroom mirror, and walked into the extra bedroom where Myra had collected items for her Christmas party: two punch bowls with cups, beer mugs, ice buckets, serving trays, and bulk packages of paper napkins and red plastic plates.

He imagined lining up the punch bowls and cups on a fence, and picking each one off with a perfect shot from his new gun. The beer mugs were safe; he could always find a use for them, but punch bowls and their little delicate cups were useless.

The thought of the gun brought an uneasy feeling to Gil. His left eye twitched, as a faint pain shot through it. He blinked and rubbed his eye. *A grown man can have a gun if he wants a gun. I'll have one. The guys at work have them. I'm not afraid of a little pistol. There are no children in the house.* His next thoughts came out loud. "So, why am I keeping it in the truck? I need that gun to defend my home and my wife." He made a gun with his right hand pointing his thick index finger at the doorway, and pressed his thumb down to shoot the imaginary intruder. *Maybe I should get Myra one, too. She has to drive downtown everyday. She can't defend herself—she's practically helpless. Where's my damn wallet?* As he walked back to the front room, the television caught his attention. *Good Morning America* was airing a segment on working women.

"Damn women," Gil complained back to the smirking Charlie Gibson, "you can't make them stay home where they belong. They get a job, and a little money in the bank, then all they want to do is run the roads. Going to the mall, going to the grocery store, going to the flea market, going to hell in a hand basket." A commercial showed a model with stay-on lipstick grabbing and kissing men to prove it. "While they're running the roads, they're putting on makeup. Shit." He clicked off the television, dropped the remote on the couch, and headed out the door.

PULLING INTO MRS. Weaver's driveway, Gil hoped she had coffee brewing. He loaded up his sprayer for the routine treatment.

"Good morning, Gil." Mrs. Weaver opened the door, and stood back. "It's good to see you."

"Yeah, I'm here like clockwork. By the way, thanks again for giving me Mr. Weaver's old pipes. They really added to my collection. You know, it's funny how some things with so little dollar value can bring so much joy." He smiled down at her.

"You are very welcome."

He didn't respond, letting the conversation lull into silence.

"Well," the old woman ventured, and then looked down at the floor.

He waited.

"Uh, Gil," she began again, "would you like some coffee to drink before you get started?"

"Maybe one cup. I got a lot of houses to do today." He followed her into the kitchen, and sat down at the small table next to the window. A box of doughnuts sat on the countertop next to the sink; he fixed his eyes on it.

"Here you go. Sugar and cream are on the table." She turned, looking in the same direction as him. "Wouldn't you take a doughnut, too?"

"Thank you. You're so good to me. My wife doesn't treat me as well as you do." He grabbed a doughnut from the box she held in front of him. "Yeah, she takes off to work in the morning as fast as she can, and now she tells me she's going to start going to the gym after work. Women just don't tend to their men like they used to."

"A little exercise is good for her—and women today are more independent than I was when I was younger." She sat down across from him. "In fact, after Albert died, I had to take over a lot of things I never thought about: getting the car inspected, filing my tax returns, getting someone to clean the gutters. I was overwhelmed."

"Women shouldn't have to deal with that stuff. It's too much for them."

"Why, Gil, are you a... What did they call it in the seventies? A male chauvinist?" She laughed a little, and patted his hand.

The old woman's spunkiness made his mind spin. She wasn't supposed to disagree with him. His mother never did. She was starting to piss him off. "No. Men are better at some things. Better able to handle stress, and deal with people—men want to deal with other men, not women."

"Bullshit. Excuse me, but that's what that is, pure bullshit." Her stern face stifled his laughter at her choice of words. "Women are doing just as much now days as men. If Albert had let me do more while he was alive, I wouldn't have been so helpless after he was gone."

"But, Mrs. Weaver, Myra doesn't have good sense. Her best friend is a faggot."

"Gil," she reprimanded.

"And she thinks that's normal."

"Oh? And what's your best friend?"

"My best friend?" He hesitated, thinking. Who would he consider his best friend? "The guys at work. They're just like me."

"Can you talk to them about Myra? When is the last time you all talked like we're talking now?" She raised one eyebrow with the question.

"Men don't talk about personal things to their friends. Only women and fags talk about feelings."

She laughed again. "My boy, what are we doing?" Becoming serious again, she said, "I think men do talk. And please don't use that mean, hateful word to refer to gays. My daughter is gay."

Shit. They're taking over. He shifted in his seat, wiping his hands on his pants. "Sorry, ma'am." *Sorry you got a dyke for a daughter.* "I need to get to work. Thanks for the coffee and doughnuts."

He stood up, and she took hold of his hand. "I don't mean to be hard on you, but try to look at your wife from her side. She's a person, just like you, with hopes and dreams. Share them together before one of you is gone, and the other is sitting alone in a big empty house wishing things had been different."

She'll never leave me. She doesn't have enough sense to survive alone. "Thanks for the advice. We're fine. Thanks."

Chapter Nine

MYRA TRIED ON another dress, midnight-blue with a pattern of faint white roses, a dress she never wore to work, but a 'church' dress. "How about this one?" She wasn't sure—the image in the dresser's mirror reminded her of her mother: matronly, ready for a PTA meeting.

Gil looked her over. "Okay. Those slacks you had on before made your ass look too big."

"Thanks. You know I lost weight," she said.

"Maybe so, but you ain't down enough to wear those." He pulled at his own pants. "Do I have to wear this? Can't I just wear jeans?"

Whose ass is too big now? She rephrased her initial thought. "Those khakis and that dress shirt look great on you. They fit you well." After looking him over again, she realized she meant it. His stomach didn't hang over these pants like it did his jeans, and the button-down denim shirt was loose enough to help hide the beer gut he'd acquired since they married. Looking at him, now, she could see the man she fell in love with six years before. His thick, black hair had body and shine. Brown, bright eyes trimmed with long black lashes seemed deep and dreamy, and when he smiled, dimples framed his straight pearl white teeth like parentheses. *I could have done worse.* But as this occurred to her, he belched and laughed.

"Try to keep that to a minimum, please," she asked.

"Okay, okay. Just wanted to get it out before company got here. It could have been the other end." He laughed, and patted her butt as he left the bedroom. "You know, I like round women," he called back.

She stepped out of the matronly dress and searched her closet for something else. Her weight had dropped some, maybe from the new workout routine, but probably more from the depression of the miscarriage and the worry of Gil's temper, but despite the unpleasant reasons, she smiled at the drape of the silk slip over her hips. For too long, the same slip had pulled at her hips leaving a grin of fabric, mocking her. Her original thought was to buy a new dress, but the time leading up to the party slipped away, and now she was stuck. Forty minutes before the party, and the midnight-blue dress made her look like her mother. Strumming through the closet, she saw a glint of silver—a lamé jacket. She pulled the dress back on and topped it with the silver jacket. She assessed herself in the mirror. *Not bad, a little flashy, but okay for a holiday party.* Finishing up with a pearl necklace and earrings, she heard the doorbell. She rushed down the hall to the living room door, checking the simmering evergreen potpourri on the stove as she passed. One last look at the apartment: ratty couch, clothed with a new sage velour slipcover, television and stand shrouded with a Christmas tablecloth holding a plate of nuts and a red candle, the Christmas tree was lighted and the presents looked festive tucked under it—even though six of them were wrapped empty boxes. She exhaled and opened the door to Topher and Alex.

"Alex?" Myra didn't hide her surprise. "Uh, come on in. Topher, it's great to see both of you." She emphasized the word 'both' to let Topher know she didn't disapprove of him being with Alex again. Topher wore black trousers and a black turtleneck; he reminded her of Cary Grant in *To Catch a Thief*. The artist in him showed by his choice of bohemian dark clothes. Alex was dressed almost identically to Gil. She wondered if they would notice—although, she appraised, his shoes probably cost more than Gil's entire wardrobe.

Topher hugged her. "I wanted to get here a little early to see if you needed any help. The place looks great—Oh, hi Gil." He nodded in Gil's direction.

"Come on in, and get a drink in your hand." Gil slapped Alex on the back, and led him into the kitchen.

"You brought Alex?" Myra whispered to Topher. "Are you two back together?"

He smiled. "I'm not sure. I couldn't think of anyone else I wanted to be with tonight, so I asked him. He wanted to come. He said he missed seeing me. Things are good. I'm happy. It's not a marriage proposal, but it's in the right direction. We have things out on the table, and dealing with them."

"Good. I'm glad." She hugged him again. The doorbell rang just as she squeezed.

"Myra? Your chest just went 'ding dong' when you hugged me." He grinned at her.

"Stop that. You're giddy—I love it." She turned and opened the door.

"Merry Christmas," Tina said as she held out a bottle of wine.

"Thanks. Come on in. Gil's in the kitchen making drinks. Put your order in, and I'll take your coat." She introduced Tina to Topher, and carried the coats back to the bedroom. As she passed the kitchen, she overheard Gil ask Alex, "So, legally, if a wife dies, and there's no will, everything goes to her parents?" *Glad he's making conversation.*

Coming back from the bedroom, Myra noticed Gil, Alex, Topher, and Tina standing around the kitchen sink, sipping their drinks and talking. "If you want to help with the party, keep it in the living room."

"Any party you have will always migrate to the kitchen," Tina replied. "We'll try to get people moving."

"Great, this kitchen is too small for people to gather in."

The doorbell rang, and panic struck Myra. She fanned herself with her hands. All her close friends were there, so these had to be the real guests.

"Okay, everybody out of the kitchen now, and start mingling with each other." Myra rushed to the door. "Someone laugh. Act like you're having a great time."

Topher rubbed her back. "Calm down and enjoy it."

"Save that line for your next date," she said and winked at him.

She opened the door to her coworker, Allen, and his wife, Phyllis. As they entered, Myra saw more people from work getting out of their cars. Topher came up to take Allen and Phyllis' coats.

Phyllis held out her hand. "You must be Myra's husband. I'm Phyllis."

"No," Myra said. "This is my friend Topher. My husband, Gil, is in the kitchen fixing drinks."

Phyllis glanced into the kitchen, and then back at Topher. "Sorry, Myra." She led Allen into the living room to look at the Christmas tree.

"What'd she mean by—" Myra started, but more coworkers walked up. The apartment was filling up, and everyone seemed to be enjoying themselves. A sigh of relief escaped her lips as she leaned against the door. Gil handed out drinks, and laughed with the guests. She hoped he used some tact in his selection of jokes. The more she watched him, the better he looked. They were seldom in a group of people, and she forgot how well he mixed. He was good at first impressions, at small talk, at making the men feel important, and at flirting with the women. She had felt so desirable when they first started dating.

GIL HAD WORKED as a carpenter on his uncle's construction crew. Twenty-seven, tall, trim, muscular, and tanned, his distant Cherokee heritage showed. The long, black hair and dark eyes melted Myra every time she took her afternoon walk. She'd taught elementary school and had the summer off. Although she worked part-time at the Belk department store at Southpark Mall, many afternoons she would be at her apartment. Her after lunch walks would take her past the new construction of another apartment building. A first, she sneaked peeks at a blond guy, but then she saw him up close, and he reminded her of Edgar Winter. Then she saw Gil.

He nailed roof joists down as they craned them up to him. As he stretched and bent in the summer sun, sweat made his bare chest glisten. Myra had stopped to watch the building of the roof. Gil worked harder and harder, nailing the joists down as fast as the crane deposited another one from the pile on the ground. He must have noticed her watching, because when he stopped to wait for the next delivery from the crane, he would lean against the last joist, and stare in her direction.

Day after day, Myra took her walk by the construction site hoping to see Gil. This routine was what Topher called a 'Hot Flash'—someone seen on a regular basis, to have fantasies about, but never talk to because getting to know them would wreck the fantasy. But the more she thought about this beautiful construction worker, the more she wanted to meet him.

"Don't do it, Myra," Topher had warned her. "One word from him and all your illusions will be blown to bits. No one can live up to the person you create in your head."

"But he's so cute. I'll wonder the rest of my life about him if I don't take a chance. Worst case, he's married. Next worst, he's gay—"

"If he is, introduce him to me," Topher said.

"I just want to give it a try. I'm tired of being on my own. Physically, I'm attracted, and he's attracted to me, or acts like he is. I want to see if there could be more."

"Be careful," he warned, "and meet in a very public place for the first date. All you know about him is he's a carpenter, and he looks good sweaty."

"I'm always careful."

After their first date, Gil would stop by her apartment after work and they would drink a beer on the balcony, or they'd go swimming in the complex's pool on Gil's day off.

"Babe, you look so hot in that bikini," Gil had purred in her ear as he rubbed oil on her by the pool. His rough, callused hands caressed her back in such a sensuous movement that it embarrassed her that they were in public. She'd slept with him within the first week, and the only reason it wasn't on the first date was her Southern upbringing.

NOW, AS SHE watched Gil talking with Allen and Tina, she wanted to pull him back to the bedroom to revive that lost passion. Her gaze shifted to Topher and Alex, talking and laughing with each other. Phyllis, Bill, Jenny, John, and Allison talked in another circle. The party floated along. Myra smiled and joined Gil.

"Myra, the party's great. You did a wonderful job," complimented Tina. "Girl, you can help me with my next one."

Wrapping her arms around Gil's waist, Myra hugged him and said, "Gil has helped so much. I couldn't have pulled it off without him."

Tina's reaction puzzled her. She had cast her eyes down as soon as Myra went to Gil, and then walked off without saying anything. Just as she started toward Tina, the doorbell rang again.

Their neighbor, Laurie, came in introducing her new boyfriend, Kyle. She handed Myra a small wrapped box. It was very fragrant, lightweight, and made a shuffling sound. Myra thanked her and placed it under the Christmas tree. "Cosmetics samples," she said under her breath as she passed Topher and Alex.

STANDING BY THE tree, Topher listened to Alex tell about a case he had finished. As Alex spoke, he smiled, and his eyes never left Topher. An invisible bubble dome had descended over the two of them, no outside sounds, no other people, no distractions. Every word between them resounded into a lyrical duet within that dome. Myra had said he was giddy, and he believed he was. He realized they were breathing in unison, like they used to just before falling asleep in each other's arms. Always, when this occurred to him, he became aware of his breathing and tried to modulate it away from Alex's. Breathing together, as one person, pleased him, but then it terrified him. So many friends had died after they could no longer breathe on their own. He remembered it was time for another HIV test. Always negative, but each time, he scanned his memory over the past fifteen or sixteen years, basically his adult life, wondering who was positive and didn't know it, and how safe could anyone be. The bubble dome began to shake. The outside world intruded.

"There's Allison Darris." Alex pointed out a tall, thin woman. "She's one of the top trial attorneys in Charlotte."

"Go introduce yourself. I'm going to get another drink. Want one?" Topher asked.

"No, thanks," Alex scratched his head and frowned, "I need to remember that last case she worked on."

"I'll be right back." Topher steered through the crowd toward the kitchen.

He walked into the kitchen, saying hello to Laurie and Kyle who talked with Myra.

"Myra," Laurie cooed, "would you give Kyle the grand tour of your apartment?"

Myra laughed. "It's just a mirror image of yours."

"That's okay. He'd enjoy it." Turning to Kyle, she nodded for him, "Wouldn't you?"

Kyle shrugged. Myra led him out of the kitchen.

Laurie slinked up to Topher. "I see you here from time to time." She had a voice like Farrah Fawcett on *Charlie's Angels*, all breathy, sweet, and tousled—a voice that soft, straight porn used to tease, to lead, to tempt. It did nothing for him.

He tried to keep from laughing. "Yeah," he replied in his best macho voice, "I like to talk NASCAR with Gil."

That hit the button. Laurie backed him against the counter. She pressed her chest against his left arm, and he felt her hard nipples rubbing his biceps and chest. "I want to get to know you better," she whispered into his ear.

Her hand ran over his chest and across his stomach. As she headed toward his crotch, he pulled away, laughing. "Sorry, I'm not interested. You're rubbing against the wrong tree."

"What do you mean?" She looked offended, so hurt, like a child who'd had her toy taken away.

Topher tried to cushion the rejection. "Laurie, you're a beautiful girl. Any straight man would love to be where I am right now."

"And..." She led him.

"And?" He struggled to understand what she wanted. "The point is I'm not straight." No response from Laurie. "I'm gay. I don't find women sexually exciting. Not even you."

"You're kidding me." She laughed a little, but stopped when Topher didn't laugh, too. "You're queer?"

"No, someone who eats dirt and thinks they live on Mars would be queer. I'm a normal, gay man."

A faint smile crossed her lips, and she shook her head. "What a waste."

Waste? Waste is the space and air someone as empty-headed as you takes up. He took a deep breath, and said, "Honey, nothing is being wasted." He laughed and walked out of the kitchen.

Myra and Kyle returned from their tour of the apartment. As Kyle joined Laurie in the kitchen, Myra took Topher's arm and asked, "You having fun?"

"Straight, single women in their twenties are the horniest people in the world," Topher said. "She went after me like a dog to a steak. 'What a waste.' I hate when women say that. I'm not wasting my life."

"What are you talking about?" Myra asked just as Alex walked up.

Topher recounted the incident to the two of them.

"I think," Alex said, "she meant that it's a waste you don't contribute to the gene pool. I'm sure she meant it as a compliment."

"I didn't take it as a compliment. She was rude."

"She's not very bright, and she can be rude," Myra said, "but she knows a lot about beauty products. And Gil says her tits are perky. Toph, you felt them. Were they firm and perky?"

Topher and Alex laughed as she acted like she was going to rub against Alex's chest. Gil walked up to their circle, "What's so funny?"

"Just talking about how friendly your neighbor Laurie is," Alex said.

Gil looked back at Laurie, and said, "Yeah, she's a little

firecracker. Cute as a puppy's nose, ain't she?"

"You're asking the wrong group," Topher said, then laughed.

"Yeah," Myra said trying to hold back giggles, "Laurie just made a pass at Topher."

Alex raised an eyebrow. "Pass incomplete."

A roar of laughter erupted from the three of them.

A faint smile crossed Gil's face, then he turned and walked away. Topher put his arm around Myra and said, "He just doesn't click in the same tracks as us, does he?"

Myra and Alex drifted away talking to other people. Topher avoided the kitchen and soon found himself in front of Gil again. A once-handsome man who acted like a contemporary version of Burt Reynolds's Trans Am-driving Bandit, Gil chewed a toothpick as he smiled at Topher. "Myra's working out at the gym."

Topher considered Gil's statement, and decided he should say something back. "Yeah, she is."

Gil just stared.

Topher added, "I think she's doing well. She's lost about five pounds already, and I can tell she's getting toned."

"How long before she looks like Laurie?" Gil chuckled.

Topher stood up straight, the disgust he held for Gil, for the abuse of Myra, for Gil's general attitude, honed into a sharp point, and he flung his verbal dart. "Probably the day she walks out on your sorry ass."

"What the hell—"

"Listen, Gil," he said, "she's the best thing that's ever happened to you. Give her some respect, as much respect as she gives you."

"I give her plenty," Gil said. "Besides, you don't know what it's like living with her. Seeing the same woman day after day. Oh, that's right, you won't ever know how a normal man feels about his wife."

"If you're a normal man, I'll be as far from that as I can."

Nearby, Phyllis grabbed Allen's hand and led him to the other side of the room.

"All I'm saying," he said, "is treat her right. Don't compare her to other women. If you have to, keep it to yourself."

Gil put his hands up like he was shooing Topher away. "Don't give me advice on how to handle women. Go back to your boyfriend, cocksucker."

"I'm flattered that you've given my sex life so much thought," Topher shot back. "Odd, I've never thought about what you do in bed. How often do you fantasize about two men having sex?"

He watched Gil's face flush and fists clench before he stomped off. With Gil gone, he realized they had caused a small scene; he hoped Myra hadn't seen it. Why did he allow someone as ignorant as Gil to upset him? He looked for Alex and saw him across the room talking again with Allison, the lawyer. He seemed to be enjoying himself, so why wasn't Topher? One answer: Gil. He had to admit that he had jumped Gil first when he made a rude comment about Myra, but he couldn't stand to hear him say things that would hurt if it ever got back to her.

Okay, forget Gil and enjoy the party.

"Hello. Remember me? I met you in the kitchen. Kyle." Laurie's date held out his hand to Topher.

"Yeah, Kyle. How are you?" He shook Kyle's hand with a firm grip, but Kyle held on longer than was necessary.

"Great. I thought you looked a little familiar. Where do you work?" Kyle stood a little too close.

"I work for an ad agency. What about you?"

"I'm a loan officer for First Catawba. I have a lot of gay clients."

Oh great, here we go again. "That's nice. Are we good clients?"

"The best." Kyle smiled wide. "No kids, lots of disposable income, love to shop, and can pay back a loan fairly easily—great clients." Kyle moved in closer and whispered, "Some of the best looking men I've ever seen."

"We do care about our appearance. Nice clothes, perfect hair, eating right, exercising, over-achievers at work—like you."

Kyle laughed uncomfortably. "So, you work out. Where?"

"The Dowd Y on Morehead."

"Me too. I don't think I've seen you there. I go in the morning before work, or to the Uptown Y at lunch. When do you go?"

Not another closet case looking for a fuck buddy. Get away from this guy quick. He's trouble. "Well, I'm not on a strict schedule," he said, trying to give Kyle no clue as to when he would be there, "but I try to go two or three times a week. You know, just enough so I can have a few beers over the weekend and not end up with a gut."

"It must be working," Kyle said, "you look good to me."

Okay, he's not taking the hint, Topher looked for Laurie. It was easier to deal with a clueless woman than her closeted date.

"Maybe we can meet at the gym and work out together," Kyle suggested.

"Can't, really, I have a hard time sticking to a...a...ah," Topher stammered, "a schedule. I'll think about it, I might know of someone looking for a workout partner. Hey, it wouldn't hurt Gil to get a little exercise. I see your girlfriend talking to him. Why not go ask him now?" He turned and maneuvered his way across the room.

Alex stood by the door, saying good night to Allison Darris and her husband. Topher joined them. After they left, he turned to Alex and asked, "How'd it go?"

"Great. Allison and I are having lunch next week. I didn't ask about opportunities at her firm, but I'm leading up to it."

Kyle walked past them on his way out. "Hope to see you at the gym. Here's my card. Call me."

"Whoa, Kyle. This is my partner, Alex. Alex, Kyle." They shook hands. "You leaving Laurie here?"

"She wanted to stay a little longer. I need to get home, but I'll be at the gym tomorrow about 3:00. Maybe I'll see you."

"I doubt it. I rarely work out on Sunday."

Kyle smiled and repeated the Y's motto, "Mind, Body, Spirit," then he added, "even on Sunday."

"My body rests on Sunday. Bye." Topher closed the door, forcing Kyle outside.

Alex smirked. "Guess I'm not the only one making contacts."

"What a sleaze. He's one of those guys who lurks in the shower, and tries to get a date in the steam room."

A FEW MORE people began to leave, citing baby-sitter's high prices and church the following day. Myra began to relax as the party slimmed down to the closest friends.

A squeaky laugh from Laurie made Myra think a cat had been stepped on, and she turned to see Gil with his arm around her bubbly neighbor's shoulders, the two of them laughing in low hushed tones.

"He can pour on the charm when he wants to, can't he?" Tina's voice startled her.

She turned toward Tina. Her motherly face told Myra they needed to talk in private. "What's wrong?"

"You tell me, Miss Thang. I have never been a big fan of Gil's, but tonight, I can see there's something wrong."

"Wrong?"

"Wrong," Tina repeated. "Wrong in how he refers to you. Wrong in how he looks at you. Wrong in the way he watches the other women at the party. You should be more to him than a meal ticket."

Myra blinked away a tear.

"Oh, baby. I didn't mean to stir up doubts in your mind. I just get so mad when I see a man not treating his woman the way he should." Tina smiled at her, and tried to lighten the mood. "He's off flirting with the women and talking football and guns with the men, and you're in here..."

Guns? Myra's mind went back to the pawnshop where they saw Gil buy the pistol. Panic set in. She felt her face flush, and tiny droplets of sweat broke out on her upper lip. "Jenny," she said to her coworker who was rifling through the cabinets looking for an ashtray, "please tell Gil I went to get more ice." She grabbed Tina's arm and led her back to the bedroom.

Closing the door to the party, Myra walked to the dresser then back to the door, stopped, and paced back to the dresser. She picked up Gil's cell phone charger then returned it to the dresser top. Finally focusing on Tina, she said, "Gil's been very nice since the miscarriage—"

"Miscarriage? What miscarriage?" Tina almost yelled.

Myra pushed the guests' coats to the side and sat on the bed, motioning Tina to join her. "The week before Thanksgiving, I miscarried. Before that, Gil and I fought...more than usual. Rougher than usual."

Tina's face tightened. "Did he cause the miscarriage?"

"No," she said. "It just happened." She looked away to collect her thoughts. "The gun bothers me. When he was a child, he accidentally shot his brother's eye out. They had been shooting at a snake in a field with Gil's BB gun. The BB ricocheted off a rock and came back to hit Buddy's eye."

"Okay, so Gil swore off guns after that?" Tina asked.

"Yeah, at least he had always said that. Buddy doesn't hold anything against him, but it's always weighed heavy on Gil." Myra stood up to pace some more. "So, it worried me when he bought one. And that we stopped having sex." She looked for Tina's reaction.

She rubbed her forehead, then looked back at Myra. "Talk to him. Find out what's going on. Guessing will make things worse."

Nodding her head in agreement, Myra said, "I know, I know, but I get scared I might bring up something to set him off. Sometimes it's better to guess than to risk asking for the truth—better emotionally and physically."

"Maybe a counselor, someone to facilitate, to keep him under control," Tina said.

"You know, that might not be a bad idea. I could say I needed counseling about the miscarriage—"

The bedroom door flung open. "Come on, baby. I'm gonna do you like you never been done—" Gil stumbled in with one hand down Laurie's pants, and the other around her shoulder hanging onto a bottle of merlot.

His face lost all color. No sound came from his mouth, but his lips formed the words, "Oh, fuck."

Chapter Ten

"YOU BASTARD! GET that bitch out of my house!" Myra's voice boomed through the apartment.

Topher looked around. Only two other people, Myra's co-worker, John, and his wife, Jenny, were left in the living room, and they quickly excused themselves out the front door. He looked to Alex as Myra and Gil yelled more. Laurie ran by them with her pants unzipped. *That son of a bitch*! Topher stormed toward the bedroom.

"Toph, wait." Alex followed him. "Stay out of it."

He stopped when he saw Tina coming up the hall. She had just closed the bedroom door behind her. She took Topher by the arm, leading him back toward the kitchen and to the living room.

As she walked, she talked in a low, soft tone. "Let them work this out. Outsiders will only make the argument worse. Besides, it will embarrass Myra more if she realizes we all know."

Topher pulled loose from Tina's grip. "He's hit her before."

"I know. I know."

"I'm not leaving this apartment."

"Okay, just sit down out here." She pushed him toward the couch where Alex had just sat down.

The dull, white walls of the room oddly soothed his nerves, but as Topher began to calm, a loud smack rang through the apartment. Before Tina or Alex could grab him, he ran down the hall, hitting the closed bedroom door at full speed. The thin hollow door splintered and swung open hard, knocking Gil down on the floor. Topher fell on top of him.

"Get the hell off me." Gil grunted. He pushed Topher off, rolling him over the matted beige carpet into the footboard of the brass bed.

Myra huddled in a corner with the stinging red outline of Gil's hand across her face. Gil pulled himself up and headed toward Myra. Topher, still on the floor, grabbed Gil's left foot and pulled back hard.

Gil teetered on one foot, and then crashed into the corner of the dresser. Blood streamed out of a gash on his chin. Kicking at Topher to get loose, he got up and continued toward Myra.

"Bitch, tell your fag boyfriend to mind his own business before I kill him!" Gil then turned to Topher.

Alex and Tina entered the room and helped Topher get back to his feet. He shook off their hold. "If you have a problem with me, don't put her in the middle of it."

"Everything doesn't revolve around you, Fag Boy. This is between me and Myra." He reached down and jerked her up by the arm. She continued crying.

Tina pleaded, "Gil, let Myra go. You're stronger than her, she can't fight back—"

"Shut up, you nigger bitch. Get the hell out of my house! All of you!" He looked back at Myra, her head down, whimpering. "Tell them to get out."

She cried.

"Tell them." He shook her. "Tell them, bitch." He shoved her back against the wall.

Topher jumped him from behind. His right fist caught Gil just below his rib cage, sinking in his side like he had punched a pile of bread dough.

With his hands free of Myra, Gil swung around with his left, hitting Topher's cheek. Alex charged at him. Gil fended him off with a right to his gut.

Doubling over, Alex went down.

Topher responded with quick left and right punches into Gil's stomach.

Gil stumbled back to the dresser, righted himself, then opened the top drawer. His hands grasped for something, knocking socks and underwear out on the floor. He turned and confronted Topher with a pair of brass knuckles. Swinging wildly, he stumbled forward.

Topher dodged Gil's swings until, out of the corner of his eye, he saw Alex getting up from the floor.

With his attention diverted, Gil surprised him with an assault of the hard cold metal striking his face. Topher found himself backed into the corner as the attack continued.

Unexpectedly, Topher felt Gil pause as if getting his second wind. He took the opportunity and all his strength to push him back. The push turned into a charge as Topher shoved Gil across the room, turning over a nightstand, and ramming him into the opposite wall.

Sheet rock cracked and fell to the carpeted floor as Gil's right shoulder went through the wall.

Topher pulled back and slammed his fists, one after the other, over and over into Gil's face.

He felt like he had left his body.

The pounding seemed effortless.

He couldn't feel his fists hitting Gil.

A high settled on him, much like the stupor of too much alcohol or pot. His mind calmed, but his body continued on its own.

He woke from this trance to find Alex pulling him off Gil's crumbled body.

"HOW COULD YOU?" Myra paced the hallway of University Hospital. "His arm is probably broken."

Topher's head ached. A black bruise covered his right cheekbone and dried blood made his stitched lower lip crusty. "He beat you up—and me. Hell, Myra, he came at me with brass knuckles. I defended myself. The only reason he has a broken arm is I got a better hit than he did. It could have easily been me—or you."

She continued her pacing. "You shouldn't have gotten involved. I could handle it."

"Shit. I saw what happened. He could have seriously hurt you." Topher stood in her path to stop the hallway circling. "I won't allow that to happen. He'll have to kill me first." He watched the tears well up in her bloodshot eyes.

"He could have. He could have killed us both. I never saw him in such a rage." She found a chair and dropped into it.

Tina returned from the cafeteria with coffee, smiling. "Girl, that was some party. I'm just glad it was at your house and not mine." She changed her tone when no one laughed. Tina sat down next to Myra and hugged her. "Do you want to come home with me?"

"No thanks. I'll be fine."

Alex walked up. "I smoothed things over with the police." He indicated the officers waiting for the elevator down the hall where he had been talking with them. "If everyone agrees not to press charges, we're good."

"I'm sorry," Tina said, "I called them as soon as I saw him standing over you, Myra. I didn't know what else to do."

"That's okay." Myra held her hand.

Alex said, "Myra, if you want a restraining order, we'll get one tonight."

"No." Her voice cracked. "I won't do that."

"Why not? You don't know what he'll do now." Topher pulled up a chair opposite Myra.

"It was bad because you all were there. I'll be fine."

Topher took her trembling hand and led her away from Tina and Alex. "Okay, no more shit. He could hurt you. You said it yourself. Don't try to cover for him in front of Tina and Alex. Stay the night with me or Tina."

"Gil will..." She lost her voice in a cough, then began again, "Gil will have a fit if I'm not here when they release him. I'm staying. He won't start anything. He knows you all know, so he'll calm down."

"I don't believe it." Topher said.

"Please leave," Myra said. "It would be better if I'm here alone when he's released."

"He'll never stop this. How long are you going to put up with him?"

Myra walked away. "Just drop it. I can take care of my life," she snapped. "If you had left us alone, it would have been a quick argument."

He put his hand to his cheek, jerking it away from the pain of the slight touch. "Yeah, I did it for the fun of kicking Gil's ass. Don't you get it? You were in danger."

"No, no, I wasn't. Mind your own business, please." Her voice had become small and quiet.

He threw up his hands. "Fine, you know where I am if you need me." Grabbing his coat and getting Tina and Alex's attention, they left Myra behind.

MYRA PACED THE waiting room alone. *He would never hurt me. Topher just made it worse.* But images of Gil knocking the bathroom door open and the pure hate in his eyes, the memory of her doctor telling her she'd had a miscarriage, and the knowledge that Gil had bought a pistol all stacked up and shook her resolve. He could hurt her. She grabbed the arm of a vinyl green couch to steady herself. A silent television flickered in the corner. Magazines littered the coffee table in front of her as she lowered herself onto the couch. The flat odor of old coffee hung in the air and threatened to bring holiday punch and sausage balls up from her stomach. The clock across the room silently jerked its second hand, hitting slightly off each tick mark between the numbers—a never-ending cycle of defects. She thought about pulling the plug, but knew the imperfection wouldn't go away.

"Mrs. Greer?" The doctor walked into the waiting room.

She turned to see a willowy woman stride up to her. The woman moved like a long reed in the river breeze. Her red hair rolled down the back of her lab coat in ringlets with a few stray strands breaking free from her plastic barrettes to dangle in front of her pale face. Myra decided she wasn't that pretty of a woman, but had been blessed with good hair and a thin body.

"Mrs. Greer, I'm Doctor Sioban Fitzpatrick." She sat down next to Myra. "Your husband is fine, just a few bruises and a slight cut to his head. His shoulder was dislocated, so it will be a little sore for a few days, but thankfully, nothing is broken."

"That's wonderful news. Thank you."

"Are you okay?" Dr. Fitzpatrick asked.

"I'm okay." Myra became a little annoyed from all the questions about her well-being. "I told your counselor, the police, and a nurse that I'm fine. People argue all the time."

"Once a pattern of abuse develops, it won't go away on its own.

There are agencies that can—"

"I don't need any agency. We had an argument." Myra realized how loud her voice had become and lowered it to a quivering. "That's all."

Doctor Fitzpatrick sighed. "Mrs. Greer, if you ever need help, call me." She reached into her pocket and gave Myra a card with her name and phone number printed on the front. "If you can't get me," she reached for the card in Myra's hand and wrote another number on the back, "call this number. That's the number where Janet, our counselor, can be reached—day or night." She smiled a gentle, understanding smile as she handed it back to Myra.

"Thanks, Doctor." Myra took the card and slipped it into her overcoat pocket.

"Your husband will be ready to be discharged in about fifteen minutes." She stood up to leave then added, "Good luck, Mrs. Greer."

SHE DROVE GIL home in silence. He went straight to bed without replying to her apologies. Myra sank into a chair next to her Christmas tree in the dark. A half-empty tray of food sat on the coffee table and plastic cups of drinks littered the room. *What would have happened if Topher hadn't got in the middle*? She asked herself that question over and over. Various answers came back; none satisfied her completely. The real question that developed as she sat in the dark was the one that brought tears to her eyes: *Would he kill me?*

SUNDAY MORNING CAME late. The sun had climbed high in the winter sky. Myra fixed Gil's breakfast, but he refused to eat. "My mouth hurts." He rubbed his shoulder, adjusted the sling, and stretched out on the couch. She cleaned up the apartment as he flipped channels on the television.

With a trash bag in hand, she collected discarded cups and plates from the party. *Why had Topher been so aggressive?* Gil lay on the sofa, a frown on his face, and she wondered how he felt about being in a fight with a gay man that left him with stitches and a dislocated shoulder.

"I was thinking," she said, gathering napkins from the coffee table, "Topher seemed out of control, like the problems he's had with Alex just erupted on you."

"Don't want to hear anything about that fag," Gil said.

"But wait, it makes sense to me. His frustration with Alex was transferred to you."

"He was crazy." Gil continued to stare at the television, the remote control resting on his stomach. "Probably on something. You know how those people take drugs."

"What people?" She kneeled by the Christmas tree and added

Laurie's gift to the trash bag.

"Fags, crazy fucking fags." He pulled himself off the couch. "I need to talk to the police, bring him up on charges." His face reddened. "He broke down the bedroom door, tried to fight me."

Tried? Myra considered his choice of words.

"And knocked my shoulder out of joint. I should put his sorry ass in jail, but then he'd probably like that."

"It wouldn't be a good idea to call the police. Topher would have to explain why he hit you."

A look came across the room from Gil that told her she was headed for a taboo subject. She knew never to bring up his treatment of her.

She covered by saying, "I just mean, it would get really involved to explain our dynamics."

"Our what?"

"The way we interact."

"Yeah, we shouldn't bring the police into our family business." Gil walked to the glass door that led to the deck. Rain puddled on the warped wood as she watched him watch the downpour. "I don't want you seeing him any more."

His back was to her, so she didn't think she heard him right. "What? Seeing who?"

He turned away from the misty glass. "Topher. I don't want you to see him again. Ever."

"But, that's not fair. He's my best friend. We grew up together. We've known each other for over twenty years— "

"And I'm your husband," he broke in. "You do what I say."

"No. I will not." Fearless determination peeked through her veil of shame when it came to Topher and her. "I will see him when I want."

"Damn you," he started to raise his hand, but cringed from the pain. "Lucky for you...or I would..." His voice trailed off. Walking toward the bedroom, he said, "Stay away from him."

"What?" She followed him down the hall. "And not see anyone? Not have any contact with other people? Stuck in this tiny apartment with you?" Her breathing quickened, and the thought of isolation scared her, scared her more than Gil's potential violence.

"You are damn lucky my arm's in this sling. But my left arm still works, so watch your mouth. This is all your fault. Now, you have to pay the price. Stay away from him. I don't want him here. I don't want you talking to him on the phone, or going over to his house. As far as you're concerned, he's dead." With his final word, Gil put up his left hand to stop her from following him.

SWEAT ROLLED DOWN her face as the instructor barked directions. Like an army of robots, the class followed the commands:

step, turn, down. Myra hated that little, hard plastic step. She snuck a look at the clock. It said 6:10, and she knew they had five minutes left. Cool down, it was the reward at the end of the class. She smiled as Wendy, the instructor, told them what a good workout they'd done. All her problems had taken a back seat for that half hour, until she saw Topher at the water fountain.

"Myra, how are you?" The stitches in his lip slurred his speech some.

"I'm so sorry." She reached up to touch the bump on his forehead, but stopped short.

"Don't blame yourself. It wasn't your fault." Topher sweated from his own workout. He hesitated a little, and then said, "I want you to move out."

She pulled him to a corner, away from the ears of other people. "He's not a danger to me—"

"Bullshit. He could snap at anytime—"

"No. All the people there made him agitated."

"So, was he agitated when he brought Laurie to the bedroom?"

Myra looked down at the floor and let a group of women walk past them before answering. "Gil and I have had problems, sexually. He loves me, and I love him. Whatever he intended to do with Laurie was strictly physical. It wouldn't have affected our relationship."

"If that's so, why did you make such a scene?"

Myra took a deep breath, considering the question. The sting of Topher's logic lodged in her heart. "I was just surprised. And a little hurt."

Topher rubbed her shoulder. "I'm sorry. We all want to be the light in our spouse's life. The hardest part is finding out we're not."

They both stood silently as the rush and noise of the gym swarmed around them.

Myra opened her mouth to speak, but the words disappeared. Finally she squeaked, "Gil said I couldn't give him everything he needs." The tears rushed to the surface, and Topher held her tight. He helped her downstairs to the lobby where they could have some privacy.

They settled into a corner of the closed snack bar. The lights were turned down, and the ammonia smell of clean tables surrounded them. Topher sat across the table as Myra cried. "I'd hoped I'd see you tonight. I didn't call because he forbade me to see you. He wants me to come home after work and not talk to anyone. He barely allows me to stop at the gym. I have to be home by seven."

"He's making you a prisoner." Topher's gaze chilled her with the truth.

"I think he's trying to fix our problems," she said. "Maybe time alone together will help?" Her voice rose with the last word, making it a question she hadn't intended.

Topher shook his head as if he were tired. "No. He's put you in isolation. This isn't the way it should be. You know that, right?"

"Yes. No." She trembled. "Who's to know what's right between two people? Who can judge?"

"You can."

"I can't. I don't know anything right now." She looked deep into Topher's eyes. "Does Alex punish you when you do something against his wishes?"

"What? No. Of course not."

"Then why did you two break up and then get back together?"

"We're not totally back together. And it's very different. Alex wants some time to decide if this relationship is working for him. I'm allowing him that time."

"Okay," she said, "what did you do just before the breakup?"

"I pushed for a commitment."

She pulled him along. "And what did he do?"

"Said he needed time."

"And, what else?"

"I threatened to break up, and he didn't stop me." Topher became quiet.

Myra made her point. "To me, being strung along is punishment. Who's to judge?"

Topher dropped his gaze for a moment. "Myra," he kept looking at the table, "I won't allow you to cut me off because of Gil. You don't want to, do you?"

"Of course not." She reached over, and lifted his chin. "I will see you here every Monday, Wednesday, and Friday after work."

He smiled at her. "It's a date."

Chapter
Eleven

LARGE SNOWFLAKES MELTED on Topher's windshield. He flipped on the wipers to clear his view of Interstate 77 in the sagging, white sunset. Christmas Eve. He was driving to Bristol, alone. His thoughts kept going back to Alex and his reasons why the Christmas ski trip was canceled.

"The Andreus case is heating up," Alex had explained. "I need to work off and on through the holiday."

"But I really wanted to spend Christmas with you," Topher had said, watching Alex avoid his stare. "I thought it would be nice to spend our first Christmas together."

"That would have been great, but I need to work. Why don't you go on to your mother's, and I'll drive up to Rocky Mount to visit my parents on Christmas Day. We can spend New Year's Eve together. How would that be?"

Resigned to the fact, Topher agreed. "I guess that would be okay. You haven't seen your parents in a while. At least, they'll be happy."

"Yeah." Alex smiled. "That's a good plan."

Topher's attention turned back to the road as he drove through Wytheville, watching other cars continue north on I-77 to the West Virginia mountains. He headed south on Interstate 81 as the snow piled up along the roadside. Hitting the Scan button on the radio didn't produce a station, so he pulled out a CD and slid it in. An old song of Sting's pleaded the line of setting free someone you really loved. "How much freer can he be?" Topher said out loud. "Everything is on his terms. I can't suggest anything without him turning it around with that smug attorney logic to make it a bad idea. Work always comes first. When do I?"

His cheeks flushed with warmth. "Myra is right. I get strung along, waiting. Waiting for him to decide when I get to be graced with his presence."

A deep sigh hissed through his clenched teeth. His hands tingled from gripping the steering wheel like a vise. He rolled down the window, and the icy air and deep breaths helped calm him.

By the time he arrived at his mother's house, she was putting dinner on the table.

"Merry Christmas, Topher. What the hell happened to your lip?" Maggie held him at arms length to look at his face.

"You should have seen the other guy," Topher joked. "I got in a little fight with Gil, but it's over with. I'd rather not talk about it."

She pulled him into her arms and hugged. A man stood behind his mother. He looked to be older than her. His thick silver hair was combed back in a rather careless fashion. His eyebrows were still dark, but his mustache had turned as steely as his hair. It occurred to Topher that if the man weighed eighty more pounds and had a beard, he would look like Santa Claus.

"Hello, Topher," a baritone voice rumbled. "Do you remember me?"

His mother grabbed the man's arm. "You do remember Coach McCormick?"

A flash back to high school brought the recognition. The rumor running the hallways then was that Coach McCormick had been caught feeling up the librarian in the media room.

He looked down at the Coach's outstretched hand, and imagined Miss 'Big Stacks' breast in it.

"Nice to see you again." Topher shook his hand despite the image still hovering in his mind.

"Come upstairs and let me help you unpack." Maggie hurried him up the staircase.

Once inside his old room, she chatted like a schoolgirl. "I met him through Billie from work. He's her cousin. Recently divorced, he's not a drunk, not lazy, has his own money, and is still quite frisky."

"Mom," Topher whined without meaning to.

"I invited him for dinner. I hope that's all right."

"Sure, whatever makes you happy."

"Sorry Alex couldn't make it." She patted his back. "Oh, try not to say anything about Alex. Ron doesn't know you're gay."

"What?" he shot back.

She dropped her shoulders. "Forgive me, but it just hasn't come up."

"Does he act like it would matter?"

"How should I know?"

"I would think you wouldn't want to date a homophobic man when you have a gay son." He dumped his clothes on the bed.

"Who said he's homophobic?" She seemed irritated, grabbing a shirt and folding it.

He sat next to her on the bed to analyze the situation with her. "Nobody. I just don't want to have to watch everything I say about my life."

"The only thing homosexual about you is who you sleep with. The rest of your life is like everyone else."

"Mom, I'm past defining myself by who I sleep with."

"Then why does he have to know you're gay?"

Topher sat in silence for a moment, untying their knot of logic. "Okay, I see your point. There's no sense in putting him on the spot with some kind of announcement, but if it comes up with something like 'Who's Alex?' or 'Why aren't you married?' then I have to explain."

"Fine. As a natural course of the conversation, that would be fine," Maggie said.

A quick smile sneaked onto his face. "You know, Mom, I remember things about him from school—"

"He's not gay?" she almost screamed.

"No, he's heterosexual and a breast man."

She looked down at her dwindling chest. "Wish he had met me twenty years ago. Time is not kind to a woman's knockers."

"God, Mom. I haven't heard the word 'knockers' in years."

"I doubt they come up much in gay circles." She laughed.

He recovered to reply, "Only among the lesbians."

"Topher!" She hid her face in her hands.

As they ate dinner, the conversation wound around work, past holiday traditions, and through Maggie's new all-crystal ornaments. (Topher called it the Ice Tree.) Coach McCormick smiled whenever Maggie spoke, and he watched every move she made.

Alex never looks at me that way. I should call him. It's Christmas Eve. Images of a warm fireplace, a colorful Christmas tree, the aroma of hot buttered rums, and Alex looking lovingly into his eyes, made him sigh. *Why doesn't he call me?*

"Topher? Are you okay?" Maggie asked. "Did that ham give you indigestion?"

"No Mom, I'm okay."

"Good. Ron and I are going for a walk in the snow. Would you be a dear and put the dishes in the dishwasher? Oh, be sure to put the ham back in the refrigerator. Thanks, honey."

The door slammed shut, and the crystal tree clattered from the vibration. "A snowy romantic night and I'm scraping mashed potatoes off plates and loading the dishwasher—alone. At least Mom has found someone." The cat, Mary Ann, rubbed against his leg. He looked down, and smiled. "Thanks, Mary Ann, but a little pussy isn't what I'm looking for." *Love, that's it, very simple—not sex, just simple love.*

For two days, he stayed with his mother, but Maggie spent most of her time with Coach McCormick. Topher spent most of his time thinking of Alex. Each night, he fought the temptation to call him—he hid his cell phone in the bottom of his suitcase. His mother and the Coach sat on the couch talking and laughing, while Topher sat in the side chair feeling out of place. Although he enjoyed his mother's happiness, he needed to get away.

After the two long days of their cheerfulness, he packed his car.

Topher hugged his mother good-bye. "Thanks for having me up for Christmas."

"I'm so glad you came." She cupped his face in her hands. Smiling, she kissed him. "I'm sorry I didn't get to spend more time with you."

"I understand completely. I have to admit, I'd liked to have spent time with Alex."

She dropped her hands, taking hold of his in a tight grip. "Don't let him run your self-esteem down. Your father did that to me. No man is worth it. Take care of yourself first, then the right people will be drawn to you."

"I will. I do," he stammered. "I try." His eyes filled with tears.

"Honey, I know you try." She hugged him hard, and the tears spilled down his face.

He wiped them on his sleeve, said good-bye, and drove away, leaving his mother with tears of her own.

ONCE HOME, TOPHER checked his messages on both his home machine and his cell phone. There was nothing from Alex. His thoughts went back to the Thanksgiving weekend and Alex's lack of enthusiasm for seeing him again. He tapped his fingers on the phone, then stood up and started unpacking his bag.

"I have to work tomorrow," he said to the washing machine, dropping in whites with colors, "and I need to get some rest. No time to see Alex, no, no time at all."

With the washer rumbling, he walked around the empty house. Few lights were on, and his paintings on the wall hung in shadows. Each footstep echoed through the open rooms and high ceilings—the space provided by the uncluttered rooms allowed him breathing and working freedom during the day, but at night the emptiness only magnified his low moods. His Christmas tree—naked without the packages—shivered in the corner dropping needles on the bare wood floor. He turned the lights on to cheer it up. Red, green, blue, yellow, and white star lights sparkled through the evergreen. Across the room, where the dining room table should be, sat his canvases, some finished, some not. One canvas sat on his easel; he hadn't paid much attention to it in the past few months. The faint gray outline of what he had started still showed around the edges of the painting, but the middle displayed bright crimson and vivid cherry reds. He leaned over and blew. Dust flew everywhere. "No wonder I'm so edgy, I haven't painted since May."

He stood in front of the painting in his flannel boxers, T-shirt, and wool socks. When he unscrewed a tube of midnight blue paint, crusty flakes dropped to the floor. The wet brush glided across the canvas and the old paint, covering what he had started the spring before.

THE NEXT DAY at work, Topher laughed and talked with his coworkers like he hadn't in months. Around the coffee machine that anchored the corner of a conference room, a group of designers and copywriters listened as Topher told them about a tiresome client and how he finally found the right layout for her ad. His new-found vitality seemed to energize the small office as writers collaborated with designers and designers talked with salespeople. Across from the row of cubicles, the design wall had current projects tacked to it, and Topher helped Dustin unravel a flow problem in his layout. Topher settled back in front of his computer to check his e-mail, when he heard Daryl humming an OutKast song on the other side of the cubicle wall.

He stood up to peer over the wall, and saw Daryl wiggling in his chair, headphones plugged in his computer. "Yo, Daryl," Topher called. "Shake what your mama gave you."

He laughed and pulled off the headphones, "Boy, you in a mood." He came around to Topher's cube. "You holding out on me? What happened over the holiday? Who came down your chimney?"

Topher said, "I started painting again. It didn't really go anywhere, but it felt great to hold the brush and smell the paint."

"You go, boy," Daryl congratulated him. "Let's have lunch over at 300 East today. I'll buy to celebrate the return of the artist."

WHEN THEY WALKED in the restaurant, Topher saw Brenda, the bartender, talking to her ex-partner, Jennifer. Topher waved, then he and Daryl took a booth at the window. Jennifer joined them. "How are you guys? I haven't seen you two in a coon's age." She looked knowingly at Topher and nudged Daryl over.

"Good," Topher said. "Are you in for Christmas?"

"Yeah, here until New Year's Day, then I'm flying back to Arizona. I had to see Brenda again. I'm trying to convince her to go back to Sedona with me, but her father's illness is keeping her here." Jennifer's beauty had always bewitched Topher. Her long, black hair fell straight down her back; her blue eyes seemed to glow as she talked. Small framed, he remembered how people laughed at her carrying the bulky massage table around in her Jetta, but she held all the power once she got her client on it. Reiki, she would explain to people, was the technique of pulling energy through the body without actually touching. She would always get upset if you called her a massage therapist.

"Having any luck with Brenda?" Daryl asked.

"No, I think she's staying here." The defeat showed in Jennifer's downcast eyes.

"Where's Sedona?" Daryl tried to change the subject.

"Oh, guys," she brightened, "it's the most beautiful place in the world. Between the desert and the mountains, beautiful red rocks surround the town, and scattered all around it are energy vortexes. It's very New Age there, and the energy vortexes are real. I can feel them in my work. The place is a little touristy, but the hiking is wonderful, work is good, and the people are very accepting. I know Brenda and I could build a life together there."

"Why'd you leave here?" Topher asked.

"I'd heard about Sedona for years, and my Reiki practice was going nowhere in button-down Charlotte, so I decided it was time to change. Of course, my plan was for Brenda to move with me, but her father got sick. She was forced to choose." Her voice dropped. "I lost."

"Sounds like a wonderful place," Topher said.

She perked up. "It is. Come visit. Please," she begged, "it would be so nice to have an old friend out there, even if it was only for a week."

Daryl excused himself, seeing someone he knew at another table. Topher took the opportunity to ask a question that had bothered him. "Jennifer, don't take offense, but how can you leave someone you love? What could be more important?"

Her answer was simple. "I am."

His blank stare brought more of an explanation. "I am more important than my relationship with Brenda. I have to be happy doing what I'm doing. Brenda adds to that, but she can't be it all."

"So, even though you and Brenda had a great relationship," he said, "you needed more...something personal, having nothing to do with Brenda."

"Right," Jennifer said.

"But didn't you sacrifice your relationship for your personal needs?"

"A relationship is part of my personal needs. Everything would have been perfect if Brenda could have moved with me, but she couldn't. And I had to. I'm trying to make it perfect, but it may take a while." She grinned at him like it was the period at the end of the sentence—ending the discussion.

Topher held her hand and kissed her cheek. "I know you've been discussing this with Brenda since you got into town. Thanks for talking with me. I'm going through some adjusting, myself."

"Want to talk about it?" she asked.

"Remember Alex?"

She nodded.

"We're still together—kind of." He wanted to say it as simply as possible. "I guess the bottom line is I love him, but he's not in love with me, but he keeps the possibility open, and me on the line."

She shook her head slowly, heavy lids covering most of her eyes.

"I know, I know. I've been warned and advised. I resigned myself to take him how I can get him. If that's seeing him once a week, okay. If it's waiting around all weekend for his call, that's okay too. I have plenty to do around the house. I don't need to be out every night—"

"Whoa," she interrupted. "Don't justify yourself to me. Look around. Decide what's right for you. Do what's in your heart. I don't think you know yourself, your mind, what motivates you. Where is your energy going? Is it doing what you need, or is it being diverted?"

Topher squeaked out, "I have no idea."

"Take a vacation from everything and come stay with me. My door is always open." Jennifer kissed him and went back to the bar.

WARM RAIN FELL on Topher as he climbed the stairs to Alex's door. The New Year's Eve's temperature allowed him to go out without a coat. Charlotte rarely had the cold weather or snow he'd grown up with in Bristol or New York. He thought about how cold he'd been a week ago at his mother's.

Alex opened the door with his umbrella in hand. "Let's not be late." He closed and locked the door without inviting Topher in.

"We're just going to Dustin and Erik's for dinner. We could be a few minutes late."

Alex gave him a look of disbelief. "Erik would have a fit if we were late. You know he's been cooking all day. Let's go."

He followed Alex to the parking lot and watched him as he went to the passenger side of Topher's Chevy and waited. "Want me to drive?" Topher asked.

"That would be great. Your car's already warm from driving over."

Topher got in and took his time unlocking Alex's side.

Arriving in the Elizabeth section of Charlotte, Topher pulled onto Greenway Avenue and into the driveway of a two-story, white frame house Dustin and Erik had bought and were restoring. Floodlights lit the front of the house, making it a blinding white.

Dustin answered the door with a hug for both of them. "Erik's in the kitchen perfecting dinner. Have a seat in the living room. May I get you a drink?" The warm house held subtle scents of bergamot, juniper, and basil, and Topher tried to distinguish the smell of dinner from the burning candles placed around the room. The refinished hardwood floors gleamed in the candle light, and when he sat down, he sank into the feather-stuffed couch. The glint of gold-trimmed china turned his attention to the dining room table. Full crystal, silver, and china were awaiting the meal being prepared for them.

Topher wondered what a formal dinner would be like in the desert. Jennifer came to mind; he imagined her sitting on a rock, eating rattlesnake that had been cooked over a campfire.

After talking a few minutes with Dustin, Erik joined them. He walked over to Dustin's chair, and sat on the arm. Dustin reached up and rubbed his back while he talked. *Alex never touches me in front of our friends. What a nice sign of affection a simple touch is.* He turned to look at Alex as the conversation flowed. He appeared to be a stranger. What was it that made him love Alex? He couldn't remember. The longer he watched Alex talk, the more he didn't recognize him. The room seemed to be a vacuum. All the air left, and voices became thin and tinny. He struggled to listen to the conversation, but couldn't tell who spoke. Rising to his feet, he excused himself, and concentrated on walking, one step at a time, to the bathroom. Once in and safe, he splashed cold water on his face, trying to snap himself out of this haze. Jennifer's words came back to him: Where is your energy going?

During dinner, he watched the interaction of Erik and Dustin. *How different it is. Why hadn't I noticed before? So much tenderness and love communicated between them in such simple gestures.*

Topher glanced at the brass mantel clock: 11:30. Half an hour until the New Year.

He didn't want to kiss Alex. He didn't want to talk to him anymore; he wanted out.

"I hate to break up the party," he explained to the concerned faces of the other three, "but I have a terrible headache—been fighting it all night. I need to get to bed."

Alex's face showed disappointment.

A moment of doubt flickered through his mind, then he took a deep breath and said, "Alex, please stay and have fun." He looked to Dustin. "Could you take Alex home?"

"Of course," Dustin said. "Do you want some aspirin? Do you want me to drive you home?"

"No thanks. I just need some rest. Happy New Year." He turned to Alex, and lightly kissed him on the cheek. "Happy New Year."

Driving home with the windows down, Topher watched the Trailblazer's digital clock hit midnight. He blew the horn, and waved at the other cars carrying people in transit on the birth of the new year.

Chapter Twelve

"ANY OF THAT fudge left?" Gil yelled into the kitchen. His stomach rumbled in anticipation of the smooth chocolate melting in his mouth, leaving nothing but the chopped pecans to chew. "Hey, Myra. You listening to me?"

She poked her head out the kitchen door. "Sorry. Did you need something?"

"Fudge."

"Excuse me?"

"Fudge."

"Oh, hold on." She handed him a butter tub with four pieces rattling around in the bottom.

"Is this it?"

"Yeah, that's all that's left from the batch I made on New Year's Day—that was Friday." She sat down on the couch across from his recliner. "Do you want me to make more? Sundays are good days for cooking." She smiled.

He couldn't tell if she was making fun of him.

He finished the fudge and dropped the container next to his chair—it landed on a potato chip bag. "Are you going to the gym tomorrow?"

Myra shifted her position. "Yeah, it's gonna be really crowded. I expect tomorrow to be terrible. All those people with New Year's resolutions to lose weight will pour into the Y. I'll be lucky to get a treadmill. I might try to leave work early to get a jump on the crowd—"

"Whatever," he ended her comments. "Don't get home late."

"I won't." She returned to the kitchen.

"Hey, do you see Topher at the gym?"

Myra poked her head out the door again. "Sorry. Did you say something?"

"Get your ass out here where I can talk to you," he yelled back. *Is she trying to piss me off?*

She sat across from him, smiling.

"Do you see Topher at the gym?"

"Once in a while, I see him and speak to him."

Gil fumed. "What did I tell you about talking to him? I don't want you around Topher." He knew she wouldn't listen to him. Why did she always have to test his authority?

"I know, honey," she said. "How's your shoulder? I know Topher's sorry for it. His lip is healing well. Maybe we could all make up and go out for dinner one night."

"I'm not eating dinner with him. If I ever have dinner with him, I can finish what he started. A few drops of choice insecticide make a nice seasoning for anyone who crosses me." He watched her look away. *Is she laughing?* "Hey, look at me. That goes for you, too. I could poison your food, your makeup, your toothpaste, even your deodorant, and you wouldn't know it."

Her eyes widened, and her face blanched. A visible shake brought her breathing back to normal. She crossed the room to him and sat on the floor at his feet. "Forget about all that stuff." She stroked his thigh. "I'll go to the store and get the ingredients to make more fudge. How would that be?"

Her touch sent a tingle up his leg. Her flannel shirt, with the top three buttons undone, revealed the gentle slope of her breast. *She's not bad.* He gazed at her white creamy flesh. He touched her face, so smooth and soft. Then he ran his hand to her neck. Her body jerked, and a flush of red splotched her throat. His hand continued down, pulling the flannel away from her breasts. *No bra, good girl.* Cupping her right breast, he pinched her nipple between his fingers. She sat stone still.

Gil's other hand moved to his crotch. Blood flowed to his cock, but he knew he wasn't completely hard. The friction from the denim of his jeans helped build his erection as he rubbed himself with one hand and groped Myra with the other.

Moving his hand back up to Myra's head, he pulled her forward as he unzipped his pants. The more she resisted, the harder he forced her head. She slowly lowered her mouth on his hardening cock, but he didn't release his hold on the back of her neck. He guided her every stroke. A fantasy formed in his mind to help him achieve a full erection, not his personal fantasy, but one from a video. He couldn't remember the bodies in the detail he needed, and he felt his erection wane.

"Myra," he said as he let go of her neck, "go put a video in—the one about the women's prison."

She stood, coughed, and started to sort through the discs in the back of the television stand. Putting the DVD in the machine, she pushed Play, got up, and headed toward the kitchen.

"Where you going?" he asked.

"I just wanted to start my grocery list."

"Don't go far." The video took his attention away from her. A male prison guard herded nude women into a room full of showers.

THANK GOD FOR videos. Myra grabbed the counter top to hold herself up. Terror still surrounded her like a serpent ready to strike. Her stomach heaved as she bent over the sink, but only hot, sour acid dribbled out. *What happened? He once loved me, didn't he?* She looked around the kitchen for something, not sure what, but for something to calm her terror. *Would he try to poison me? Could he?* She smiled, trying to relieve her tension. *He's never in the kitchen, but he leaves for work after I do and comes home before me.* The smile faded. He would have the opportunity.

Why? The question floated through her mind, passing images from the past few months. His abuse had gotten worse. *He hates me. Why?*

"Get out." The sound of her own voice startled her. "Just until he's calm again." *What if he wants me back in there?* Tears flowed down her cheek. *The grocery store—that will be enough time.*

She wrote her list with trembling hands, recalling the items she had formed in her mind while Gil had used her. Making lists was her form of detachment when he wanted her to have sex without asking or building up to it. She recalled the early days of their relationship. He had been so verbal—telling her how beautiful she was, touching her with genuine love and desire. She had enjoyed their physical relationship then. Maybe it was her, maybe she couldn't give him what he wanted now. Although she had been what he wanted, she knew she had, back in those early times.

Chocolate chips, pecans, marshmallows. Her list flowed out onto the back of an envelope, and her tears dried.

Gil walked past the kitchen, and she heard the bathroom door slam shut. She went into the den to turn off the video. Two women were having sex with each other while the prison guard jerked himself off. *He hates gays, but loves to watch lesbian sex. I don't get it.* She watched for a little while, hoping she might be a lesbian and not know it. But the thought held little appeal to her. *If sexual orientation were a choice, I'd choose another woman, but I can't change who I am.* She sighed and imagined how nice it would be to have a partner who knew her body and liked the same things she did, instead of some fumbling clumsy man who was only interested in his own satisfaction. She wanted to crush the terrifying serpent that threatened her and put an end to living in fear.

She grabbed her list and pocketbook. "Gil," she yelled toward the bathroom door, "I'm going to the grocery store." *Poison me?* Her mind chewed on it, then swallowed.

TOPHER KNEELED IN Saint Peter's Episcopal Church and stared at the stained glass windows. The winter sun filtered through in deep, rich colors of cobalt, emerald, and ruby. The heating system rumbled, blanketing the building in the comfortable scent of dust and incense. The rest of the congregation recited the Lord's Prayer, but Topher's mind was numb, blank. This time of year, the church seemed so plain. With Christmas over, going to church was almost dreary.

He closed his eyes and envisioned what he wanted from life. His prayers could never be put into words; they came in pictures, like personal paintings he sent to God, and in return, he knew God sent paintings back that ended up on his canvases.

He looked up and saw the choir lining up for Communion—friends he knew outside of church, writers, artists, accountants, old and young, gay and straight, not only in the choir, but in the pews. The community of this church reflected the loving side of Charlotte. He smiled and bowed his head again.

Unsettled, he asked himself, *What have I missed?* The Christmas sermons and readings formed the story of preparing for a change in life as it was known, a hope of peace and rebirth. With Christmas over and the new year begun, what was his change? No more Alex? Going through it all again with someone with a different name and face? The question "Why?" formed on his lips.

A voice, full and deep, rattled through his mind: The voice of one crying out in the wilderness.

His head jerked up as if he'd almost fallen asleep. The choir reclaimed their seats, and the first rows of the congregation lined up to go to the altar for Communion. The gift, the sentence still rang in his ears. Tears filled his eyes. John the Baptist, a wild man in the desert, heralding the coming of Jesus—the beginning. *Is this my cry in the wilderness? Am I starting a new beginning? Is this what I've prepared for?* Chills ran over his arms. He stood and followed the line to the altar and knelt. The priest placed a piece of bread in his hands.

He felt the bread in the palm of his hand. When he raised it to his mouth, it tasted yeasty and sweet.

A soft rustle of the priest's robe stopped in front of him again. A gold cup sparkled in his eyes.

He waited, but the priest did nothing. Topher lifted his head to see a true fatherly, loving smile from the priest. *Help me, please.* He bowed his head again.

"The Blood of Christ, the cup of salvation." The priest lifted the cup to Topher's lips.

"Amen." The wine burned his throat as he swallowed. He looked up at the priest, but he had moved on to the next person. A shaft of light from the stained glass created a shimmering violet circle on the altar rail in front of him. He turned to see the image of John the Baptist with fierce sunlit eyes. Topher made the sign of the cross and stood.

Turning, he saw the rose window glowing on the back wall. *More, there is more.* He walked down the aisle and out the door, not stopping until he paused at the gate of the churchyard. He knew what needed to be done to save himself. The first step, he'd accomplished on New Year's Eve. Now, he needed to find out where he belonged, where his energy should be channeled. Only one truth gleamed in his mind like stained glass: he needed to find that place, and leave Charlotte far behind.

Chapter Thirteen

POISON MY FOOD? Myra took the cap off the milk jug and started pouring it into the kitchen sink. The white liquid swirled around and down the drain. *But he has to eat, too. He can't put poison in his own food. Anything in a common container should be okay. Anything he doesn't eat has to be thrown out.* She dumped her low-fat honey mustard salad dressing in the trash along with the bananas, lettuce, apples, oranges, grapes, and cottage cheese.

She had claimed she had strong menstrual cramps so that Tina would give her the afternoon off—a time when Gil would be out of the apartment. She hated to lie to Tina, but she felt too foolish and paranoid to tell the truth.

Myra pulled new makeup and deodorant out of a shopping bag and stuffed them into her pocketbook. *I'll leave what's in the bathroom as decoys.* She made a list of everything she used in the apartment and duplicated it with products in her purse, car, or in her desk at work. Finally as 4:30 approached, she felt secure. After dumping the trash in the building's dumpster, she straightened any signs of her afternoon activities. Gil would be home within thirty minutes, and she didn't want him to know she wasn't at work. She headed toward the gym, hoping to see Topher.

The YMCA's parking lot swarmed with BMWs, Mercedes, assorted sport utility vehicles, and minivans. Myra finally parked two blocks away on the street. Once inside the dressing room, she found an empty locker and changed clothes, while the 'temps,' as the Y veterans called anyone who started working out in December or January, stood in front of the mirrors checking their makeup before appearing in mixed company. Myra pushed her way past them. She felt like a veteran. She didn't stand around flirting and giggling. Her purpose was to get her workout done, and today, it also included finding Topher.

Scanning the Free Weight room, she didn't see him. She walked upstairs and through the Circuit Training area; no Topher. She went up another level to the cardiovascular equipment. She thought he might be on an elliptical trainer or stair climber. *He's usually here. Maybe it's a little early.* She considered calling his office. *This is just stupid. He'll think I'm overreacting.*

The waiting list for a stair climber had five people ahead of her, so she grabbed a magazine and plopped down on the floor. The gray sky filled the small casement windows behind the machines. She stood to look out over Morehead Street to downtown Charlotte and its constantly changing skyline, dominated in the south by the Carolina Panthers' stadium.

A smile emerged as she remembered the first time she and Gil had been to the stadium.

"GUESS WHAT?" SHE had found it hard to disguise her excitement.

Cell phone static made hearing Gil's voice difficult. "What?"

She knew he had been working hard in the August heat and could use the treat. "Tina just gave me two tickets to the exhibition game against the Bears." She sat back in her desk chair and waited to hear Gil's yahoo.

"Yeessss!" Gil honked his truck's horn and yelled again. "I always wanted to see the Panthers play. Have I told you how beautiful you are?"

"Would I be as beautiful if I weren't holding two Panthers tickets?"

"Oh, now," he stammered, "you know I love you and think you're beautiful—with or without tickets. But, this just adds points."

The game was played on a steamy Saturday night. Gil parked the car several blocks away. He had insisted on wearing his Carolina jersey, which she knew was too heavy for the night. Halfway up Stonewall Street, he started to sweat.

"Damn, humid tonight."

"Let's slow down. We have plenty of time to get there." The crowd heading up Stonewall thickened while buses full of fans crept up the street among hundreds of cars trying to get a close parking space.

A crammed parking lot ahead of them housed several tailgate parties. Gil looked at Myra and winked. "I need a beer."

He strode to the middle of the parking lot, held both fists above his head, and yelled, "Panthers rule!"

The tailgaters responded with shouts and hoots. A balding, beer-bellied man walked over to Gil and slapped him on the back. "How about a beer, man?"

"Hell, yeah. Myra, let's have a beer."

She joined the crowd at the back of a minivan, where a folding table had been set up and loaded down with fried chicken, potato salad, chips, and beer. Gil laughed and talked with the strangers as if it was a family reunion, and he was the long-lost relative.

During the game, they made friends with the people sitting around them. Gil bought rounds of beer. Yelling at the referee for a bad call and cheering touchdowns, he and the men around them seemed to possess the enthusiasm of young boys playing their own football game.

Myra sat next to another wife. As they looked through the program, picking out the cute players, the wife smiled at her husband and Gil, and said to Myra, "I can't say I ever saw Larry have such a good time. Your husband is just a party waiting to happen."

"YOU'RE UP." A younger woman in a Bank of America T-shirt tapped Myra's shoulder.

"Thanks." Myra mounted the stair climber and set the controls. *Why has he changed?* Her thoughts rehashed what she had worried about for months. *I don't know if I can save our marriage.*

She kept looking for Topher as she worked out. By the end of the thirty minutes, he hadn't shown, so she decided to get dressed and call his house.

The phone rang and rang, then finally, the machine picked up. "Topher? This is Myra. I'm at the gym. I thought I might see you here tonight. Guess not. I'd like to talk to you," then she added quickly, "but don't call me at home. Call me at work tomorrow. Love you, bye."

She hung up. Her feet seemed made of concrete, not because of the workout, but because of her doubt about what to do next. She dreaded going home, but knew she had to, had to keep going like everything was fine, had to act like she didn't fear for her life, had to act like she didn't take his threats seriously.

"HEY, I'M HOME," she called as she came in the door. Gil sat in his recliner, watching the news.

"You go to the gym?"

"Ugh," she grunted, "me go to gym." She forced a laugh and kissed him on the head.

He ignored her joke. "What time will dinner be?"

"About seven? Is that soon enough?"

"Yeah."

She didn't attempt any more conversation, but went to put her gym clothes away and start dinner.

She slid the tray of rolls in the oven just as the phone rang. *No, Topher, I said not to call here.* Her stomach churned, and her mouth dried. The smell of the peas cooking on the stove sickened her. The phone rang again. She crossed the kitchen for the phone, but Gil had already picked up the extension in the den.

"Hello?" Gil answered.

Myra shivered when he looked into the kitchen at her.

"I told you there was nothing to talk about," he said into the receiver.

She waited for more.

Gil shifted in his chair, and ran his fingers through his hair. "Listen, Buddy, if Mama wants to go, then you got to take her. I can't get off work."

She sighed and leaned against the counter.

He hung up the phone, and turned the television back up.

"That was Buddy?" Myra yelled into the den.

"Yeah, Mama wants to go to Aunt Geraldine's in Spartanburg, and he wants me to take her. He needs to get off his lazy ass and drive her there. I don't have time. I work for a living." He crushed his empty beer can. "Babe, can you get me another?"

"Sure." She took him a beer and went back to the kitchen.

THE NEXT DAY, she waited for Topher's call until eleven o'clock. Wondering why he hadn't returned her call, she dialed his work number and waited. He didn't answer, but the call went to his voicemail. She hit zero, and waited for someone to answer.

"Proof 2 Print. This is Patti." Her voice bounced as she pronounced her Ps.

"Hello, Patti. This is Myra Greer. Is Topher in?"

"He's not in today. Can someone else help you?"

Myra hesitated then said, "Daryl. Is Daryl in?"

"Yes, hold please."

Myra heard the Carpenters singing "Close To You." Remembering her preteen days when the song was popular, she grinned and sang a little.

Daryl picked up with a click.

Myra kept singing.

"Hello? Karen? Karen Carpenter? Are you hungry, dear? Eat something. You're nothing but skin and bones."

Myra laughed. "Daryl. It's Myra. Have you seen Topher?"

"Girlfriend, I ain't heard from him in days. The boss says he called in to take a few days off. He isn't returning my calls. I bet him and that handsome lawyer are up in Blowing Rock snuggling in front of a fireplace. Caressing each other, drinking champagne, rubbing their—"

"Whoa, Daryl." Myra said.

"Sorry, girl. It's just been so long for me that I like to have these little fantasies of what a romantic getaway would be like."

"You and me both," she said. "If you hear from him, have him call me at work."

"Sure thing, Miss Thang."

She hung up the phone, glad that Topher might be enjoying himself.

As noon approached, she slipped on her overcoat to go to lunch. Her hand felt a card in the pocket. She pulled it out and read the name: Dr. Sioban Fitzpatrick. Myra flipped it over to see the name and number of the counselor Dr. Fitzpatrick had written there. *Maybe I could call her, not use my real name, but just talk.* The idea made her nervous. She stuck the card back in her pocket and left for lunch.

When she came back to her office, she closed the door behind her and dialed the number on the card.

"Janet Vinson, may I help you?" Her strong voice clipped each word into distinct sounds with the silence between the words speaking louder than the words themselves.

"Uh, yes, this is, uh," Myra searched for a name, "Tina. I'm having some trouble with my relationship with my husband."

"Yes, Tina. Would you like to make an appointment to come in and talk about it?"

Myra didn't want to talk face to face, not yet anyway. "This is real quick—probably something I shouldn't really be concerned with. You may be able to help me with this one call."

Janet laughed a short staccato chuckle. "Tina, that would make my day."

"Well," Myra said, "it's like... Have you got time now?"

"Yes. Yes. Go ahead."

"You see, my husband and I have been having arguments. A couple have gotten a little physical."

"Go on," Janet said.

"And, in the heat of an argument, really in an offhanded remark, he said he could poison my food and makeup without me knowing it. Is this possible?"

"Tina? Are you asking me if it's possible to poison someone without her knowledge, or are you asking me if it's possible for your husband to do such a thing? Either way, get out of that house. I mean today."

"I can't do that. On one hand, I don't think he was serious, but on the other—"

"Listen to me," Janet interrupted, "any time your life is threatened, you take it seriously. Come in and see me. I can help you get out of this situation."

"No," Myra almost yelled into the phone, "this is moving too fast. I just wanted to know if this is a common, empty threat men use."

"Tina, you took the first step. You need help, come in and let's talk. I can let you talk to other domestic violence survivors. It will help you understand your feelings—"

Myra hung up the phone. *This is too fast. I can't leave.* She considered her options: Tina had her own family and her mother to take care of, and Topher was busy with his own life. *I can't impose. My family? No one's really left but Granny, and she's so old. No.*

Her eyes filled with tears. *I'm on my own. Without Gil, I'm on my own.*

THE PHONE ON Topher's desk buzzed, breaking his concentration.

"Where have you been?" Myra's voice came across the line like a slap to his face.

He moved the phone to his other ear and replied, "Nowhere."

"Come on, you haven't answered your cell or home phone or gone to work for a week." She paused then asked the question in a slow measured voice full of concern and fear. "Are you okay?"

Okay? He knew what she intended; consciously or not, she always worried about HIV. "Physically, I'm healthy. Mentally and emotionally, I have a long road ahead."

"What happened?"

He realized he hadn't talked to anyone except Dustin and Erik about the breakup since it happened. "Alex and I aren't together anymore."

"I'm sorry."

"No, I think it's what I wanted. I broke it off, not Alex. I spent the past week at Dustin and Erik's house avoiding everyone. I'm sorry, I should have called you, but I was so crazy, I just wanted a place to crash where I could lock myself up and still get meals and maid service." He chuckled, then the veil fell again. "I phoned Alex once, but I kept it brief. I feel like I've been shot through the heart, no pain, just a sudden realization that there's no longer anything there. Maybe a vacuum is there. The rest of my life seems to have followed that loss. But you know the odd part?"

"What?"

"It was my choice. I honestly believe Alex would have kept going like it was—no love, no commitment, no friendship. But I have to give him credit, he was always honest. He never made that verbal commitment of saying he loved me. Although, he did everything but that, so he left open his one loophole."

"What can I do?" Her voice held him in tenderness.

"Thanks for the offer, but I need to do this on my own."

She sighed. "I know what you mean. Some things can't be accomplished faster with two instead of one. This is your recovery." Her voice dropped to a low whisper. "I'm working on one, too." She took a breath and continued. "Remember, I'm here when you need me. In fact, let's meet after work and talk. Would that be okay?"

Topher felt the urge to hide again. Talking over his feelings for the past week with Dustin and Erik had left him exhausted, but he wanted Myra's perspective. "Okay. I'll see you at 5:30."

AFTER TALKING WITH Myra, his mother, Daryl, and other friends about his breakup, Topher felt the urge to get on with his life. Erik and Dustin sat across the table in their dining room, passing the steamed salmon and grilled vegetables.

"So, Topher, it's almost time for that mid-winter fling—the Red Party." Dusty smiled like a kid talking about Christmas.

"Oh, great," Topher said, "the Red Party. I'll wear black. I don't think I can stand the Valentine's excitement."

Erik took another drink of chardonnay. "I think you should go. What you need is someone new. Someone dark, moody, passionate, Spanish or Italian, an accent would be wonderful, maybe a large, hard—"

"Hey!" Dusty pounded the table. "You better be thinking about someone for Topher and not for yourself."

"I'm happily married. I just want Topher to have what I have." Erik smiled at Dustin with genuine affection.

Dustin put both hands on the table and pushed his chair back. "I don't have an accent. I'm not Spanish or Italian. But I do have one thing you didn't mention in your brief, but very telling fantasy, I have a blackberry cheesecake. Get your happily married ass in the kitchen and bring out the coffee."

Erik obeyed, and Dustin turned back to Topher. "You'll have to meet the second best man in Charlotte. I have the best."

Topher laughed, gathered up the dishes, and followed them into the kitchen. "I don't know if I'm ready to meet anyone new. God knows, though, I'm tired of seeing the same old faces."

Dustin and Erik stopped in mid-motion.

"No, I didn't mean the two of you," Topher said. "I just mean I'm tired of seeing the same people who bring back memories of Alex, or know Alex and ask where he is. By the way, will he be there?"

"Probably," Erik said.

"Of course, he'll be there." Topher paced the kitchen floor. "A place to make contacts, maybe further his career, small talk about fashion, cars, furniture. He's so damn gay."

"Ouch," Dustin grabbed his chest, "that little arrow hit me. What do you mean 'he's so damn gay'—what are you?"

"Sorry, I just wanted to call him something."

"Call him a jerk or an asshole if you're mad." Dustin's face flushed. "As long as we use 'so gay' and 'faggot' to insult each other, how can we expect anyone else to stop doing it?"

Erik put his hand on Dustin's shoulder. "Let's don't argue. Stop being so politically correct, Dusty."

"I'm sorry," Topher said.

"No, I'm sorry. I just hate to hear it. I hear it enough whispered and chuckled in the background at the grocery stores and the restaurants."

"I know." Topher changed the subject. "I'll go to the party. It's for a good cause. Last year, they raised a lot of money for AIDS. I might ask Myra to go, if Gil will let her out of the house."

"That Neanderthal's still around?" Dustin carried their cheesecake back to the dining room.

"Yeah," Topher said. "And he's worse than ever. I talked to Myra yesterday, and she's just about had it. She could do so much better."

"She has such a pretty face."

"Erik, that's what everyone says about fat girls," Dustin scolded. "I really like her. If we could just get her to Dion for a make-over..."

"Guys, Myra's my best friend. She's fine the way she is. She doesn't try to change me, I don't try to change her. Acceptance, remember what we want? Acceptance. Stop being so gay." Topher laughed and punched Dustin's shoulder.

"Owww! You hurt me. You brute." He slapped Topher's arm with an exaggerated limp wrist. "Stop being so butch."

"Okay, so we're set," Erik stopped their play. "Next Saturday is the Red Party. We'll meet here and go together."

"Fine. I'll see if Myra wants to go."

"TOPHER," MYRA'S VOICE sounded tired, "I'd love to go, but there's no way Gil will let me—especially if he knows I'm going with you."

"That's okay. We'll have lunch on Monday, and I can tell you all about it." He hung up the phone as Daryl walked into his cube. He carried in a large cardboard heart-shaped candy box, the top decorated with red satin ruffles and a floppy satin rose glued to the middle.

"Like my big heart? I want to make it into a hat for the party." He placed it on his head and smiled his Miss America smile. "I'd like to thank all the little people who helped me along the way. Let's see," he placed his index finger on his chin and rolled his eyes up, "there's Ted, he was small; Malachi, for a black man, he was tiny; Eddie, small-framed, created an optical illusion he was bigger than he was— "

"That's enough," Topher stopped him. "I don't have all day to listen to your list."

Daryl dropped the box on the floor, sat down, and whispered. "Last weekend at the bar, I met the most handsome man. But you know the cosmetic effect of darkness, and I have been known to go home with a prince and wake up with his ugly stepsister, so I whipped out a flashlight and put it right in his face."

"No. You didn't?"

"Sure did. You know who it was?" He paused for dramatic effect. "It was your ex! I almost slept with Alex. But, being the loyal friend I am, I just gave him my phone number, and asked him to call me after the appropriate mourning period."

"No!" Topher felt his heart sink into his stomach. "Are you making this shit up? Really?"

"I swear on Donna Summer's grave."

"She's not dead."

"Might as well be."

"Seriously, was Alex at the bar last weekend?" Topher had to know. *Could he be so cold? Did the break-up mean nothing to him?*

"Yes, he was, but no, I didn't talk to him. I saw him across the room. He leaned against the bar and talked to a few people. Willie and I played the Hardy Boys and followed him as he left."

"You followed his car?"

"Of course, dear. The bar was dead. He drove up Freedom Drive, Morehead, by the stadium, and back to Fourth Ward. Damn, he's boring. Straight home without so much as a cruise through the park."

Topher realized he'd been holding his breath and let it out in a long sigh. "He's free to do what he wants. But the bar, so soon."

Daryl picked up the Valentine's box and held it on his head again. "Forget about it. There's a huge party this weekend, and you'll meet someone better."

"Yes, I will." He reconsidered. "No, I won't. I'm fine on my own. I would just like to talk to Alex one more time."

A smile uncurled on Daryl's face. "Should I prepare for a cat fight?"

"No. I just want to finalize things."

TOPHER ARRIVED AT Dustin and Erik's house wearing all black. He couldn't bring himself to wear red—no romance, no passion, no energy to try.

Dustin answered the door. "Black? Come on. You look like death, and that's not a good thing for an AIDS benefit."

"Sorry, it's all I could do. Look at Erik, he's in brown."

"No," Erik said, "it's brick. It's a shade of red."

"He doesn't think red is his color," Dustin whispered. "And you know, it isn't. With that fair skin, he looks pink."

"Red's not my color either."

"Whatever," Dustin said and pushed him toward the door. "Let's go before all the single men are taken. We need to get you married off."

Erik's Mercedes glided down Monroe Road to the site of the party. A large tent had been constructed in an office park. Heaters rattled outside the tent almost as loud as the music coming from within, while a stream of red-attired people filed into the front of the billowing tent from the parking lot.

"It's outside? I'll ruin my shoes." Dustin pressed his nose against the fogged up window of the car.

The winter night's cold wind blew the musty odor of damp, decaying leaves across Topher's face as they got out of the car. A light drizzle remained from the afternoon's rain, coating everything in a light mist. "Great night for a party."

"Oh, Topher, it will be fine once we're inside." Erik led the way to the tent.

Two large folding tables flanked the entrance, and volunteers gathered money and distributed red ribbons. An elderly woman gave Topher his ribbon and a second glance at his black clothes. "It makes the ribbon show up better," he said with a smile.

Crowds of people stood around talking and drinking, a few danced on the temporary wooden floor laid down next to the deejay's stand. Topher scanned the tent for Alex, but didn't see him.

"Let's get a drink." Dustin pulled Topher toward the bar.

"In a way, I hope he's not here," Topher said after they claimed their drinks.

"Who? Oh." Erik glanced around. "He might not come. Last time I talked to Alex, he wasn't sure."

"You talked to him?"

"Yeah."

"How is he? Did he say?"

Erik took another sip of his beer and looked at Dustin, then back to Topher. "He understands the break-up and just wants what's best for you."

"Typical," Topher said. "That's just typical of the whole relationship."

"Hey, hey, hey, boys. Glad you made it." Daryl, clad in tight, red, pleather pants and no shirt, entered their circle with his cardboard Valentine's hat cocked to one side of his head.

"That's wonderful." Dustin patted him on the back. "Good job. I wasn't sure you were really going to wear it."

"You talking about those pants or that hat?" Topher asked.

"Bitch, don't get jealous on me." Daryl hung onto Topher's arm. "At least I'm not dressed like Johnny Cash."

Topher smiled and tweaked Daryl's nipple. "Okay, let's see your masterpiece."

Daryl tilted his head and raised an eyebrow. "You talking about my hat, right?"

"Yes, ma'am. I'm still amazed you wore it."

"Have you ever known me not to carry through on a fabulous idea?" Daryl made a graceful turn so they could see it from all sides. A large tag hung from the back.

Erik grabbed the tag. "Hold it. What's this?" He read it and laughed.

"What does it say?" Dustin turned Daryl around to look and read it out loud, "Single and looking."

"Very subtle, Daryl. Good luck with it." Topher smiled and then asked, "Have you seen Alex?"

"Yeah, he's over there." He pointed in the direction of a crowd of people near the opposite corner.

The wind blew through the tent like a hurricane, but no one seemed to notice except Topher. He turned and walked away from his friends, looking for a place to disappear. Facing Alex wasn't something he looked forward to doing. *What if those feelings come back? I haven't seen him in over a month. Am I ready?* The thoughts swirled in his mind with the chill of the wind. His head throbbed, and his eyes stung. He looked up to find Alex standing in front of him.

"Hello, Topher."

"Hey."

"It's good to see you. You look well. I saw you from across the room—the black shirt and pants make you stand out in a sea of red. Of course, you always stood out from everyone else."

Topher stared at the muddy ground. "I hear you've been hanging out at the bars."

Alex's face turned to cranberry, matching his cashmere sweater. "I went out to meet Scott and Doug. They wanted me to get out of the house."

"Well, good. You need to get out and meet some people. I probably held you back from making the contacts you need." He didn't intend for it to sound as bitter as it did.

"You didn't hold me back. I enjoyed what we had. It just didn't work out." Alex shifted his stance. "It was a good experience for both of us. Besides, what else would we have been doing over the past year? It was fun being together for a while."

"Fun?" Topher looked him in the eyes. "That's all it was to you, fun?"

"What more did you want?"

"Love. I wanted someone to love, to care about, to share my life with. How can you be so cold?"

"I'm not being cold. It's just the facts. Do you want me pretending? Years going by with doubts about our true feelings? We had fun together. Let's just leave it at that."

"No, I feel like I wasted a year of my life on you. I changed to suit you—"

Alex interrupted, "I never asked you to, did I?"

"Not in words, but in actions. I tried to be everything you wanted. We started dating because you liked the idea of dating a painter, but then you never asked about my painting or took an interest in it. I'm willing to bet the painting I gave you isn't above your bed anymore."

"Yes it is," he said. "I was interested in your painting. I was interested in you. You never seemed to be interested in my life."

"What life?" Topher shot back. "You did nothing but work and talk about work. You never read anything but legal briefs, and when we would go to a movie, you had no comment on it afterwards. It was so hard talking to you. If we ate dinner at your house, it was in front of the television, and dinner at a restaurant was a nightmare—you wouldn't talk. You responded to my questions with one-word answers. Wasted. No, stolen, you're a thief. You stole my affection and kept leading me on. I believed there was something special between us. You knew there wasn't, but you kept playing the game, taking, taking, and taking—"

"Hold on. I did no such thing. Do you expect me to know from day one that I love someone? It takes time and effort to get to know a person—"

"But a full year?" Topher asked.

"Who can put a time limit on that?"

"I did. Yours ran out."

"Then it's my fault. I'm sorry I failed you. I'm sorry I wasn't what you wanted me to be. I can't change. I won't change to please you or anyone else. You wasted your energy on me."

Topher calmed and smiled. "Yes, Alex. I did."

"I'm sorry it took so long to see it."

"So am I. I'm sure, in time, I'll be grateful." Topher thought for a moment and repeated Alex's words back to him. "What else would we have done over the past year?"

A puzzled look fell over Alex's face.

Topher smiled and walked away.

THE NEXT DAY, Topher got in his SUV and drove four hours to Sunset Beach. He hadn't thought about going to the ocean, he had been on his way to the store for cigarettes, but he kept driving. By the time he got there, it was close to dark, and he walked down the beach of the small island staring into the distance. The weather had cleared, but the air still held a chill. The Atlantic stretched into the horizon, and he imagined walking out into it. The salty, crisp smell of the sea and the gusty winds surrounded him as he stood at the water's edge, arms outstretched and his coat whipping around him. Salt crystallized on his face and clothes as he sat behind a dune, surrounded by thoughts of his life, the relationships, the mistakes, the losses, the problems, the bad decisions, and the circled reasoning of what he should have done differently and the inevitable question of would he do anything differently next time. Darkness shielded him from the few hardy beachcombers and surf fishermen going home for the night.

Cold, hunger, and thirst had no hold on him, but sleep claimed him near three in the morning.

The dream came fast: Alex leaned against a palm tree with the wind thrashing its feather-like leaves. The sky churned black with steel gray clouds; lightning flashed and cracked around the bobbing wooden crate Topher floated on just off shore. He wanted to get to land and yelled for Alex to help him, but Alex stood still, leaning against the tree, a slight smile on his lips. The waves grew and crashed against the crate. He clung to the edge to stay on top of it. He looked around for a way to get to the beach, but the waves took his attention back to struggling for his own survival.

Another glance at the shore revealed Alex walking away. Topher yelled for him to come back and help him to land, but he didn't acknowledge him. Myra's voice floated across the wind. He couldn't understand her. Turning away from the beach to look for Myra in the stormy ocean, he squinted and shielded his eyes from a ray of glistening sunlight from the west.

A bright sky and squawking gulls woke Topher from the dream. His stomach rumbled for food. Covered with damp sand and salt, he looked out to the ocean and thanked God for the new day.

Chapter Fourteen

MYRA SLID DOWN into the warm soapy water and exhaled while the soothing, comforting fragrance of lavender swirled around her body. With eyes closed, she gently glided the bar of soap over each arm and across her chest. Warm, soft, water lapped across her breasts, splashing her nipples with rhythmic waves. Her mind floated and calmed. A smile emerged as her hand traveled across her stomach and down to the silkiness between her legs. Invisible hands caressed her. Invisible lips kissed her with tenderness. She relaxed as her own hands massaged and explored her body.

"Myra?" Gil knocked hard on the bathroom door.

Her eyes sprung open, and she felt her face flush. "Yes?"

Gil opened the door and walked in carrying something behind his back. He grinned at her like a mischievous kid. With one swift motion, he revealed a box of chocolates. "Happy Valentine's Day, babe. I got you these chocolates—your favorite." He extended the box to her.

She reached up with a dripping hand to take them. "Thanks, Gil. That was sweet of you." Not knowing what to do with the candy while in the tub, Myra set them down on the toilet lid.

"Go ahead and have one," Gil urged.

"I will, once I'm out of the tub."

"Nah, have one now."

"But, my hands are wet and soapy. I'll get one later. Thanks again."

Gil bent over and pulled the lid off the box. "I'll feed one to you."

"Thanks, but that's not necessary. That box wasn't even wrapped in plastic." Her anxiety began to rise: *Why is he so insistent? No, it can't be... Poison?*

Smiling down at her, Gil held a dark chocolate cream in his hand. "I unwrapped them for you. Open up."

She shivered even though the bath water steamed around her. The chunk of chocolate came toward her mouth, and she obediently opened up. The sweetness lay on her tongue. She could feel it melt and fill her mouth. Gil stood smiling at her. The chocolate dripped down the back of her mouth to her throat, but she fought the urge to swallow.

"Well, happy Valentine's Day, again. I love you." Gil bent over to kiss her. One hand fondled her right breast, while the other, on her shoulder, held her to him. She stiffened. His lips parted hers. His tongue forced its way into her mouth, exploring, probing. He pushed the melting chocolate to the side and ran his tongue over hers. He released her, stood up, and smiled. "Good chocolate. I'll be waiting in the bedroom." He closed the door behind him as he left.

Myra took the box off the toilet, lifted the lid, and spit out the candy, then calmed her mind in preparation to have sex with a possible madman.

THE NEXT DAY, Myra took a few of the chocolates out of the box and dropped them down the disposal. She checked the box from time to time to see if Gil was eating any of them, but the only ones to disappear were what she took. *Did he poison the candy? Or maybe just one or two of them?* Her thoughts kept going back to those questions. With her growing suspicion, she became more distant to Gil, but he seemed to grow fonder of her. As they sat in front of the television, eating a dinner of lasagna she had fixed, Gil scraped his plate and Myra picked at hers.

"You look great," Gil said.

Myra, a bit shaken by the praise, smiled back at him. "Thanks. I guess the gym is starting to pay off."

He leaned back and patted his stomach. "If I wasn't so full, I'd throw you down on the floor right now and have my way with you."

"Thanks." Myra meant it for not acting on his words. She couldn't think of anything she hated more than having sex with him, except his violent fits. She tried to discourage him from touching her in any way. Her mind associated any physical contact from him with abuse.

The compliment hung in her head. The next morning, she looked in the mirror to determine what change Gil had seen in her. She could actually see the inward curve under her cheekbones and her collarbone showed under her skin. She noticed her pants didn't pull at her waist anymore, and some of her clothes were actually too big for her.

She walked into her office smiling. Tina yelled after her, "Looks like Ms. Myra had a good weekend."

"It was okay."

Tina came into Myra's office and sat down. "Things going better for you?" The implied question of Gil's abuse swept the smile off her face.

"Oh, yeah. He hasn't been violent at all. I think he's changed," she said, not wanting to get into her biggest fear about Gil's behavior. "And I changed too. I feel like the gym is working."

"You do look good. What all are you doing?"

"I go to the Y just about every day after work. I take an aerobics class and lift some weights to tone. Also, I cut down on eating at home. A late dinner can be a killer." A nervous laugh escaped her lips.

"Well, girl, whatever you're doing, keep it up. In fact, make me start doing it. I could stand to lose a pound or two." Tina patted her butt, then amended, "or ten or twenty."

Myra's phone rang, and Tina excused herself.

"Human Resource Development, Myra Greer."

"Myra, this is Buddy. How are you?"

"Buddy Greer, where have you been? I haven't talked to you in—I can't remember when." She had always liked Gil's younger brother.

"Yeah, it's been a while. I talked to Gil a while back about taking Mama to Spartanburg, but he wouldn't. Can you talk to him for me? I have a new job at a machine shop in Florence, and it's too soon to ask for time off. Mama's bitchin' and moanin' about how nobody loves her, and she's too old to drive herself." His voice sounded so much like Gil's. She liked hearing it in a friendly tone.

"I don't think I could be much influence on Gil. When he decides something, it's set in concrete."

"Just like Daddy. Gil's just like Daddy."

Myra thought back to the old man who died a year after she and Gil married. He was rough and harsh. Constantly, he would pit brother against brother on any task. "Gil makes more money." "Buddy has a better truck." "Gil's smarter." "Buddy's better to his mama." The old man passed judgment on everyone and everything, and never changed his decree. Myra agreed with Buddy, "Yeah, just like Mr. Gilbert Greer."

"Don't ever say that around Mama," he cautioned. "Gil's her pride and joy, but she couldn't stand Daddy."

"I never realized that."

"Yeah, boy. Daddy would whip us as soon as look at us, and he would do the same to Mama. That temper is what put him in his grave. That old redneck's hate was more than a weak heart could take."

"Your daddy beat you and Gil? And your mama?" Myra asked with caution. Since Gil would never talk about his father, she had thought the whole family was just as silent.

"Yeah, but nothing we didn't deserve." He changed the subject. "Are you sure you couldn't talk to Gil and get Mama off my back?"

"I'll try." She hung up the phone and looked for the number of the domestic abuse counselor.

TOPHER MET MYRA for lunch at a small deli tucked in the basement of a gleaming downtown skyscraper. Little thought had been given to the décor, just the basic linoleum floor and tabletops with plastic daisies in glass vases. The draw was the food. The Greek man who owned the deli employed all his family to run the restaurant. Topher liked the idea of eating with a big family.

"I think I know why Gil acts the way he does," Myra said to him.

"He's mentally disturbed," Topher insisted, but he could tell she was serious.

"No, well, maybe a little," she laughed. "I talked with his brother this morning, and he says that their father did the same thing to them and their mother."

"Just because it happened to him is no excuse for him to repeat it. He knows better."

Myra shook her head. "No, I don't think he does." She dropped her gaze to her plate. "I called a woman at the domestic violence center."

"Great." He was glad she was getting help.

"She said it was common."

"What else did she say?" He hoped the counselor had had better luck convincing Myra than he had.

"That's all I asked. I didn't want to get into a long conversation with her trying to get me in to talk to her."

Damn, what is it going to take? "I think you do need to talk to her. Tell her the whole story. She can help. Did she say Gil needs counseling?"

"Of course, but Gil would never do that."

Topher took a sip of iced tea and tried to get her to a conclusion. "So, if he won't go to a counselor, and you won't talk to anyone about this, what are you going to do? This won't fix itself."

She rearranged the lettuce in her salad. "I'm not sure." She looked him straight in the eyes, her face smooth and eyes wide exposing honesty and uncertainty. "I'm not sure if I want to try."

"What?" he almost yelled. "You want to keep on living like this?"

"No, I know I can't keep doing that. I'm talking divorce." Her brown eyes reddened and filled with tears. "But I feel like I failed in some way. It's hard to explain." When she blinked, the tears spilled down her cheek.

He reached across the table and blotted her face with his napkin. "You always helped me, and I'll always be here for you. You're my family. I don't think you failed. No one could've lived this long with him. You should get an award."

She sniffed and wiped her eyes. "That's why I'm considering divorce. I feel so bad dumping this all on you. How are you doing?"

He shifted in his seat. "I feel like you do. Something needs to change, but I'm not sure what it is. I'm so restless. I'd like a new job, lose the responsibility of the house, different surroundings, new faces, leave the money-making power-hungry attitudes of Charlotte behind, and start over."

She smiled as she listened.

"Alex is over. I'm going nowhere with my paintings. I feel so weighted down here. Not that my job is that intense, or that I don't care about my friends—I just want to love my life. Right now, I don't." He looked at her and guilt filtered through him. "Damn, Myra. I'm saying this to you, and you're living with a psycho killer."

She laughed. "Topher, we're both riding the same runaway train. I think you just know to jump off before it wrecks. I keep thinking it will glide to a stop. I'm not sure which one of us is right. One thing I do know is I don't want you leaving Charlotte. You're my best friend. I don't know what I would do if you weren't here."

"Thanks." Topher rubbed her hand.

"No, no, I don't mean to put that on you. Do what's right for you. That's what's important, you leave Charlotte if you feel you need to. Don't stay for me, or your other friends, or anything else. You're free. Nothing binds you here."

A sense of lightness overcame him. She was right. He was free to do whatever he wanted.

THAT AFTERNOON, TOPHER called a real estate agent, the mother of an old boyfriend.

"Rose, this is Topher Langston. Remember me?"

"Of course, dear. How are you?"

"Great. I was wondering if you could give me some advice?"

"Sure, what on? You know me, sweetie, I'm a wealth of advice on any subject: financial, gardening, shopping, sex, divorce, cosmetics, furs, jewelry."

"I'm more interested in real estate. You've been to my house. What do you think I could get out of it, and how fast do you think it would move?"

"You're selling that well-maintained, quaint bungalow?"

"Thinking about it."

"How many bedrooms and baths?"

"Three bedrooms, one and a half baths. About 1600 square feet."

"How are the schools out there?"

Topher laughed. "No kids, remember? I don't know anything about the schools."

"That lot is about half an acre, right?

"Yeah, still in the county."

Rose bubbled. "Sounds wonderful. Let me check the comps, and I'll get back to you."

He hung up with his hands shaking. *Am I really going to sell my house? Can I drop all these material things and start over?*

THE COLD RAIN fell in sheets outside the window. Myra rinsed the dishes from dinner and stacked them in the dishwasher. *Would I really leave him?* She looked into the den where Gil aimed the remote at the television; he flipped channels so fast he couldn't possibly know what was on each one. *That's all he does: eat, sit in front of the TV, and sleep.* She sighed and closed the dishwasher. *There has to be more.*

"Have you given any more thought to taking your mama to Spartanburg?" she asked, walking into the den.

"The old woman doesn't need to go. She needs to keep her ass at home." Gil kept flipping through the channels.

"It might do her some good to get out and see some of her family."

"Sounds like you been talking to Buddy."

Myra looked out the sliding glass door at the rain freezing on the deck. "Yeah, he called the other day. He just started a new job—"

"Buddy's working? It's about damn time."

"And he doesn't want to ask off to take her. I think it would make your mama happy if you offered."

"Nope. I'm fine here. Don't need to be running her all over South Carolina. She bitches the whole time. When I took her to Orangeburg to visit her brother, all I heard was 'Gil, you drive too fast. The law will get you. Slow down.' or 'I need to stop. I gotta pee.' That old woman's got a bladder like a peanut. Why should I put myself through that?"

"Maybe because it would be a nice thing to do?"

"Nice? Shit," he huffed, "let Buddy be nice."

She let the subject drop. He settled back and left the channel on an old movie, a western with John Wayne. She picked up a magazine to read, but after staring at the first paragraph of an article on keeping your husband happy, she walked into the kitchen and dropped it in the trash. She ambled back to the glass door, looking over the deck and to the darkened parking lot. Laurie's CR-V wasn't there. *Bitch, you can have that lump on the recliner.*

Gil came and stood behind her. "Sit down," he said. "You make me nervous standing around, looking out the window."

"I'm just a little stir crazy. I feel like I want to do something, but I'm not sure what." She felt his hands wrap around her waist. She tensed.

"We could go back to the bedroom," he whispered in her ear.

The stale smell of beer on his breath made her stomach churn and the acid bubble up her throat. "I think I'm starting my period."

"Shit! You're either on the rag or getting ready to be."

"Guess it's an effect of the miscarriage." She didn't look at him.

"Sorry," he mumbled, going back to his movie and beer.

She knew he never kept track of that sort of thing and didn't really want to know. "Excuse me. I'm going back to lie down for a minute." She went to the bedroom and pulled her portable stair climber from under the bed and started working out. As she worked, she imagined climbing a stairway with Gil falling farther and farther behind her. After she finished, she took a shower and went to bed, leaving Gil in the den with his television, beer, and ten o'clock snack.

THAT SATURDAY NIGHT, Myra searched through the drawers of the dresser, dismissing clothes as she dug.

"Why don't you wear those black jeans?" Gil asked.

She looked at him with confusion. "I could."

"They look good on you since you lost weight."

"Thanks. That's nice of you to say."

She watched him getting ready for his bowling night. He stood in front of the closet in his white briefs, with his stomach hanging down like a pregnant woman's. He tried on his jeans, but he couldn't get them fastened.

"These have shrunk in the wash." He pulled them off and his underwear came with them. "Oops, the monster's loose."

"Maybe cold water will help," she said.

"What? Oh, the jeans." He tugged up his briefs and grabbed his bowling shirt off the hanger.

"Yeah," she sighed, "maybe I should wash them in cold. They wouldn't shrink so much." *Shrink? You never considered you're getting fatter?* "This will be a real treat. I haven't been with you on a bowling night in years."

"I thought you might like to see some of the guys again." He pulled on another pair of pants, taking a deep breath as he buttoned them.

She slid on the tight-fitting black jeans and a white blouse. In the bathroom, she applied makeup and hairspray. Not quite a skinny, boyish beauty queen, she appraised, but more womanly with the curves in the right places—firm and tight. She smiled and went back to the bedroom where Gil tied his shoes.

"Wow, babe. You look wonderful." Gil stood up and kissed her, patting her butt.

AT THE BOWLING alley, Gil made sure everyone knew Myra was with him. He introduced her to his coworkers and friends from the leagues playing that night.

"Okay, Myra, go sit up there." He pointed to a line of red plastic chairs lined up behind his lane. "You can see good from there, and our scores will be up on that screen."

She looked up at the scratchy projected image. "Honey, I've bowled before. I know how it works."

"I know that. Just sit here and look pretty." He set a Diet Coke in front of her and returned to his bowling partners.

Why is he treating me like an idiot? Myra watched the men bowl. They talked and laughed, but every few minutes one would turn and look at Myra, then slap Gil on the back or shake his hand, laughing the whole time. *What are those dimwits laughing about? Why is Gil the center of attention?* She looked to the left and right of her chair, underneath it, and behind her. Then in a blinding flash of the obvious, she realized she had been set on the trophy platform. Other women sitting in the same chairs watching their men, all had that same made-up, teased and sprayed hair, look. The overweight and older women bowled on the floor with the men. *Can't he just treat me like another person, not like some possession?*

She walked down to the floor and pulled Gil to the side. "I need to go get some tampons at the drug store. Can I have the keys?"

"Well...uh, sure," he stammered, handing her his truck keys.

She grabbed the keys and headed for the door. As soon as she saw the truck in the parking lot, she stopped and looked at the keys again. *I have his keys. Find the gun. Get rid of it.* Instead of going through his truck there, she drove it to a shopping center down the road and parked it under a streetlight.

The harsh light helped her look through the cab of the truck, but she couldn't find the gun. She got out and started unlocking and checking each storage cabinet built into the bed of the pickup. "Damn," she said out loud, "nothing. Where?" Myra got down on her hands and knees to look under the truck. She stood back up, opened the door, and popped the hood. "Has he moved it to the apartment?" Fear shook her whole body.

The stores in the shopping center began to shut off their lights. Myra checked her watch. It read 9:15. She had to get back to pick up Gil. He would probably be waiting for her.

As the truck squealed into the bowling alley's parking lot, Myra searched the entrance for Gil. He wasn't there. She parked and hurried inside where a line of people waited to settle their bill. Gil wasn't in the line. She noticed a few of his friends leaving.

"Good night, Myra. It was good seeing you again," Arnie, another exterminator, yelled as he walked out the door.

She waved back, trying not to draw too much attention to herself. *What will I tell him to explain why I was so late getting back?* She listed excuses in her mind: I had to go to another drug store, because they didn't carry my brand; I ran into someone from work, and we talked for a while; I had car trouble; I left my pocketbook and had to retrace my steps.

Turning a corner, she caught sight of him. He bowled in the far lanes, just where she had left him. *Maybe he didn't notice how long I was gone.* She slipped back into her seat. Before his next turn, he stood up and looked back at her. She smiled. He looked at the wall clock and back at her, shaking his head.

He noticed. Sweat broke out on her upper lip. She stood up and paced a little. Noticing the rows of bowling balls, she patted one and rolled it around to look for the size. *Casual, casual, casual.* She sighed, a long exaggerated sigh, then walked back to her seat.

Gil was almost finished with his game. He walked back up to her chair. "Sorry, it takes so long. We're about finished. I noticed you walking around. No one tried to hit on you, did they?"

"No, Gil...I was just checking out the place. After I got back, I sat in the snack bar and watched a little TV." She waited to see if he believed it.

"Good. I just didn't want you to get bored."

Jackpot. She held a faint smile and said, "No, I wasn't bored at all."

THE NEXT NIGHT as Myra came home from the gym, she unlocked the door and heard Gil talking on the phone. He turned to look as she walked in.

"Yes, Mama." Gil held the receiver away from his ear and rolled his eyes at Myra.

She smiled and went to drop her gym clothes in the washer.

Gil continued with his mother. "Mama, I don't owe Buddy nothing. Yes, I remember the BB gun accident. How long do I have to pay for that?"

Guilt? She uses guilt to make him do things? Myra considered it. *No, he's over any guilt with me within an hour.*

"No, don't put Buddy on the phone; I don't want to talk to him...Dammit." He slammed the phone down. "Son of a bitch."

Myra closed the laundry closet door without a sound and went to the bedroom to allow Gil time to cool down.

Who's out there? She considered her options, places and people where she would feel safe. She lay on the bed, curled her legs up, and hugged them to her. The home she had always imagined didn't include fear, but it did include a husband, and some day, children. Depression settled as she mourned the life she had planned—no husband, no children, no home, no family.

As she reexamined her decision, she knew she had made the only choice: no man—even with his potential to give her children—outweighed her need for security and self-respect. She smiled as she realized, that now, the only thing she treasured in Gil was his sperm. *And that's not even an attractive gene pool.*

"Oh, God," she whispered to herself. "How do I tell him?" Thoughts of the poison, the gun, the beating, and the shouting, swirled around her body, sending chills over her skin, and penetrating her lungs. It stole her breath. *I can't...I can't tell him. He'll kill me for sure.* She sat up and looked at the door; the clomping sound of Gil's footsteps came down the hallway. Wiping her eyes, she straightened the bed to erase signs of her presence, then stood by the dresser, braced for his anger.

The door flew open. "When's dinner?" Gil asked. "I'm starving."

"Um," her mind raced to find words to answer him, "in a few minutes. I'm trying to get organized."

"Good." Gil turned and closed the door behind him.

A long slow breath escaped her as she sank back down to the edge of the bed. Her arms and legs had filled with lead, and she didn't have the energy to move. *I can't do it...I can't not do it.* She looked around the bedroom and tried to decide what she actually needed. She practically lived out of her pocketbook and car since she replaced all her potentially poisoned toiletries. *A couple of suitcases of clothes. Everything else, he can have.* The lead feeling began to lift from her body.

MYRA FINISHED HER aerobics class and then started looking for Topher. Excitement, like the bouncy energy of a junior high school cheerleader, washed over her. She bounded up the steps to the stair climbers. Topher read a magazine as he climbed. "Topher, Topher, guess what?"

"What? What are you jumping around for?" He laughed as he watched her.

Looking around at the other people nearby, she decided to wait for some privacy. "How much longer before you finish?" She jumped up to see his control panel.

"Five more minutes."

"I'll wait for you downstairs in the cafeteria." She headed toward the stairs, then turned and yelled back, "Hurry, I have great news!"

Topher met her in the nearly deserted cafeteria. She finished a cup of water and smiled as he approached.

He sat across from her. "So, girlfriend, what are you so excited about?" Sweat rolled down his face, and his hair, wet and dripping, glistened in the dim lights.

Trying to contain her excitement, she told him, "I've decided to leave Gil."

"No? Really? That's great." He hugged her across the table, then stood and wrapped his arms around her in a strong embrace. They held each other so hard Myra almost lost her breath. They let go, peeling their sweaty shirts apart. "When? How? Have you told him?" His questions flew like fireworks.

"First off," Myra said, "I haven't told him. I know I should, but I'm afraid. Secondly, I thought I would go to my grandmother's in Tennessee. It's been so long since we visited her, he's probably forgotten she exists. I just want to get out of state as soon as I leave. I can stay there for a while until I decide what to do."

"When are you planning to do this?"

"As soon as I get my nerve up. I just feel so relieved to have a direction. I want to take my time, but it won't be too long. I'm sure of this. I know it's the right thing to do. There is nothing to salvage from that relationship—nothing at all."

Topher grinned. "Funny, how we arrived at the same place. I hadn't told you, but my house is on the market. I'm selling it to simplify my life. I could easily— Damn, is this something you feel you need to do on your own?" His enthusiasm caught Myra by surprise.

"Not necessarily. Why? I thought I'd take off and learn to stand on my own two feet."

"This is a huge step. I really admire your self-confidence to even consider this." He took a deep breath and smiled. "What if we go together? Starting over with new jobs and a new place would be so much easier with someone else."

Her heart raced at the thought of starting over with Topher. "I would love to have you along for companionship. I know I'd feel more secure in a new place with you nearby, plus I have a feeling that Gil might not accept this easily." She hesitated to voice her fear, but the words came on their own, "He might actually come after me."

He guided her back down into the chair. "Gil would try to track you down? Do you really think he'd do that?"

"Yes, I do. You know how upset he got at the Christmas party. That was nothing compared to what he would do if I left him. His family would die of embarrassment. He wouldn't want to tell the people at work. It would look bad on him." She shivered, thinking about it. "He once told me about an aunt who left her husband, and the whole family went after her."

"You could get a restraining order," Topher said.

"Yeah, but it won't help if I'm dead."

He looked at her with a shocked expression she recognized as the realization of genuine danger. He shook loose the look with a single word. "Don't."

"Don't?"

"Don't say anything to anyone. Don't let him know what we're planning. If we don't leave a trail of people knowing where we're going, he can't find us."

"That's going to be hard to do. How do we just disappear?"

He thought for a moment. His expression lightened like he knew he could solve all her problems. "Oh, Myra," he grinned his little boy grin, "that's the adventure."

Chapter Fifteen

HEARTY GOLDEN DAFFODILS pushed their blooms up toward the warming March sky. Topher picked a few and placed them in a paper cup on his kitchen counter. Boxes littered the floor of his house. Sorting into three stacks, he labeled the boxes 'garage sale,' 'donate,' and 'ship to Mom.' A portable radio played in the corner since his stereo sat packed in its boxes and labeled for the garage sale. The doorbell rang, and he looked through the kitchen window to see his banker, Brad "Bam Bam" Williams. The "Bam Bam" came from his habit of gulping beer at Hotel Charlotte and slamming his mug down for another round.

Topher opened the door and took a deep breath. His attraction for Brad still stood—his Italian looks and his hands got to him, just like always. Topher loved his strong hands and the pattern of dark hair on the back, like an arrow pointing to Brad's ring finger. He shook that hand and invited him into the house.

Brad laughed at the piles of boxes. "You don't mess around when you say you're selling."

Topher offered him a stool at the kitchen counter. "The house sold right away. I'm so glad. I'm closing on the 29th."

"And your plans?"

Topher squirmed a little. "They're kind of undecided." He watched Brad rub his forearms, a nervous habit. "You know, I'm sorry things didn't work out between us all those years ago." Topher's mind flashed back to the time when they had first met almost ten years earlier, had a brief relationship, and then remained friends.

"Yeah," Brad said, "but it was for the best. We both grew into people so different than we were in our twenties. How did we stand each other? I know I wouldn't want to date anyone who acts like I did back then."

"Me neither. Hey, let me get you a beer, Bam Bam." Topher handed him a beer, then lit a joint and passed it to Brad. "Totally, dude, a beer and a joint on a Saturday. Good thing we're not like we were in our twenties."

"So, what do you want to do with the money from the sale?" Brad asked.

"To be honest, I need your help and your confidentiality. I'm leaving town. Alex and I broke up. He never loved me, and I was too infatuated to see it."

"So...you're running?"

"No, I just want to start over. I don't feel good about Charlotte anymore. I've done all I can here. Also," Topher decided to tell him everything, "do you remember Myra?"

"Myra? Yes, she was the girl who was in love with you." Brad laughed and patted him on the back. "Congratulations. She got her wish. You've been converted, and you're getting married."

Topher took another hit from the joint. "Not quite. Her husband abuses her, and she wants to leave him, but she's afraid he'll track her down and kill her. Personally, I think she's over-reacting. I know he physically abused her, but I don't believe he cares if she goes or not. Anyway, we've decided to travel together, so I need you to not say anything to anyone about me and where I might be—for Myra's peace of mind and for mine. I really just want to dump everything and make a new life."

"Sure, you know you can count on me."

"That's why I called you. I want my money to be available to me no matter where I am—"

"Credit card," Brad said.

"How would I pay the bill? I won't have an address."

"Pay it on-line."

"I'm not carting a laptop with me—new life, remember?"

Brad took another hit from the joint and a gulp of beer. "Your debit card. The money comes directly from your checking account. I can have your bank statements sent to my branch, then you can call an 800 number to get your balances or you can always access your accounts on the bank's Web site when you get to a computer." He thought some more. "We have branches almost all over the country. If you need anything go to the local branch and have them call me. I'll okay all your transactions."

"Let me get you another beer." Topher handed him another bottle. "You make this so easy. The only concern Myra might have is that Gil will be able to find us through the statements and where we use the debit cards."

"Tell her not to worry. He can't get access to your account information. You're safe. In fact, Myra needs to work this out with her own banker, someone she trusts."

Topher interrupted, "I'll have her get with you. The fewer people involved the better."

"Just one thing I ask in return...take me with you!" he yelled. "I don't want to stay here. I want to go. Please, please, please!"

"Tell you what, Bam Bam, once I get settled, you've got a place to stay. Come for a visit. Maybe help me get set up."

Brad rubbed his unshaven chin. "Let me encourage you to run toward Hawaii or Palm Springs. Maybe Aspen. I wouldn't mind a vacation in any of those places."

The thought hit Topher. "Damn, I honestly don't have any idea where we'll end up. I guess we'll head west, not much room to head east. I lived in the north, maybe...I don't know."

Brad held up his beer in a toasting position. "Here's to spinning the wheel and living life."

THAT NIGHT, TOPHER dialed his mother's number and took a deep breath. By the time she answered on the third ring, he had already composed a message for the machine.

"Oh, Mom, you're there. I thought you might have gone out."

"No, Ron is coming over for dinner. I'm in the process of getting ready."

"Sorry, I won't keep you. I can call you tomorrow."

"We're going to Cherokee for a flea market tomorrow. He has a friend with a booth there, and I'm taking some old furniture to sell."

He laughed. "I boxed up some stuff for a garage sale. I should just get the two of you to come take it all up to Cherokee."

"What are you selling? Why? Do you need money?"

"No, I need to lighten my load." He took another deep breath. "I sold the house."

"What? Are you crazy? Why?" She calmed a little and asked, "Are you moving in with someone?"

"No. I just hit a wall here. I want to sell everything that isn't essential in my life. And you know what? I don't need much."

"You'll see," she warned, "you will need more than you think."

"Maybe so, but I just want to be free for a little while. The house was a good investment. I made some money on it—"

"Don't blow it all. You'll never get another house."

"It's going straight to the bank. I can live light until I find where I want to be and get a job."

"You quit your job?"

"I'm leaving town. I can't commute," he said sounding more sarcastic than he intended. "I know this is sudden for you, but I've thought about it for a while. I need to do this."

"If you need to do it, come stay with me."

He smiled. "Thanks, but that wouldn't work, Mom. I want to live, have adventure, see what's out there. I'll keep in touch. You'll probably hear from me more while I'm on the road than you do now."

"You taking your cell phone?"

"No way. I already cancelled it and threw it away. I hated that thing."

"How will I contact you? How will you contact me?"

"Hotels have phones," he said. "There are still pay phones along the road."

"I know you're safe now," she said in a low steady tone. "When you go on this little adventure, I won't know from one minute to the next if you might be lying dead along some highway."

Topher knew she was worried. "I can take care of myself." He resisted telling her Myra would be with him. Gil would probably phone looking for her. "If you don't hear from me, assume I'm having the time of my life and am too busy to call—like college."

She sighed. "You aren't being responsible. Everything you worked for... You can't just leave troubles behind. The problems will go with you. Maybe it isn't Charlotte and the people there—"

"Hold on," he interrupted, "isn't that exactly what you did in New York? Dad left us, and you packed up and moved to Virginia."

"I didn't find any answers here." Her voice held a tinge of defeat.

"I'm not looking for answers. I just want to shed some chains, and as long as I'm here, those chains get heavier."

"Don't expect miracles when you leave the city limits." She paused, then added, "Just be happy, that's all I ask."

"Thanks, Mom. Now go get ready for your date. I'll call you later." He hung up the phone and finished packing.

THE NEXT SATURDAY, Topher got up before daylight to set up for his garage sale. Daryl arrived to help. He staggered into the garage and fell on the couch.

"Hey, that's for sale. Don't make it look too used," Topher said. "Thanks for coming over to help."

Daryl lifted himself up on one arm. "Too used? If this couch could talk, it would be the hottest ticket in town." He got up and started looking through the items for sale. "Would you take ten dollars for this lamp?"

"Daryl, you can have anything here. Take it."

"No, no, I want to contribute to your cause. Besides, I'm the Garage Sale Queen. I love hunting for bargains." He flipped through a stack of albums, "Bee Gees, Madonna, Olivia Newton-John, KC and the Sunshine Band, Duran Duran, Super Tramp, the Commodores, Wham, Bruce Springsteen—before the muscles, K-tel's Dyn-o-mite," he held one up and smiled, "Gloria Gaynor. 'I Will Survive.' Let's play it."

"Sorry, the turntable is boxed up."

"How will you sell it if no one knows it works? Let me set it up." Daryl began unboxing the stereo equipment. "You get so much more out of it if it's set up and playing."

Within minutes, a scratchy disco diva began singing. As the music swelled, Topher hit the garage-door button and the door slowly rattled its way up. A group of early shoppers stood outside and clapped as the opening door revealed Daryl lip-synching into a rolling pin. He took a bow and announced, "Welcome to the disco garage sale."

The music played for another half hour before Daryl felt he got the top price for the stereo and records. To Topher's surprise, the furniture moved quickly, and by noon, they were sold out.

"I'm going home to take a nap." Daryl yawned and stretched. "What are you going to do? You sold your bed."

"Sleep on the floor until Wednesday when the house closes, and then I'll stay with Erik and Dustin for a few days before leaving." Topher counted the money in his shoebox.

Daryl's eyes teared up. "I'll miss you."

"Oh, Daryl," he got up and hugged him, "I'll miss you too, buddy. I'll write to you as soon as I'm settled. I promise."

"I'm afraid you'll get lonely or hurt on your own."

Topher almost forgot about his pact of secrecy to Myra and corrected Daryl, but instead, caught himself and said, "I'll be fine. In fact, I'm glad to be getting out of this little incestuous community—no more dating ex-boyfriends of ex-boyfriends. The world will be mine. I'll make new friends."

"One last thing, have you told Alex?"

"No. I'm not telling many people. In fact, you, Dustin and Erik, and Myra are the only ones who know. I don't want a lot of people asking questions. I just want to slip out of town quietly. I didn't tell Alex, because I didn't think he would care, and if he did, I didn't want to talk about it."

"Okay," Daryl said, "I'll take it to the grave, or at least till you're out of town."

"It's a deal. Tell everyone you want after I'm gone." Topher patted Daryl on the back. "Take care of yourself."

ON WEDNESDAY, TOPHER packed all his belongings in three suitcases, a couple of cardboard boxes, and a backpack. He stashed CDs around the TrailBlazer for easy access during their journey. Then he headed for the lawyer's office. The young couple buying his house was almost as excited as he was. He handed them his house keys, and the lawyer handed him a check.

He walked out the front door of the office onto the sidewalk of Fourth Street. He looked up at the sky and laughed. *For the first time in my life, I feel mobile, free, like I could float away.*

Brad met him as he walked into the bank's lobby. "Hello, Topher." He shook his hand with a firm grip and led him into his office.

"Here it is." Topher handed him the check. "I want to put that in my savings account. Now, can I transfer from savings to checking over the phone?"

"You need to go to a branch to do that—or call me. I can do it for you."

"Thanks, I'll stay in touch. Has Myra come in to see you?"

Brad shook his head. "Not yet, but I did talk to her yesterday. She said she'd try to get in this week. When are you two leaving?"

"As soon as she gets her shit together. I'm ready today. The job is done. My last paycheck is on direct deposit and should be in my account by next Friday. I'm ready," he repeated. Then he looked Brad in the eye. "I hope she's not losing her nerve."

Chapter Sixteen

MYRA LEFT BRAD'S office smiling. *I have a new account that is all mine. Gil won't miss my part of our money until after I'm gone.* She had cashed out her portion of their joint checking account and her own savings to get new accounts she could access through her debit card and with transfers through Brad.

The first day of April shone with a bright, warm sun. She leaned against her car and watched the people going into and out of the bank. Her hands, clammy and cold, shook, and she rested them on the warm car to soothe her nerves. The uptown skyline loomed in the distance, her office tower at the southern end. *Can I do this?* She slid into her car and pulled out into the noontime traffic heading back up Kenilworth Avenue. A thought occurred to her, and she laughed out loud: *if I don't leave, I will have a hell of a time explaining to Gil why all my money is in separate accounts now.*

Back in the parking deck of her office, Myra checked the trunk of her Honda. Two suitcases bulged with clothes that she had sneaked out of her apartment in her gym bag. A list of other things she wanted formed in her mind: her mother's wedding album (Gil could keep theirs,) her yearbooks from first grade through college, her diploma, an iron—just in case they needed one on the road—a few family pictures, and maybe a few books to read. *The car!* She tried to decide if she would leave it for Gil or sell it just before she left. *Damn, it's in Gil's name. I can't sell it on my own.*

Still thinking about the car, Myra didn't hear Tina speak to her as she entered the office.

"I said, 'hello.' What's got you so distracted?" Tina asked.

Myra looked up and waved the bankbooks. "Just doing a little banking."

"Hold it. That isn't our bank. You been banking with our competition across Trade Street?" Tina teased.

Myra followed as Tina went into her office. She closed the door behind them and said, "I need to take a leave of absence."

"Excuse me?" Tina propped her hands on her hips as if she was ready for a fight.

"I need some time off."

"That's okay. I was just kidding—of course you can take some time off. Now, the bank will grant leaves for certain circumstances: family illness, maternity..."

"No, no. It might not be a leave of absence I need." She paused, not knowing what to say, but wanting to tell everything, to yell across the concrete and glass canyons of Charlotte, to let everyone know she had the courage and the strength to take control of her life. Tina's bold chestnut eyes drilled into her, and she looked down at the carpet.

"Myra, look at me. What's going on?"

"Please, don't ask a lot of questions." Myra stood up and looked out the window. Boeing 737s circled the airport to the west, like a swarm of yellow jackets defending their nest. "I'm going on a trip...soon. I need to make sure that my profit sharing and final paycheck get to these new accounts."

"Final paycheck? What is Gil making you do? Where is he taking you?" Tina stood and leaned across the desk, the veins in her neck strained, and her eyes darted from side to side as if calculating a battle plan.

"He doesn't know anything about it," she said. "In fact, I don't want him to know anything, not where my bank accounts are, not where I might be, nothing. A lawyer will contact him with divorce papers. I just want to get away and start over."

Tina settled back behind her desk. "You know you can always work at one of the branches or some of the divisions scattered around D.C. and Delaware. I hate to lose you. You're one of the best team players I have."

"Thanks. Can I use you as a reference once everything settles?"

She smiled. "Of course. And I'll do everything I can to help you. That includes getting you contacts, and if needed, money while you set up in your new place."

Myra felt some of her anxiety lighten with Tina's volunteered support. "That's awfully kind of you. I might take you up on it. But, for now, I just want to get everything changed to these new accounts."

"Sure, we can get that set up today. Are you going to be okay?" Tina asked.

"Yes. I think I'll be the best I have ever been."

THE DOUBLE RING of an outside caller on Myra's phone startled her. *Gil?* She looked at the phone. No visible physical movement as it rang again. She expected it to shake like a cartoon phone delivering bad news. *Has Gil noticed the balance in our checking account?*

"Hello?" Myra's voice quivered.

"Hello?" Topher laughed. "What kind of way is that to answer the phone at work? What happened to 'Myra Greer, Human Resource Development'?"

"Sorry, I forgot where I was." She relaxed back into her chair.

"Are we still on for tomorrow?"

She smiled. "Yes. Everything is ready here. I'll leave for work as usual, and meet you here in the parking garage. Did you tell Dustin and Erik that tomorrow's the day you leave?"

"Yeah, but I didn't say anything about you going with me. It's hard, isn't it?" His voice lowered.

"I'll miss a lot of people," she said. "Don't feel like you need to go with me. I can do this alone— "

"No," he cut her off. "I want to leave, and I want you to go with me."

Tears came to her eyes, and she swallowed hard. "I can't think of anyone I would rather be with."

"Thanks. Now, get home and finish packing. Oh, and say 'bye' to Gil for me!" He laughed riotously.

She noticed the sweat from her palms on the phone as she hung it up. All her work was in order. She turned off her desk light and hugged Tina good-bye.

GIL'S TRUCK SAT in front of the apartment building when Myra drove in. She parked next to it because it would shield her car from being seen from their apartment in case she had to put anything else in the trunk that night. Walking in, she smiled and said, "Hey Gil. Did you have a good day at work?"

"I had two termite inspections today."

"How'd it go?" she asked.

"Good. We should get business from both of them. I wrote up the standard report about finding debris under the house with termite damage. Damn people believe anything. They pay me eight hundred dollars to scare them into a treatment contract."

"It seems so wrong that the inspectors are the same people who make a living fixing the problem."

"That's our little perk from North Carolina." He laughed. "So, what's for dinner?"

She decided to make the last night as easy as possible. "Well," she ran her fingers through his hair, "since you had such a good day, why don't we eat out?"

He looked up from his recliner, grinned, and said, "Hooters."

"The food is terrible. What about the restaurant at the Hilton?" She wanted one good meal before going on the road.

"I'd have to get dressed up for that."

"Okay," she compromised. "That NASCAR restaurant. They have a little of everything, and you don't have to dress up."

Gil thought about it and then said, "Sounds good to me."

The crowded restaurant smelled of tangy, sizzling steaks, cold beer, and cigarettes. The noise of the crowd and the televisions didn't allow them much conversation, but that lifted the burden off Myra to talk about ordinary things when her mind raced with thoughts of a new life. *I'll never sit here again. He won't be across the table from me anymore.* Regret still hounded her, but her expectations kept pushing her forward. Freedom. Hope. Dignity. What would it feel like to be able to relax at night? Not to be afraid to sleep?

After they returned home, Gil settled back into his recliner with a full stomach. Myra gathered some clothes together and carried them through the den toward the door.

"You leaving me?" Gil laughed. "Cause you know I'd have to hunt you down like a dog." He laughed again like it was the funniest thing he'd ever said.

She recovered her breath and chuckled, "Oh, no. I'm going to put these in my car so I don't forget to take them to the cleaners tomorrow." Closing the door behind her, she leaned against the cold brick. Her head throbbed. *He was joking, just joking in his own odd way, trying to be funny—yes, that's it. He doesn't know. He can't know.* She calmed down, but her nagging instinct didn't let her forget his words. She unlocked her car and hung the clothes in the back seat, then she popped the trunk to add a few more things she had smuggled out.

Gil remained in his chair when she returned. He had almost fallen asleep, so peaceful, like the man she had married years ago. Myra went into the kitchen to write up a week's menu for him. Not knowing how or if he would cook, she wanted to help him a little. After finishing the menu and grocery list, she wrote her good-bye letter:

> I know it is no surprise to you that we have had our share of problems. Frankly, I am afraid of you. My bruises may heal, but I can't keep living in this state of fear. I never know when you might explode and hurt me—maybe kill me.
>
> My love for you has vanished. It started going away the first time you hit me and continued to fade with each hurtful word or smack. You killed our baby with your temper. I will not be next.
>
> I want to be left alone. You can have everything. All I need, I will take with me. My car is in the parking deck at work—the keys are under the mat. Please don't try to find me. I will be in touch when I feel safe.
>
> I once loved you and think you loved me. But people who love each other don't hit, don't threaten, don't kill. I just want to find peace, and that's where I have gone. I hope you find it one day, too.

She folded the letter and placed it in her briefcase. Gil still slept in the den. His face didn't look like the face of a killer, his hands didn't look like they could crush bones, his mind seemed too simple to plot a murder. But he had beaten her, humiliated her, and dragged her down into a hole of self-loathing. She knew this was the first step in pulling herself out.

In bed, she couldn't get comfortable. Her stomach churned and cramped. Panic gripped her mind. *What did I eat? Anything here?* She had left the table at the restaurant. *Would he have put something in my food in public?* Stabbing pains twisted her as she huddled under the covers. Bile rose in her throat. She started to heave, and ran to the bathroom. Kneeling on the cold tile floor, she vomited her dinner and bitter greenish-yellow fluid into the toilet. The pain in her stomach subsided, but her mind wouldn't allow sleep to come.

Gil staggered into the bedroom about midnight, and she pretended to sleep. The bed dipped as he lowered himself under the covers. His hand, under her gown, rubbed her outer thigh, and then, slipped up and over to the crotch of her panties. She held her legs together tight as he stuck his thumb under the elastic. He stroked her a few times. She didn't move. Finally, he gave up, rolled over and went to sleep.

His steady breathing comforted Myra. She stared at the dark shadows on the ceiling as she had done so many times before and cried, not the past months' tears of fear, but tears of release and hope.

When the morning light streamed through the blinds, she was still awake. Beating the alarm and Gil, she took a shower and dressed for work. As she used her toothbrush, toothpaste, makeup, and deodorant she placed them back in her pocketbook or briefcase. She heard Gil getting up and yelled into the bedroom, "I'm clearing out of the bathroom. Your turn." She passed him in the hallway. His eyes half closed, he headed for the shower.

Myra finished packing her car while Gil was in the bathroom. She made coffee and waited for him.

He walked into the den, dressed and ready for work. "I thought you'd be gone by now."

"I heard the Interstate was backed up going downtown, so I thought I'd have another cup of coffee and wait it out here."

"Well, I need to go." He put on his coat, jingling his keys.

Myra dumped her coffee in the sink. "Hold on, and I'll walk out with you." He stood in the den at the door waiting, while in the kitchen, she opened her briefcase and left the letter and grocery list for him inside the refrigerator on top of his beer. "Okay, let's go."

As they drove out of the parking lot, she watched Gil's truck follow her. He stayed with her until she took the I-77 interchange. He flashed his lights, and she waved good-bye.

Chapter Seventeen

"WHAT'S ALL THIS shit?" Topher laughed at the items in her briefcase. "You won't need makeup, pantyhose, hair spray, a curling iron. Remember, we're free."

She transferred it to a suitcase in her trunk. "Okay, I'll leave the pantyhose, but I need the hair spray, conditioner, styling gel, eye liner, mascara, eye shadow..." Her voice trailed off then she looked at Topher. "I really need this stuff. I want to look good—I might meet a trucker. Besides, how much hair gel, after-shave, cologne, and other assorted boy cosmetics did you bring? I bet you have a full suitcase of beauty products."

"Two suitcases," he said. "Besides, I might meet a trucker too."

"You'll probably meet one before I do."

Topher smiled and moved her bags to the back of his TrailBlazer. "Anything else? Do we have all our worldly possessions in the back of my SUV?" He made a face.

His mock expression of horror unnerved Myra a little. *Everything I own is in the back of the Blazer.*

"I'd better not wreck or we'll be homeless. Wait, we're already homeless." He laughed, but Myra felt a tinge of panic.

She reassured herself that she had money in the bank, if she needed it. Material things didn't matter. She knew items could be replaced, but her safety and peace of mind were hard to regain. That was why she did this. *Yes, for me. But are we homeless? Technically homeless?* The vision of her in dirty clothes, begging money from strangers plagued her mind. *I always looked the other way, ignored them. What if they started out just like this?*

"Jump in. We're on our way." Topher opened the door for her.

As they drove out of the city, Myra looked for the homeless people who always seemed to be around, but she couldn't find them. *Do they become invisible if you look through them long enough?*

THE BRIGHT SUNSHINE gleamed on the windshield and warmed the inside of the vehicle so much that Topher considered turning on the air conditioner, but instead, he rolled down his window an inch or two. Driving south on Interstate 85, they crossed the Catawba River into Gaston County, and he turned to Myra. "Well, we're out of the county. Soon, we'll be over the state line. Are you sure Atlanta is okay with you?"

"Of course, any place to get out of state." She settled into the passenger seat.

He recounted his reasoning for her, glancing over from time to time, but keeping his attention on the traffic. "I thought about people I knew within a four or five hour drive. Richmond was a possibility, and that amount of time would have put us in DC, Baltimore, Philadelphia, Jersey, or New York, and we went to college with a lot of people living there. But, it's still cold. So I thought about Charleston or Savannah—too hemmed in by the ocean. I want room to go in any direction. So that left Atlanta."

"Atlanta's fine." Myra patted his shoulder like a weary mother soothing her hyperactive son.

"Atlanta has some nice parts."

"Buckhead," she mumbled.

"Buckhead?" He repeated the word like he'd never heard of the place, trying to get some energy flowing in her.

"We could stay at the Ritz Carlton and walk to Lenox Square." Myra laughed without moving her head or looking at him. She stared out the windshield.

"Yeah, right, and blow all our money in three days," Topher kidded her. "I called Chris Davidson. I used to work with him, remember?" He glanced over, but Myra made no sign of recognition. "Anyway, he's a great guy, lives in the Virginia Highlands area, and he says we can stay as long as we want. That way we can take a breath and look at a map." He looked at her again, hoping she liked the plan.

"Good, but I know one place I have to go."

"Where?"

"Tennessee. I want to see my grandmother." She rolled her head on the headrest to look at him.

Topher started to worry about her state of mind. Usually, she talked more. "Tennessee is good. When we leave Atlanta, we can take I-75 straight up to Phillips Bluff...or is it Sweetwater?"

"Phillips Bluff." She smiled at his ability to recall that detail of her life.

"Are you okay?"

"I'm fine. I just need sleep. I was so scared I didn't sleep at all last night. Such a relief. This is such a relief to be out and away from him. I feel so new, just like an empty diary ready to be filled up with a new life. I can hardly believe it. Thanks." She leaned over and kissed his cheek. "I couldn't have done this without you."

He felt the heat come to his cheeks as he blushed. "Yes, you could have. You're making it easier for me to leave, too. I don't know if I'd have really left without you."

"From the way you talked, you would have left Charlotte even if Alex begged you to stay."

"Well, he didn't. I'm so glad to be starting over. Okay, time for a quiz: if you could live anywhere in the world, where would it be?" Topher shoved his hand toward Myra like he held a microphone.

She dipped her head and rolled hers eyes up at him, batting her eyelashes. "Well, Sir, after I achieve world peace, feed all the hungry children, stop those nasty drug dealers, and invent a cure for cancer—"

"And AIDS." Topher added.

"And AIDS," she said, "I want to turn in my tiara and sash, and go to Disneyland."

"Good answer, Miss Cotton Products. You won the talent competition with your rendition of 'God Bless America' played on your cello, but please remember to wear a longer dress and panties next time."

"Oh," she giggled in a little girl voice, "I thought I felt a draft."

"Okay, really, where would you like to go?"

"Anywhere away from Gil. I'm a little scared he will come after me." She turned and looked out the back window.

Topher laughed. "He's still at work. It's not even ten o'clock yet. We'll be in Atlanta well before he gets home and finds out that you left him."

"I feel like I played a terrible joke on him. I know he'll be hurt."

"Hurt? He beat you. You were afraid for your life."

"I still am. I never told you this, but I miscarried before Thanksgiving. Gil hit me, and," her voice cracked, "I lost the baby."

"Oh, Myra, I'm so sorry." He didn't know what else to say. *She should have left after the first time. She should have reported him. How did she stay so long?* "It won't happen again. You're safe."

She finally drifted into a deep sleep and slept until they crossed the Georgia state line. Clouds had moved in as they drove through Greenville, and a misty rain turned into a spring thunderstorm. Rain spewed across the windshield so fast the wipers couldn't keep pace. He strained to see the road, not wanting to slow down, not wanting to lose time.

"Damn trucks throw water over everything," Topher muttered.

"Where are we?" Myra rubbed her eyes.

"Sorry. Did I wake you up? It's raining—must be Georgia. I never drove to Georgia when it didn't rain. We have about two hours to go before we're in Atlanta," he said.

"How's traffic?"

Topher shrugged. "Not bad, except for the spray coming off the trucks. But traffic will get worse as we get closer."

She stretched and ran her fingers through her hair, twisting it into a loose ponytail. "Why don't you let me drive the rest of the way?"

"Thanks, I'm okay. The only problem is I can't find a radio station. See what you can come up with."

Myra pressed the Seek button over and over, nothing but static came from the radio. "Okay, I give up. What CDs did you bring?"

He grinned and pointed to a box behind her seat. She unbuckled her seat belt and turned to dig through the old computer monitor box. Topher had filled the box with trays of CDs, stacked into rows, and alphabetized by artist. Myra turned back around. "You must have three hundred CDs."

"Closer to four hundred. I couldn't sell them or give them away." He cleared his throat. "Uh, that other big heavy box is my magazine and video collection. I couldn't get rid of it either. I would look at each centerfold and say, 'We had such good times. I can't throw you in the trash.' I have an emotional attachment to each and every one of those men."

"What? I was trying to get my life to fit in five suitcases, and you bring all your CDs and all your porn?"

He shrugged and smiled at her. "It might get lonely on the road. Besides, I'll share them with you."

"Porn doesn't do anything for me. Women aren't visually stimulated."

"Oh yeah, get in that box and pull out the December issue—the one with the fireman on the cover. Look at page 42."

"Got the page memorized, huh?" She found the magazine and opened it up. "Big deal, naked men, I want to know minds, personalities... Oh my God!" She looked at Topher. "Is that real?"

"You mean Gil didn't look like that?"

"Gil looks more like me than he does this guy." She folded the magazine and stuffed it in her pocketbook. "I might want to take a second look at that later."

Topher laughed. "Help yourself to anything I have." He noticed she blushed, so he kept his eyes on the road. "See if you can find a B-52's CD, since Athens is just up ahead. I always like to listen to them while driving by the Athens exit."

"Got it." She held up the disc. "We should be in Atlanta soon."

"In time for lunch and a few beers."

She slid the disc in the player and turned up the volume.

"GOD DAMN SON-OF-A-BITCH!" Gil threw one of the dinette chairs at the wall cracking the sheet rock. "That fucking bitch." The refrigerator door stood open; her note lay on the floor. He kicked the dishwasher and paced the floor with an unopened bottle of beer in his hand. When he realized he still held it, he flung it against the wall where the chair had made its impact; glass and brown, sticky liquid splattered the white wall.

He grabbed the phone and punched in Myra's work number, then pressed zero to talk to a real person.

"Good morning, sorry, afternoon," the receptionist corrected herself. "How may I direct your call?"

"I need to talk to Myra Greer," he hissed.

"Just one mo—" She clicked him on hold before she finished the word 'moment.'

He looked at his watch: 12:15. *She can't be at lunch yet.* He looked around at the mess in the kitchen and kicked the refrigerator door closed. *I need to keep her here. I need to make her stay at home. She got her way too much. I didn't keep her in her place. Tonight, she will pay for this stupid note.*

The receptionist clicked back on. "I'm sorry, sir, Ms. Greer no longer works here."

"What?" Anger flared in his head.

"She no longer—"

"I heard what you said. Put her boss on," he demanded.

The sound of typing on a computer keyboard ended with the receptionist announcing, "That would be Tina Matthews. Hold, please."

Tina answered the phone, and Gil yelled. "Where the hell is Myra?"

"Is that you Gil? How are you?" Treacle dripped from Tina's voice.

"Cut the shit. Where's Myra? I came home for lunch and there's a note here saying she's..." He didn't want Tina knowing his business.

"Saying she's what? Gil, what did she say she did?"

"Nothing. They say she doesn't work there anymore."

"That's right. She quit yesterday."

Gil couldn't speak. His mind seemed suspended, on pause. *Gone?* Stuck on one thought: *She's gone.*

"If that's all you need, I'll be going. I have work to do." Tina's voice began to wake his mind.

"Hold on." His brain started firing again. *Tina knows where she is. I need to see that bitch face to face to get it out of her.* He controlled his voice to make it soothing and calm. "I'll come in and pick up her final paycheck."

"Oh, no. You can't do that," she stammered. "It's not allowed."

"Why not? She's my wife. I can pick up her paycheck for her."

"It's on automatic deposit. It will go electronically to her account. A check won't be cut. I need to go. Good-bye, Gil."

Damn, damn bitch. He slammed the phone back in the cradle and looked at the list of people on their speed dial chart. *Topher, he knows where she is.* Gil pushed the button next to Topher's name; the phone dialed, and then squawked back that the number had been disconnected. "Disconnected? Where the hell is he?" His thoughts linked. "It's him. He made Myra do this. She wouldn't do this on her own." The heel of his right hand hit the cabinet. "Damn it."

"YES SIR, I want to report that my wife has been kidnapped by a faggot friend of hers." Gil shivered as he held the phone. Any encounter with authority scared him and talking to the police left him panicked.

A deep, full voice boomed across the line. "Hold on. Let's get the facts down. Is this an emergency?"

"Well, she's gone."

"How long has she been gone?"

"Since this morning. I left for work with her."

"She's not at work?"

"No. She was kidnapped."

"What time does she usually get home at night?"

"I don't know. Maybe, seven o'clock if she goes to the gym."

"Sir, it is only 4:20— "

"She isn't at work. She isn't coming home. She was kidnapped by that queer. His phone is disconnected."

"Calm down. You aren't making sense. I can send an officer over. Are you at 5406 - H Meadowview Lane?"

"Yes," Gil said, glad to have someone coming to talk to him.

Within ten minutes, the police officer knocked on his door. Gil opened it to find a thick woman built like a Dixie Crystal Sugar bag packed into a dark blue uniform—no curves, just stuffed, hard and thick. Her haircut, along with the fact that she didn't use any makeup, made her look like a teenage boy. The lines under her eyes and around her mouth gave her the look of a woman with troubles. He stepped back to allow her to enter the apartment.

"Mr. Greer?" Her voice scratched the still air of the room. "I'm Officer Morelli. You reported your wife missing?"

Gil backed up into the room, felt for the recliner behind him then guided himself down to its comforting embrace. "She was kidnapped."

Morelli placed one hand on her holstered gun as she scanned the room. "How long has she been gone?"

"Since this morning."

She finished her visual inspection and turned her attention back to Gil. "Why do you think she was kidnapped?"

Gripping the arms of the chair, he rolled out his tale. "We left here together this morning. She was happy. I got home for lunch and called her office—she was gone and they don't know where she is. I called this gay boy she's friends with, and his phone is disconnected. So," he concluded, "I figure he kidnapped her."

A warm, motherly smile came from the strong Morelli. "I think you might be jumping to conclusions. I don't think she's kidnapped. Is there a ransom note?"

"No, no note." His voice—like his bulky body—dropped deep into the recliner. *Damn lesbian. She's probably in on it.*

"What exactly did the people at work have to say?"

"I don't remember exactly."

She moved toward the phone in the kitchen. "I'll call them. What's the number? Never mind. Here it is on your speed dial." She looked through the pass-through window at him. "Mr. Greer? You have a mess in this kitchen. Was there some problem in here?"

"No, no problem."

"Looks to me like a fight. Did you and your wife have an argument? I know a couple of officers were out here before for a domestic dispute."

"No, nothing happened."

She picked up the phone and called Myra's office. After a few minutes, she walked back into the den. "Tina Matthews, your wife's manager, said Mrs. Greer quit work yesterday and said she needed some time away. The good news is, she's fine. The bad news is, she's gone for a while." Morelli opened the door to leave. "Take care of yourself. Hopefully, she'll call soon to let you know she's okay." She closed the door leaving him in the darkening apartment.

She can't leave me. I'm the best thing she ever had. What will people say? I'll get her back if I have to drag her ass back in a pine box.

Chapter Eighteen

MYRA AND TOPHER exited the Interstate before it flowed into downtown Atlanta. Following residential roads lined with budding maples, oaks, and flowering dogwoods, Topher maneuvered the SUV onto Virginia Avenue. Myra compared the houses to the same bungalows and old mill houses found back in Charlotte's Dilworth neighborhood. "This is so much like home." One house caught her eye where the dogwoods floated their flowers around the house like low-hanging puffy clouds. Blood-red azaleas bloomed along the foundation of the gray house, giving it an important air, like it had been underlined in red. "That house looks like the one I like on Berkeley Avenue. So comfortable, so homey, but I bet these are more expensive."

"I don't know. They're close to downtown, but it's a neighborhood that's turning around. You'll love Chris's house. He's remodeled a lot and really gotten the house in shape."

"Is Chris just a friend or an ex-boyfriend? I don't remember hearing much about him." Myra posed the question carefully.

Topher laughed. "Chris is just a friend. When we worked together, he was in a long-term relationship. Then they broke up, and he moved here. He's quite handsome, but I never considered him as anything more than a friend, really like a brother."

"Just wanted to know the deal before we got there."

He pulled into a driveway. "Good timing. We're here."

The one-story brick house had a long front porch with ivy growing up the rails. The large windows showed no signs of life. Myra noticed a white Mercedes parked in front of a detached garage in the back yard. They walked up the path to the front door, and Topher rang the bell; a dog barked.

"Get back, Buster," a voice yelled from behind the door. Chris opened the door holding the black Labrador by the collar. The dog jumped and wagged his tail so hard the rest of his body shook, too. "Sorry, we were in the den watching television. Come in, come in." He switched on a lamp. "It's so damp and rainy today that I just hibernated in the back room. Topher, so nice to see you." They hugged, and Buster got loose and went straight to Myra's crotch.

"Sorry, he likes to gather all the information he can when he meets someone new. Hi, I'm Chris." He held out his hand.

"Myra." She shook his hand. *Handsome, but too short for Topher.* She knew his taste in men. "Thanks for letting us stay here."

"No problem. I bet you're both hungry. After you freshen up, let's walk down to the corner. There's a great deli there."

CHRIS AND TOPHER talked about people she didn't know or knew only by name. As they caught up, she played with Buster until they left for the corner deli. The drizzle and the gray sky loomed over her. *Was this such a good idea?* They settled at a table in the restaurant and ordered beer, and she began to relax. The presence of Topher and being in new surroundings helped lighten her mood, then the sandwiches and beer anchored her in a mode of security. *Yes, this is right.*

They spent the rest of the day getting settled at Chris's house. That night, they opened their road atlas on the kitchen table. Myra scanned the map of North America and sighed. "Maybe we should have planned out exactly where to go."

Chris placed a bottle of wine on the table, along with three glasses. "Try this. It's a Spanish wine my friend Arden brought back from her trip." He poured it into the crystal and they clinked glasses.

"Waterford?" Myra asked.

"Right."

"I left mine behind." She said, and added, "Of course, all I had was what we got for wedding presents. We never spent the money to complete the set. I had five white wine glasses. Waterford. I love it." She looked at Topher. "I thought we wouldn't have room to bring anything but necessities." She stressed 'necessities' by drawing it out.

"I told you my magazine and video collections are necessities."

"Right," she said. "I can see that. At our age, your libido should be declining, while mine is just starting to peak."

Chris spoke up. "Uh, maybe I shouldn't put you two in the same room."

"No, that's fine. Myra and I can sleep together—we're like brother and sister."

Sweat broke out on her upper lip. *God, it's been years since we slept in the same room, back when we would go on trips and couldn't afford two rooms. I can do it. I'm an adult. Do I want him to see how I look in the morning? Shit.* She looked up. Chris and Topher were still talking, not aware of her mild panic attack.

"So, the third bedroom is a wreck with all the projects I'm working on. A landscape design bid is due by Friday, and there is a mess of layouts and planting charts all over the room. Of course, I know where everything is, but if you really don't mind, you can both sleep in the front bedroom." Chris turned to Myra. "It has a queen-size bed."

Her smile trembled, she hoped not noticeably. Bringing the sweet red wine to her lips, she tried to still them.

"Fine. That's fine," Topher leaned back in his chair, put one hand over his eyes, and held the other one over the map. "Boom." His finger landed, and he uncovered his eyes. "Deadwood, South Dakota? No way. Let me try again."

"Let's be a little logical about this." Myra turned the map toward her. "After Tennessee, where? Do you know anyone close?"

Chris poured more wine. "You are welcome to stay. Atlanta is a great place. Lots of opportunity."

"Thanks, but we were thinking of a change of scenery. Atlanta is too much like Charlotte." Topher pulled the map back in his direction. "Okay, Tony is in Dallas."

"Tony? Still in Dallas? You gained ten pounds dating him," Chris teased. "Never date a chef."

"We broke up as friends. Not a lot of chemistry, so the relationship just fizzled out," Topher said.

Myra considered Texas. *Cowboys, boots, flat land, why not?* "Do you think he would mind if we stayed there a few days?"

Topher scratched his head, messing up his hair. "I haven't talked to him in a couple of years, well, before Alex and I started dating. Although, I did get a Christmas card. He didn't say much in it." He looked at Myra like he was asking her for permission.

She shrugged.

"Okay, I'll call him tomorrow."

"Great, we have a strategy: Tennessee, then Texas. After that, we can determine later." She felt a slight relief from setting the plan. Glancing at the clock over the oven, she wondered what Gil had done when he got home. *He can't find us. No way.*

The bottle of wine and then another were emptied as they laughed and talked. Chris stood and said, "I need to get to bed. I have a meeting at Peachtree Tower in the morning. If you aren't up when I leave, bagels, eggs, and juice are in the refrigerator, and cereal is in the cabinet above it. I'll make coffee when I get up. Do you need anything? Pajamas? Extra toothbrush?"

"No thanks, I have my toothbrush," Topher winked at Myra, "and I sleep in the nude."

The mental image of him lying on crisp white sheets, beckoning her to bed made her cheeks burn. "Now, now, Mr. Langston, keep your shorts on if you sleep with me," she laughed, a little artificially. "No telling where that thing has been."

"Girlfriend, I could take you around the world in one night—show you things you could never imagine."

"Enough." She stood up. "I don't want you riled up before

bedtime." She started down the hall.

"I'm only teasing." He followed her. "Your body is safe with me."

It doesn't have to be that safe. She considered the possibilities. A little snuggle wouldn't be too bad.

She slipped on her long nightgown and climbed into bed. Lying as far as she could to the right, she felt a little silly, so she scooted over toward the middle. Topher came in from the bathroom without his shirt. She picked up a *Southern Living* magazine from the nightstand.

He sat down on the bed and pulled off his shoes. "I'm worn out. I'll sleep well tonight."

Lowering the magazine, she said, "I know I will, too." She looked back to her *Southern Living*. The metallic sound of a zipper caused an involuntary reflex in her to look up as Topher dropped his jeans to the floor. He had his back to her, so he couldn't catch her staring. He wore white knit boxer-briefs. *A compromise between the little boy image of briefs and the old man boxers. He looks good.* She put the magazine back up as he turned around. He slipped under the covers and clicked off the light on his side of the bed.

"Go ahead and read. I'm going straight to sleep. Good-night."

"No, I'm ready too. Good-night." She turned off her light and rolled over facing the edge of the bed.

Less than a foot separated them. She could feel the heat from his body, warmth radiated across the bed that reminded her of Gil's complaint that the bedroom was always too hot. She pulled her hair away from her neck then pushed the covers down. The bed warmed a little too much. She rolled onto her back, trying to get comfortable. Steady, deep breaths came from Topher. Glancing over at him, she watched him lying on his back, mouth partly open, sleeping. She rolled back over on her right side. *I hope I don't wake him tossing and turning. I just can't get comfortable.*

He began to snore, softly at first, then a few loud breaths caused him to stop for a moment, then he started again after repositioning himself. She turned on her back and let her hand fall toward him. She calculated her hand had landed within inches of his right thigh. Over the span of several minutes, her little finger rested against his leg. He shifted again and stopped snoring. *Is he awake? Does he know what I've done?* She took long, slow breaths, and held her eyes shut. His snoring resumed.

The hairs on his thigh tickled her finger; she wanted to move it. *What if I wake him? Damn, why did I do it?* Slowly, she pulled her hand back toward her. Inch by inch, trying not to make any sudden movement or noise, she slid her hand back a safe distance. Every position she tried left a cramp in some part of her body. The clock's red numbers glared 2:42 in the morning. Finally, she drifted into sleep.

BACK ON THE road, they headed for Tennessee. Myra slept most of the way, waking in time to help Topher find the exit to Phillips Bluff.

"Things have changed so much since the Interstate was built." She watched the gas stations and fast food restaurants go by. "Dad would drive Highway 11 from Bristol. It seemed like it took forever to get here, but we spent every Easter and Thanksgiving at Granny's. Turn up here." She directed him to her grandmother's house.

An old, white mill house stood on a corner lot, a block from the railroad tracks. Her grandmother had kept the house in good repair. Myra noticed new paint, and the yard had been mowed. A carport to the left housed the ancient, brown Oldsmobile she remembered, along with her mother's tricycle—55 years old if it was a day, and still sitting next to the side door. They pulled in behind the Olds, and Myra ran to the door and knocked.

"Granny? It's me, Myra."

The old woman hobbled through the living room door and into the former office (now a storage room) of her late husband to the carport. "Myra! I'm so glad you're here. Give me a kiss."

After hugging and kissing her, Myra stepped back to look at her grandmother. Her eyes sparkled like a young girl's, but her body seemed to be shrinking, leaving the skin hanging and her once-thick hair thinning. "I'm so glad to see you. Sorry we didn't give you more notice. This is my friend Topher."

He shook her hand. Granny laughed and pulled him to her for a hug.

"So, where's Gil? You leave him behind?" She looked out at the TrailBlazer for him.

"Kind of." Myra stammered. "He's not on this trip. Topher and I are going to Dallas to see a friend of his."

"Dallas? That's awful far. You've lost weight. I'm going to have to feed you good to get some of that back on you."

"That's okay. I want to keep it off."

"Well, don't just stand there. Come on in." She led them into the house, filled with Myra's childhood memories: blond living room furniture, a blue curved couch. "Now the boy," Granny said, "can sleep on the divanette."

Topher looked around the room for it. Myra pointed to the couch.

"And you can sleep in your mama's room. Come in the kitchen and let me get you a dope and some ham."

Again, Topher looked to Myra.

"A Coke. She's always called them dopes," she said.

After their late lunch, they helped Granny clean up. The old kitchen looked the same, with a heavy oak table with mismatched chairs pushed against the paneled wall. The sink Myra used to wash the dishes was part of the ceramic counter, and the wobbly faucet required that the hot water handle be turned three full turns before water flowed. A range wedged in the corner was the only appliance less than forty years old, and it was a Christmas present from Myra after that Thanksgiving years before when Granny's turkey never quite cooked in the old oven. When they finished, Myra suggested they go for a walk.

"You young'uns go on. My story is coming on," Granny said.

"We won't be long. Just after riding for so long, we're a little stiff." She and Topher walked toward the railroad tracks and downtown Phillips Bluff a few blocks beyond.

Large oaks and maples lined the road, with other small houses and mobile homes in their shade. Just across the tracks stood a large brick house with two tall windows flanking the double door and two identical windows above on the second floor bordering a small balcony over the front porch.

"Who would build a big house like that around all these little ones?" Topher asked.

"That was the mill owner's house—or maybe the manager's. This whole town was built around the mill. Granny worked there until she retired back in the early eighties. I remember me, Wanda, and Mama coming down here to see her after Dad died. We would get in before she was off from work and walk over to the mill to get the house key. She worked on a big knitting machine, making tube socks. Every year, for Christmas, Wanda and I would get tube socks." Myra laughed and pointed to a burned-out building. "That's the old mill. Come on, I'll show you downtown."

They turned down a short street that ended in a paved square, like a large, unkempt parking lot with gravel and dead leaves scattered by the occasional car. On the right were the remains of the mill, to their left was a line of three two-story storefronts, all closed and boarded up. At the far left, facing the mill, were the post office and another boarded-up building, and the square topped off with the railroad tracks running on toward Louden, Lenior City, and Knoxville.

"Up the road are the two white churches: Methodist and Baptist. The black churches are back behind the Square. Granny goes to the Methodist church, and her sister goes to the Baptist. In the summer, they open the windows, and the congregations try to out-sing each other." Myra smiled then looked around again. "I had such good times here when I was little. I hate to see it this way. My great-uncle Stanley ran that hardware store." She pointed to one of the old storefronts. "The mill closed, then burned. All hope of jobs left. Now, only retired people and a few farmers are left."

"Too bad. I bet it was a nice place. Still is." He grinned at her.

She sighed and sat down on the broken sidewalk. "Just seems like my history, my memories are decaying in front of me. Granny will be gone soon. This might be the last time I ever see her." Tears flowed.

"Am I doing the right thing? I left my husband. Everything I own is in the back of your car."

"SUV," he said with a wink.

"SUV, truck, car, whatever the hell it is. I know I had to go, but..."

Topher sat down next to her and hugged her gently. "Don't start second-guessing yourself. You did this to survive. If you want, we can stay here for a while."

"No, if Gil comes for me, this will be one of the first places he looks."

"Don't worry about Gil. He couldn't find you across the street."

"He's smarter than you think, and he's vengeful. I know he's mad and hurt. His mother's father was half Cherokee. He told me once that it was a dishonor for a wife to disobey her husband, and that his grandfather had threatened his mother not to ever complain about how she was treated by her husband. She did once, and only once. Gil never would say exactly what happened."

Topher put his hands up in distress. "That was just another way he had to keep you under his control—another thinly-veiled threat. Do you think that old Indian is going to come after you? Come on, let's be logical about it."

The warning still haunted her. Gil didn't make idle threats, but she knew he couldn't track them down—or at least she told herself that. "I guess you're right. Let's get back to Granny's."

"YOU LEFT HIM? You get right back there and apologize. Maybe he'll take you back." Myra's grandmother paced the kitchen floor, wringing her hands.

"He beat me. He caused a miscarriage. I'm not going back." Myra sat at the table with her head in her hands.

"Marriage is forever. You didn't try to make it work. If George hadn't been killed in a car wreck, we'd be still married. Things weren't always good between us, but we stuck it out. He was always away from home, traveling, selling, but I stayed here and raised your mama."

"I don't have children, and even if I did, that wasn't a good environment for them. Or me."

"So, you just run off with this other boy. People will talk. A married woman running off with a strange man."

"Topher and I have been friends since high school." She let her voice drop. "Besides, he's not interested in me—that way."

Granny sat down next to her. "Honey, all men are interested in women that way."

"He's gay, Granny. He doesn't like women."

She turned and looked at the closed door leading to the living room where Topher watched television. "Not him? He's not. He's a big healthy man, not a sissy bone in his body."

"Not all gay men are florists or hairdressers. They don't have to hide anymore. Trust me, he is."

"Well," she considered, "that just makes it worse. Why are you running away with a man that doesn't want you? Leaving a perfectly good husband."

"He cares for me, as a person, as an equal, and Gil isn't a perfectly good husband. He's a wife beater."

"Baby doll, you know I want you happy. But why not give Gil another chance? He's learned you won't take it. He'll be better."

She took her grandmother's cold wrinkled hands and looked in her watery eyes. "Would you rather have me beaten to death..." she caught the look in her grandmother's eyes, "yes dead, or alive and away from Gil and happy?"

Her grandmother sat stone still for a moment, then said, "He wouldn't do that."

"Promise me that if Gil calls, you won't tell him I was here," she said.

Granny replied, "He has the right to know his wife is alive and okay."

"If you have to tell him anything, just say I called, and I'll be in touch with him in a few weeks." Myra stood up and looked down at her grandmother. "Please?"

"BUDDY, WHAT THE hell are you doing here?" Gil stood in the doorway blocking the entrance.

Buddy bent his lanky body to look under Gil's obstructing arm and into the apartment. "Mama said to come up here and bring this material to Myra." He held up a paper bag. "She's going to make curtains for Mama. I called Myra at work yesterday, and they said she quit. What's up?" He looked around Gil again. "She home?"

"No. Since when did Myra sew curtains?" He kept his arm barring the door.

"Since forever. Myra made these curtains." He indicated the valances over the miniblinds in the apartment, and adjusted the patch over his left eye. "You ain't going to ask me in? I just drove two hours to get here."

Damn. He doesn't have a life of his own, always wanting to know my business, too. "Get your skinny ass in here."

"What happened? The place is a mess." Buddy pulled his cap off as he walked in. "Where's Myra?"

"She went to visit a friend." Gil followed him in, watching him scan the room. "Is that all you want to know?"

"She quit her job and then went for a visit?"

Gil thought for a second, looking down at the floor. "If you and

Mama have to know, she got a better job at another bank. She took some time for a vacation before starting the new job." He grinned, proud of his quick thinking.

"Hey, do you mind if I spend the night?" Buddy sat down on the couch without an invitation. "I don't know if I want to drive back tonight. I don't see so good at night."

A storm grew, clouding Gil's mind. *It's not my fucking fault you only got one eye. It was an accident.* "Why the hell did you drive up here after work? You could have called first."

"I called Myra."

"Dumb ass, she isn't here."

"Then where is she?"

The storm burst open. "What is this thing you got for Myra's whereabouts? She's not the fuck here."

"Okay, man. I just wondered. I like Myra. She reminds me of Mama."

"What? She's nothing like Mama. Sometimes she's a bitch, mouthing off, doing things I tell her not to, pissing me off."

Buddy grinned. "Who we talking about, Mama or Myra?"

Despite himself, Gil chuckled and sat down in his recliner. "Yeah, sometimes all women act up."

"Makes you just want to slap them, doesn't it?" Buddy lit a cigarette and passed the pack to Gil.

"Thanks. Yeah, Myra needs to be put in her place—a time or two." He inhaled the cigarette and exhaled a long slow column of smoke, "Yeah, a time or two. Hey, run in the kitchen and get us a couple of beers."

Returning and taking a few sips, Buddy settled into the couch. "Gil? How often do you have to hit Myra to keep her in line?"

An icy stare met Gil's eyes when he looked over at Buddy. "Oh, I don't. We have a few arguments, but nothing bad." He waited for a reply, but silence filled the room. He took another drink and a drag on the cigarette. The cold, bitter taste followed by the dry, smooth breath of the tobacco reminded him of the tension and release of a fight with her. He looked back at Buddy, who still held him in his gaze.

Finally Buddy spoke. "Mama would tan your hide if she knew you had hit Myra. I believe I would kick your ass up one side and down the other if she asked me to."

"What the fuck are you talking about? I just said I didn't hit her."

"You know Mama was beat by Daddy, and you remember we pledged to her never to raise our hand to a woman."

"And I don't," said Gil.

Buddy posed the question like fact. "Myra left you, didn't she?"

"Get the hell out of here." He stood up and waited for Buddy to leave.

With the patience of a priest, Buddy set down his beer and ground out his cigarette. "I know she's gone. Look around. Not long gone, but still gone."

"Get the hell out, and don't say anything to Mama. I'm going to take care of this."

Buddy looked back at his brother with a pleading eye. "Let her go, Gil. Let her be. Don't hurt her anymore."

"She can't do this to me. I'm bringing her back." He slammed the door, locking Buddy out.

IF I CAN just pass this truck, Topher steered into the left lane of the Interstate—*Got to get past him before this hill.* The Blazer inched up beside the speeding, silver trailer, and then past the cab. He pulled back into the right lane. *Yes! Great!* He looked over at Myra and grinned at his accomplishment.

"You know," she said with still water calmness, "you don't have to pass everything on the road."

"Naw, I didn't want to get stuck behind that truck as he goes up this hill. I can drive in the right lane. No problem." He stuck out his lower lip. "Sorry, I didn't mean to scare you with my driving. Anyway, I was going with the traffic flow."

"Right, and if everyone jumped off a cliff, would you do it too?" She mocked the warning of the archetypal mother.

A sigh that seemed to rise from his right foot resting on the gas pedal swelled through his body and exited through his nose relieved the tension of competitive interstate driving. *Old women drive in the right lane.* "I can do it. I can relax and let other cars pass me."

"Topher, I want you to relax, that's the whole point. Don't poke along, but there's no need to get a ticket. We're in Alabama now, then," she checked the road atlas, "Mississippi, and Louisiana. These are not the best states to get caught speeding in."

"Okay, okay. I'm envisioning us on a train. The Interstate is a large train running on tracks, and nothing I can do will make it move faster."

She turned to look out the back window. "Maybe we could take some side roads. You know, see the country."

With the slopes of Lookout Mountain still in his rearview, he glanced over at her and said, "We're coming down the ridge of the Appalachian Mountains. There aren't a lot of parallel roads. If you want to see the country, look over the edge of that cliff." The back window seemed to draw her attention again. Topher knew what she was thinking and tried to ease her mind. "He's not following us."

"I thought I saw a truck like his. I know it's stupid, but I'm a little paranoid. Of course, this car is easy to find: a gray, Chevy SUV, loaded down with our stuff, North Carolina license plate, and a gay pride rainbow sticker on the back window. Not hard to find that on an Interstate."

"Okay, here's the deal. We switch license plates with an Alabama car at the next rest stop," he said, narrowing his eyes into a squint. "I'll get some spray paint and change the color of the car from gray to green, and slap a NRA sticker over the rainbow."

"That'd do it." She smirked at his plan, then said, "A baby seat in the back would make us look more Republican."

"That's enough on scary, old Gil. How about some music? Get the *Grease* Soundtrack out of the box. You can be Olivia, and I'll be John Travolta."

"Okay, but don't you usually do the Olivia part?" she joked.

"Bitch," he grumbled under his breath.

After singing the *Grease* Soundtrack, they switched to Bruce Springsteen, Emmylou Harris, The Smiths, Elton John, Pink, and the Pet Shop Boys. Their voices, raspy and hoarse, finally gave out as they pulled into a motel outside Jackson, Mississippi, just before midnight.

"Sorry. I didn't realize when we crossed the state line it would take us so long to find a decent motel." Topher unlocked the door to their room. He walked in and threw his backpack on one of the double beds. "My back is killing me. I'm not used to sitting in one place for that long."

"Why don't you soak in the tub," Myra said, then added, "after I use it to get ready for bed. I'm worn out."

"Be my guest. I just want to lie here with my eyes closed. If I never see another cotton or peanut field, that will be fine with me."

"Me too." She headed to the bathroom with her overnight bag. "Give me about fifteen minutes, and it's all yours."

"Take your time..." his voice trailed into silence.

He woke from the creak of the bathroom door opening as she came out. "Finished already?" He yawned.

"Yeah, I ran a tub full of hot water. It's ready when you are." She patted her hair dry in a towel.

He noticed her nightgown, different from the past two nights, not loose flannel this time, but body-hugging silk. "That looks nice. Guess it's warm enough down here to switch out of the heavy stuff." Pushing himself up, he dropped his shirt on the floor next to his bag and walked into the bathroom. "Hey, thanks for putting the bubble bath in."

She laughed. "Thought you might like it. I'm going on to bed. Goodnight."

"Goodnight, Myra." He closed the door and pulled off his socks, jeans, and underwear. The hot water burned his feet when he first stepped in, but he soon adapted, until he began to sit down in the tub. "Oww," then "ooh," as he glided the rest of his body in. *Wonder where a young gay man could find some company in a town like this?* He frowned at the thought. *Probably in the shadows. It's not a very accepting part of the country, from the looks of things. If only this place had room service, and a handsome waiter to deliver it...* The steamy water relaxed his mind so that the thought escaped.

After he realized he'd been in the water for over twenty minutes, he pulled himself out of the tub, dried off, and wrapped the towel around his waist. Myra was still awake when he came into the room.

"Feel better?" she asked.

"Much." He pulled back the covers of his bed and climbed in, then threw the towel out and onto the floor. "Burrr. This bed's cold. That hot bath made me horny, but this cold bed has extinguished that fire." He looked over at Myra. "Remind me when we're at Tony's how that relationship didn't work, cause I feel like I'll fall in lust with the first gay man I see." He winked at her.

"Maybe you need a cold shower," she said.

"I'm just kidding with you. But I think men have a harder time controlling their sexual urges than women. The blood leaves your head and flows to your dick—that explains a lot of masculine behavior."

"About ninety-nine point nine percent of masculine behavior," Myra said.

"I'm just a little worried about seeing Tony again. First, I haven't had sex since December, that is, with another person. Secondly, Tony has a killer body, hung like a horse, and is really handsome and funny. We just never had anything more. Nothing but great sex and wonderful meals. If I could paint the way he cooks, I'd be the most successful artist in the country."

"Great sex and great food. How long did that sustain you?"

"Several months," he admitted, "but I was much younger."

"I'll remind you. Of course, a good meal isn't too much to put out for. I've done it for less."

"Oh, really?"

She clicked off her light. "Go to sleep. That's none of your business."

THE NEXT DAY, they took Interstate 20 across the Mississippi River into Louisiana. Myra helped drive, but as they neared Monroe, she took an exit to Highway 80.

"You need a rest? I can drive for a while," Topher said.

"I'm okay. Just getting a little bored, thought I could drive this road for a while. It runs parallel to I-20." She kept looking in the rearview mirror.

Topher noticed her wipe the sweat off her lip.

She caught him watching her. "I honestly thought I saw Gil."

He worried about her "Gil sightings." Turning around in his seat, he looked out the back window; two cars followed them, a beat-up Ford Mustang and an orange Plymouth Duster. Back about a quarter of a mile, he could make out a pickup truck pulling off the I-20 ramp. All he could distinguish was the shape of the vehicle. It was a full-size pickup, but he could not tell the color, or even if it had toolboxes mounted on it like Gil's truck had. He watched the cars behind them. The Mustang passed them and sped away. The Duster stopped at a convenience store. The truck stayed a constant distance behind them; even when Myra had to stop for a traffic light, the truck didn't get any closer. A slight, slithery, suspicion crept into his mind: *Could he have found us?*

"No, no way." He looked at Myra. "There's no way Gil could track us this far. Hell, I don't think he could have found us on the other side of Charlotte, so there's no way he could find us in Louisiana. Even if he wanted to track us and knew we were headed for Dallas, this is not the most direct route from Charlotte. I-40 is the most logical way to go west." They both turned to look back. The truck had disappeared.

"I just want to be careful." She lessened her grip on the steering wheel and sighed, "I get a little obsessed, sorry."

His own paranoia dissipated as she shrugged off her suspicions.

"You're right. Gil couldn't find us," she said. "Let's say he found us early on, and has been following us since."

"Okay."

"He follows us, but keeps a safe distance. Why? We've been on some really deserted roads late at night, but nothing ever happens."

Topher agreed. "You're right. He would have done something if he knew where we are. I think we're home free."

"Yeah, let's get back on the Interstate and get to Dallas. I have a horny gay man in the car, and I'm not sure if that's good or bad."

IN DALLAS, THEY found the restaurant where Tony worked, Le Chateau in the West End of downtown. The West End was a historic district of old warehouses that had become a tourist attraction, with the old book depository building, famous for the President Kennedy assassination, as its main draw. Le Chateau sat on Lamar Street and served a mixture of French and Texan food. The culinary combination packed in the locals and tourists. Surrounded by the elegance of a French country chateau with a smack of Texas twang, Topher studied the waiting area: Louis XIV-styled chairs had been upholstered with calfskin; an armoire housed a large ceramic rooster and French country china in vivid tones of yellow, blue, green, and red, all with the rooster design.

"Looks like," Topher nodded toward the rooster-themed armoire, "this is the house of cock."

"Stop," she said, "and think wholesome thoughts, instead."

They waited until Tony could get out of the kitchen to talk to them. He walked out and greeted them wearing his white, starched chef's uniform, appearing like a tall, muscled super hero—Chef Man! His black hair was slicked straight back underneath his tall hat. The baby-pale skin of his face was made rugged by the thick, dark, five o'clock shadow.

"Tony, you look great. Head chef?" Topher asked.

"Yes. Things are crazy here. A convention of computer people hit town, and we're barely keeping up."

"Hey," Topher cast a devilish grin at Myra and then turned to Tony, "how can you tell who the Head Chef is?" He didn't give them the chance to answer. "He's the one with the dirty knees."

Myra shook her head, and Tony instinctively looked down at the knees of his white pants. He finally got the joke and smiled. "Stay for dinner. I'll get you the next available table. Then, you can go back to my house. I'll be there after we close."

The dinner was the perfect combination of light French flavors and hearty Texas portions. Tony gave them directions and the key to his house. His small, brick house stood just out of sight of the Dallas skyline, off Cedar Springs Road. All the comforts were there, especially a large gourmet kitchen.

"You would think after cooking in a restaurant all day, the last thing he would do is cook at home," Myra said while going through the refrigerator.

"Find any milk?" Topher called from the adjoining dark-paneled den.

She poured a glass and set it on the coffee table in front of him. "What time did he say he'd be home?"

"A little after midnight."

"I don't think I can make it until then." She stood up and stretched. "Thank him again for me, and apologize to him, but I have to go to sleep. Good night." She kissed Topher's forehead and headed back to the guest room.

Glancing around the den, Topher noticed some pictures on the mantel. He scanned each one, looking for Tony or any other familiar face. A photograph of the ocean caught his attention. It was a picture of him. He and Tony had taken a long weekend in Hilton Head, he had almost forgotten about it, but there was his image, in a Speedo bikini emerging from the surf. He was much younger then, and he cringed at the shadow of his youth. "It's nice that he has that out," he said to the empty room.

After watching television for a while, he fell asleep on the couch. He woke when Tony came in the back door.

"Sorry to wake you. You should have gone to bed." Tony sat down next to him and kicked off his shoes.

"Long night?"

"Yes. It was constant chaos." He unbuttoned his shirt and leaned back.

The smell of orange marinade and barbecue sauce mixed with sweat invaded Topher's head. He took a deeper breath. Running his fingers through his hair, he stretched then let his hand fall on Tony's shoulder. "Thanks again for letting us stay here."

Tony turned to him and smiled. His deep brown eyes bored into Topher. "I'm glad you're here. It's been a long time." He leaned toward Topher, and they kissed, soft and slow at first, then with more passion. Soon, clothes began to fall to the floor. Tony's white uniform lay in a heap, as he frantically started unbuttoning Topher's jeans.

"Whoa!" Topher sat up, gasping for air. "We need to cool off." Tony sat in front of him totally nude looking like a Donatello sculpture in an Italian piazza, except this statue sported an erection. Topher began to laugh. "Sorry, you look wonderful, and I'm crazy to stop, but I just can't do this right now."

"That's okay." Tony scratched his hairy stomach, then let his hand rest on his thigh. "Would tomorrow be better?" He grinned, and Topher couldn't tell if he was kidding or not.

Topher's hands trembled as he picked up his shirt. The sight of Tony sitting there and the memory of what he could easily have again raced through his mind. Sexual desire boiled up, blocking all reason, but he kept trying to lead himself to a logical thought pattern. *I haven't been around him in years. I'm too old for purely physical relationships. I want more. This could turn into another Alex. Oh, God, he looks good. Why not? I've been on the road for four days; why not grant myself one indulgence, or maybe a couple days of indulgence.* He smiled at Tony, and said, "I need to get some sleep. Let's both calm down, and consider this before we jump back into bed together."

Pulling on his shorts, Tony laughed. "You have changed. We used to never think twice about it. We just did what felt good."

"That was a long time ago." He stood, and kissed Tony's cheek. "I'll see you in the morning."

Sleep took its time claiming Topher. He tossed and turned, thinking about Tony and what could have happened. Thoughts ricocheted around his head: *I have a responsibility to Myra. Would she go on without me? Is this where I want to stay? Maybe staying for a few days to see how I really feel wouldn't be a bad idea. This could be the place.*

THE ODOR OF sizzling grease made Gil's stomach growl. He shifted his cell phone, and tried to block out the noise of the truck stop diner.

"Some boy in Dallas..."

He was losing his patience with the old woman. "Listen, you said his name was Tony. Did you get a last name?"

Granny's voice started to quiver. "I just can't think—something Italian."

"Did you get an address or phone number?"

"I made her give me a phone number. I think it's where that boy works."

"Yes, yes," he encouraged her, "that will do." Sweat rolled down his brow. *Finally, time to settle this.*

Chapter Nineteen

THE TELEVISION CHANNELS flashed by. She stopped at a talk show, but the people were yelling at each other, and Myra couldn't take it. "Here." She tossed the remote to Topher. "I can't find anything."

"I didn't see anything either. Want to walk over to Cedar Springs Road and get a beer? Maybe go to a movie?"

"No," she said, but she didn't want him feeling bored. "Why don't you go on for that beer?"

"No," he said with a sigh. "What time did Tony say he'd be home from work?"

"By three, but he goes back at five for the dinner shift." She looked over at him staring at the television as he mindlessly flipped the channels. "Have we run out of things to say to each other now that we aren't driving? It's only been five days."

"What?" He looked back at her.

"Have we run out of things to say to each other?" she repeated.

"No. Of course not."

"Well?"

"Well what?"

"Are you bored? I am." She stood up, and glanced around the room, the paneled walls pressed in on her as if she were caged. The previous days on the road had been long, but the changing landscapes, the other cars, the stops for gas and bathroom breaks provided steady stimuli for her. Now, she roamed someone else's house looking for something to do. "I want to get outside." She thought for a moment, as he watched her. "I know, let's go for a jog. I haven't been exercising, and my blood has slowed. That would do us both good."

"Okay," he said. "It couldn't hurt."

They changed clothes, and took off down the street. Myra felt her heart beating harder after the first block. "Wow," she gasped for air, "I can...really tell...I haven't...worked out...lately."

"Me, too." Topher slowed his pace a little.

Myra watched the houses as they ran by, wondering if she would have her own house one day. *A house and family—will that happen, or did I throw it all away? Was he really that bad? Could we have worked things out?* A flash of someone behind the corner of a gas station caught her eye. She slowed to try to make out the familiar sight, dark straight hair, bright eyes... *Dimples?* She stopped to try to catch the figure again.

Topher turned to look back at her, and yelled, "You okay?"

"Yeah, sorry." She jogged up to where he waited. "I thought I saw someone."

"Who?" Then his face changed expression. "No...Gil?"

"I'm not sure. No, it couldn't be."

"Come on. Stay with me. It was just your imagination." Topher jogged on with her at his side.

Looping back around the neighborhood, they arrived back at Tony's house. "I just got a glimpse, but I swear it looked like him," she said.

They sat on the back patio. Topher brought out water for both of them. She settled back and tried to relax. "So," she wanted to change the subject, "have you forgotten about your last relationship with Tony? I noticed things are very cozy between you two."

"I know," he said with a slight whine of a child caught swiping his finger through a cake's icing. "I asked you to remind me, but I think we're both different now." He took a gulp of water and looked away from her.

"Want to talk about it? I know you have been sleeping in his room, of course that doesn't necessarily mean you're having sex," she teased, "but usually..."

"Okay, yes, I have given in to my dick. I said I wouldn't, but I did." He glanced at her. Topher gulped his water, and it dribbled down the sides of his mouth. "Yeah, can't seem to get control back from the little guy." He laughed. "Okay, not that little of a guy, but you know what I mean."

"I'm glad you're happy. Enjoy yourself." She tried to sound like she meant it.

"I didn't want another relationship so soon, but..." Topher looked down and ran his finger along the edge of the table. "Tony's excited for me to be here. We talk all the time, and there is a physical attraction. I can't deny that. We have a history."

A cool breeze swept across the patio. Myra watched a black ant climb the leg of her chair, circle around the armrest, and back down to the concrete. "Aren't you going in a circle?" She looked at the ant, but Topher answered.

"Maybe, but I...I don't know." He rested his elbows on the table and buried his face in his hands. "It's not everything I want. Honestly, I don't want to end up with that empty, dull ache, realizing I should have been more selective."

"I wish I could give you some wise words, but I can't claim success with my relationship." She trembled on the breezy patio.

Could this be the end of the line? I could go on without him, maybe... This is not good. I can't let him make a mistake. Where is his excitement about adventure, starting over? Myra reached over and rubbed his head like she would a small boy. "You say it isn't everything you want. What do you want?"

He glanced up, leaned back in the chair, and sighed. "If I knew that, I'd be one happy man." He thought for a while then said, "I want how I felt about Alex, plus that returned to me." He laughed. "I want someone like me in love with me."

"Don't we all?"

"Do you mind staying a couple more days?"

She smiled. "We don't have a schedule. In fact, we don't have a destination. Dallas is good—for now." She reached across the table and rubbed his head again. "Take all the time you need. No hurry, unless Gil shows up." A nervous laugh escaped.

He winced. "Keep thinking he's around the corner, and you'll will him here."

TOPHER WAITED UP for Tony to get home. Topher let him settle down before beginning.

"Tony, I think I should sleep in the guest room tonight."

"Why? What's the problem? My bed's been big enough for both of us the past few nights." He leaned back on the sofa, gazing intently at Topher.

The unreadable stare bothered Topher. Anger, disappointment, rejection, or indifference? He couldn't define the stone look. Of all the possibilities, he feared indifference. He fought indifference with Alex, and knew, of all opponents, it was the one that couldn't be changed. "I...I just think I need time. I left a relationship back in Charlotte. It wasn't a good one. I'm prone to repeating the same mistakes, especially when it feels good doing it. Like 'Can I eat that whole gallon of butter pecan ice cream?' Then I gobble it down, am sick for a week, but when another gallon is dangled in front of me, I do the same dumb thing. I always have a hard time remembering the week of sickness that comes after the hour of pure pleasure."

Tony kept quiet.

"You're the hour of pleasure," Topher said, "and I'm forcing myself to remember that sick feeling from my last hour of pleasure. That's why I want to slow down, back off a little. Do you understand?"

Tony shifted on the sofa, exhaled, and grinned. "You're completely right. I don't want us to rush into any serious emotional thing. I'm available, you're available. We're in the same house, my house. A little physical stimulation isn't too much to ask."

Topher, stunned, lit a cigarette to help him organize Tony's statements.

"You and Myra have been here for five days—"

"We'll gladly pay you something. Myra and I have cleaned the house, done laundry, bought groceries."

"The two of you have done enough housework, and I don't need any money. What I want is your ass in my bed."

"What?" The heat of rage boiled up from Topher's churning stomach.

"Hey, you're a friend. We slept together. We've done it before. While you stay here, you can take the role of a houseboy. No working, just be available when I want you."

He stood up and ground out his cigarette with slow, measured twists. "Why would you think I would go for something like that?"

Tony remained seated. "You called me and said you needed a place to stay." He opened out his arms to indicate his house. "Here you are. This satisfies your need. I just want mine satisfied, too."

His patience went. "You are so fucked up. We're not friends. You don't know what a friend is. If you stop your dick from thinking for you, you might survive. But the way you're going, I doubt you will."

Tony lost his grin and leaned forward. "You hit the nail on the head. I won't survive. I stopped my medication because nothing is working. The virus has adapted to everything the doctors have tried."

"You have AIDS!" Topher dropped back down to his chair. Tiny white lights flickered in front of his eyes. *My life passing by...*Then as the lights faded, his mind gained control. The heat of anger raised him back to his feet. "AIDS! You didn't tell me?"

"Why concern yourself? I'm gone in a year's time."

"But you could have exposed me!" Topher felt panicked. He had never knowingly been with anyone HIV-positive. A tight rope stretched across his future, with him teetering to keep his balance. "I should beat the shit out of you."

"Calm down. We were safe, and besides you were on top, and we always used condoms."

"Safe? It's never safe." Topher wanted to hit him, to knock the arrogance and rashness out of him.

"Are you upset because you now know you bedded death? Or is it because I put the truth in front of you?"

"You dumb fuck. Just because you're dying doesn't mean you have to take everyone with you."

"No, everyone went before me. I'm the last. My circle of friends is all gone. The love of my life died fifteen months ago. I watched him go from a strong young man to nothing more than a skeleton. He couldn't see, walk, or even make it to the bathroom on his own. Now, I know what my future holds." He began to tremble with agitation. "So, excuse the fuck out of me if you get offended when I ask for what I want."

Topher rubbed his forehead. "I'm saying you should have told me."

"I'm lucky, so far. It doesn't show. I can stay in the closet. I tried telling people, but they made the proper excuses and disappeared."

Topher watched him settle back into the sofa. "This is not the way to get someone to stay with you."

"If men know you have AIDS," Tony explained, "gold-diggers come out of the woodwork, just waiting for you to die. I had friends who had young men come into their lives and steal from them...change their wills...abandon them days before they died, then return to claim everything. So, letting someone know up front is not financially smart. Wouldn't you be suspicious if you had a man drawn to you because you had AIDS? Why in hell would anyone want to go through that?"

"Maybe some people are caregivers." Topher tried to think of other reasons, but they all led back to Tony's description. "Okay, how about another HIV-positive person? Like a team effort to battle the disease."

"That's what Bill and I had. Seems that the lucky one dies first, in the arms of someone who loves them. I'm left alone. Friends and lovers, all dead." Tony began to cry.

Topher hesitated, wondering how he could help fix things for Tony. Forgiveness hadn't developed, but compassion had. "Have you gone to any support groups?"

"When Bill was really sick, I did, but they didn't do much for me, so I quit."

"Go back. Make new friends. Start living again."

"Easy for you to say," Tony fumed.

"What the hell is the alternative? Trying to trap someone to take care of you?"

He began crying again, and Topher moved over to the couch and put his arms around him.

SHE MADE UP her mind to allow Topher the choice. She wouldn't try to get him to leave if he wanted to stay, for a few more days or forever. Rustling from the other guest bedroom led her to believe Topher had not slept with Tony the night before. She fixed breakfast and waited for him to appear.

"Good morning." He headed straight for the coffee. He wore boxers and socks; all modesty had evaporated between the two of them.

"I want to talk to you," she said.

"Hold on while I get a couple sips." He slurped the coffee like it fed him liquid energy. Setting his cup in front of him at the kitchen table, he opened bleary eyes to Myra and said, "Okay, I'm awake."

"This can wait until after your shower."

"No, no. I'm okay. I just had a long night last night."

"This wasn't such a great idea." She started with a statement she hadn't planned. "I mean, maybe I should be in Charlotte, trying to work things out with Gil."

"Oh, shit." Topher sighed.

"Really. I have some doubts."

He glared back at her. "Myra, we are not going back to Charlotte."

"But if you want to stay here with Tony, I don't want to be in the way. It's really time we each go out on our own."

"No, no, no, no," he crescendoed, looking wide-awake. "We are leaving Dallas today, together." He recounted his late-night conversation with Tony.

Poisoned. Myra hated the thought. *He could have easily poisoned Topher's body with a killing virus.* She wanted to escape, with Topher safely sealed in a glass jar, out of any harm. Take him and hide from everyone: Tony, Gil, strangers, and friends.

"We can't give up the dream of starting over, being free." He lit a cigarette and paced the kitchen floor. "I've been thinking. I have my portfolio of my paintings." He turned to look at her. "I want to try making it as a painter."

A smile erupted across her face. She could feel it stretch her cheeks. "Wonderful, I'm so happy you want to do it." She hugged him, hard.

"I feel so much energy now that I know my direction." He sat back down, hands fidgeting with the cigarette lighter, the sugar bowl, and anything else within his reach.

She envied his excitement. What did she want to do? Nothing came to her, just silence. *Stable, reliable, sure money to live on.* Her thoughts defined the security she wanted. "When we leave, which direction will we head?"

Topher smiled, almost laughing. "I thought about this last night. Wait here." He grabbed his keys, still in boxers and socks, and ran out the back door to the TrailBlazer. He returned with the road atlas, flipped through it, and pointed to New Mexico. "It's a long drive, but it is the largest art center in the country—Santa Fe!"

Her mind had settled on somewhere like California, but Santa Fe sounded all right. "I haven't been to Santa Fe."

"Me either, but I've heard so much about it. Look." He flipped the page back to Texas. "We're right next door to New Mexico. It might take a couple of days, but I'm excited and ready."

A thought hit her, dampening her excitement. "What about Tony?"

"I'm still pissed he didn't tell me. He's in such a hard situation, but I won't get dragged into it. I want to help, really I do, but I'm not a caregiver. I just can't do it. Just because I'm gay doesn't mean I have to sacrifice my life to this virus. I need to look after myself."

She sensed he wasn't being completely honest. "Yes, you need to take care of yourself, but you *are* a caregiver. You take care of me, of

Daryl, your mom, a lot of people. I think if you loved Tony, you would be there for him. I know that if anything happened to me, you would be by my side through it all, and I'll be there for you. I know we have each other to lean on, and if anything were to...develop...to happen," she choked on her words, "I'll be there to take care of you." She held his hand across the table.

"I know you would." A tear slid through the stubble on his cheek. "I don't think I'm in any danger. Maybe that's why I feel guilty leaving him alone. But I did get him to agree to join a support group and to get involved in the local AIDS groups."

She shook her head and said, "Good. That should help. You gave him a direction he didn't have before. He can get the support he needs. You're a good friend." The smile crept back to her face. "I think I'll get my stuff packed up."

"I want to wait for Tony to wake up before we leave."

"Does he know?" she asked, concerned there might be an argument over it.

"Yeah, we talked about it last night." He paused, then said, "Are you sure I'm not being a jerk for leaving?"

"Topher, you would be a bigger jerk to stay."

He laughed. "Remember that line the next time you start thinking you should have stayed in Charlotte.

"WHERE THE FUCK is Topher's truck?" Gil scanned the yard and neighboring driveways. *Enough pissing around.* His thoughts ricocheted, collided, exploded. *She's had time to change her mind and come home. Take control. Take, take, take it.*

AFTER A DAY and a half to cross the Texas panhandle and the mountain ranges of New Mexico, Topher and Myra pulled off Interstate 25 north of Albuquerque, just outside of Santa Fe. The hills rolled with scrub brush and low-lying cactus, a scattering of pinyon pines, and a lone aspen. The cool wind came from the north, along with a few steel gray clouds tumbling over each other like fat children playing leapfrog. Myra instinctively glanced back at the road—no trucks followed them.

"This is the Turquoise Trail, Route 14. The bed and breakfast should be about a mile south. They say you can see the lights of Santa Fe on the horizon." Topher grinned like a little boy looking in the window of a toy store.

"You found it in a gay guide book?" She wasn't sure what to expect.

"Right, but it's mixed; more gay-friendly than strictly gay. Don't worry. There won't be drag shows or old queens cruising the halls."

Embarrassed, a little, she laughed. "I just want to know if I need to fight the men off you."

"More like I'll have to fight the women off you," he teased. "It's run by a lesbian."

Myra's expression gave her away.

"No, no," Topher said. "I'm kidding. It's not any different than staying at a straight bed and breakfast, if there is such a thing."

They drove south, looking for the turn. After driving too far, they turned around and found the sign. About a mile down a rutted, dirt road, they pulled up to a one-story adobe with a long, covered porch and a tan mutt of a dog sleeping next to the front door. Betty, the owner, answered their knock. Myra gauged her age to be early forties. She was dressed in jeans and a denim shirt, with turquoise earrings. She used no makeup, and her hair was cut short, but stylish. *Very independent and strong looking,* Myra appraised.

Topher touched the thick adobe walls and Navajo rugs as Betty showed them around.

"The original adobe," she explained, "went back to there." She pointed to the back wall of the living room. "Formerly, it was the living room, this entrance hall, the large front bedroom, and part of the kitchen. I added on my bedroom, behind the kitchen, and the other three bedrooms down the north hall."

"How old is it? Who were the original owners?" Topher fired questions.

"It started as a small ranch house in 1926. I'm still surrounded by grazing land. I don't think I know who was the first one to call it home."

He went back to look into the courtyard through floor to ceiling glass. "Which way is Santa Fe?"

"That courtyard catches the morning sun from the east. Santa Fe is to the north. You can see it from your room." She led them to the corner room and opened the door. Two rough-hewn timber twin beds sat on either side of a window, woven rugs covered the wood floors, and a rust-color tiled bathroom connected to the right. Thick burnt-orange-hued adobe walls rounded from the floor and up into the beamed ceiling. Betty pointed out the window. "On the horizon, now that the sun has set, you can see the lights of the city."

Myra and Topher joined her at the window.

Topher turned to Betty. "I can't wait to see it tomorrow. We're considering moving here."

"Wonderful. I'll tell you all you want to know. Now, I'll let you get settled. Breakfast will be at eight on the table outside your door. Goodnight."

Myra set her suitcase on the bed. "I'm so tired of riding in that car."

"Just wait until we go into Santa Fe. Museums, galleries, shops, all like this. I love this atmosphere. This is definitely different from Charlotte."

Myra unpacked her suitcase. "First impressions: I like it. I'm really interested in town and what kinds of jobs are available."

"It's the state capital. You should find lots of opportunity." He kept looking out the window.

"Yeah, but what kinds of jobs are available, what are housing costs, what are the taxes, and is it better to live within the city limits or out here?" She glanced over at Topher and knew he wasn't listening to her. A glow seemed to radiate from him that wrapped her in its warmth, a feeling of safety, refuge, harmony, serenity. Love. She knew she loved him, but her affection had grown beyond what they had in Charlotte. She craved his presence. Driving for eight to ten hours a day wasn't too much because he was beside her. She knew he wanted someone to love. Maybe... *I know he's had sex with women before, and we love each other...*

"Hey," he woke her from her thoughts, "I'm going to find Betty and talk to her about the art scene here. Want to come?"

"No, go ahead. I want to take a long shower." She started to unbutton her shirt, and he turned and left.

A few of his clothes hung in the open closet, so when she finished her unpacking, she turned her attention to his bag on the floor. "Okay, I can help by unpacking for him." Looking back at the door, she carefully unzipped the bag, and started to set folded clothes on the bed. *Not that I'm looking for anything, I just want to help.* Shirts and pants were added to the closet. She stacked underwear and socks in a drawer of the large, pine chest. In a separate pocket of the bag, she found the clothes he had deemed ready for the laundry. *Wonder if Betty has a washer and dryer we can use?* She absentmindedly refolded the T-shirt he had worn the day before. The cotton felt smooth and cool in her hands. Without thinking, she held it to her face and inhaled. Remnants of his cologne had a citrus smell, and the faint stale odor of cigarette smoke lingered there. *I need to get him to quit smoking.*

"Okay, I'll talk to you in the morning." The sound of Topher's voice let her know he was approaching the door.

Stuffing the T-shirt back in the bag, she tossed everything onto the closet floor and headed into the bathroom. *How silly. I was just smelling it to see if it needed washing.* She looked in the mirror. *I can't force anything between us. I'll let him know I'm willing if he is. That will allow him the choice, with no pressure.*

She checked the room, but he still stood in the hallway talking. She left the bathroom door ajar, and started the shower. The water steamed as she got in.

The hallway door slammed shut, and Topher yelled, "I'm back."

She pulled the shower curtain open a little.

"Sorry, I have to pee," he said coming into the bathroom. "I won't flush."

Myra pulled the curtain back, knowing her breasts would show, and replied, "What?"

He repeated, "I won't flush." Then he turned his head toward her, looked, smiled, and said, "Nice knockers, girl."

She jerked the curtain closed in embarrassment. "Sorry," she yelled over the roar of the shower.

"That's okay. You've got a nice set of tits. Be proud of them."

She heard him close the door as he left the bathroom. *Oh God, what have I done? I put my body out there. I feel like such a fool. He didn't sound mad. I hope he isn't. He acted like it was no big deal. Maybe, he didn't realize... God, I hope he thought it was an innocent accident.* She let the water run over her as she banged her head gently on the tile wall.

She came out of the bathroom in her bathrobe, hoping he wouldn't say anything about the incident. Scattered on his bed were several brochures, maps, and guidebooks. Topher sat in the middle of them, drinking a beer.

"Betty gave us a couple of beers. I set yours in the ice bucket to keep it cold."

"Thanks. What did she have to say?"

Topher looked up and waved some of the paper. "She gave me all these guides. I'm amazed at the number of galleries in this town. Also, she said south of here is a town called Madrid."

"*Mad*-rid?" She repeated his pronunciation of the name.

"Right, that's how they say it here. It's an old mining town that hippies took over in the sixties, and now it has painters, potters, and all kinds of stuff going on. Betty said we really needed to see it for ourselves."

"Sounds good." She sat down on her bed and looked at one of his brochures.

"In Santa Fe, the main areas are the Plaza in the middle of town and Canyon Road. She said to check out Canyon Road for more contemporary art."

Relieved that he didn't bring up her breasts, Myra popped open her bottle of beer. "Here's to your new career as a major art presence in Santa Fe."

THE NEXT DAY, they drove into downtown Santa Fe. The outskirts of the city looked like many they had passed through where convenience stores, malls, fast food joints, and gas stations lined the road. But, closing in on the Plaza, the buildings took on the regal air of heritage, strength, and survival. Few structures stood taller than three stories, which made Myra think of the small towns around Charlotte, but the strong adobe architecture entranced her as much as it did Topher.

"I love it." She squeezed Topher's arm. "Let's stay and live in an adobe in the desert with bunches of red peppers hanging from the rafters. I could wear silver and turquoise jewelry, denim skirts, and boots without pantyhose. In fact, I would never have to put on pantyhose again!" She pointed out the car window. "There's a parking space."

They parked the SUV and agreed on a time to meet up for lunch. Topher headed for the galleries to check out the art and talk with the gallery owners. Myra decided to get the feel of the city. She walked toward the Plaza, stopping at a souvenir store with lots of Indian rugs and dolls. The dolls, Kachinas made by the Hopi Indians, caught her eye. A stout, white saleswoman with garlic breath explained how the Hopi believed the Kachina dolls held the spirits of their ancestors. Myra kept trying to get away from the woman, but she followed her around the store explaining the carving techniques and talking about the "investment potential" of the craft. When she saw the price tags, Myra excused herself from the saleswoman and left the store.

After wandering into a few jewelry stores to look at the silver and turquoise, she found better prices from the local Native Americans selling their own silver displayed on mats on the sidewalk. One elderly woman wrapped in a red, orange, and black patterned blanket held up a silver necklace with a small turquoise desert quail on the end. Her dark, wrinkled face folded into a faint smile. "A charm for the flight of your spirit."

Myra bent down to look at it. "It's very beautiful."

"Wear it close to your heart and your spirit will fly free."

"I feel pretty free right now." The weight of her North Carolina accent twanged, and she cringed, realizing how out of place she must look and sound.

The old woman seemed to catch it, too, and her smile broadened, showing a few lonely, yellow teeth. "For you, I sell for ten dollars," she stared over Myra's shoulder then looked back into her eyes, "because you will need it."

She turned to look where the woman had looked, but saw nothing. Myra paid the woman and put on the necklace. As she walked around the Plaza, she wondered if the old woman said that to every tourist who stopped.

A few shops held furniture and rugs that she arranged in her fantasy desert adobe, with a playful cat batting at Topher's feet as he stood in front of a canvas working on his next show for the Museum of Fine Arts. After looking at more black clay pottery and sand paintings than she thought possible, she headed back toward the car to meet Topher for lunch.

At twenty minutes after their arranged time, he walked up behind her. "Hey. Are you hungry?" he asked with a low, graveled tone.

"Yeah, let's go over to the Coyote Café. I saw it over there, only a block that way." She started in the direction, and he followed. "How'd it go?" she asked as they walked.

"They weren't very encouraging. Most of the art that sells here has a Southwestern theme. Did you see all the Indian stuff? Even white artists do Hopi and Navajo art to make ends meet."

To enliven his attitude, Myra bought a round of margaritas before lunch, then a couple more during the meal. By the time they left, mid-afternoon, they were a little drunk. They walked around town and visited a couple of historic buildings and churches. Myra showed him the new necklace and told him about the old Indian woman. He laughed and agreed it was probably her standard bait to seal a tourist sale.

By five o'clock, most of the businesses had closed, along with the restaurants. They couldn't find a drink in the town, so they headed back to the bed and breakfast.

Betty was feeding her dog as they drove up. "Did you have a good time?"

"We spent the day around the Plaza." Myra patted the dog when he ran over to her.

Topher said, "Yeah, the art wasn't what I expected. Well, it was a little, but so much Southwestern stuff."

"Check out Canyon Road tomorrow," Betty said. "I think you'll see more variety there, and there's always Madrid. A lot of artists live there and sell out of their houses and studios."

The next day, they wandered up and down Canyon Road, Topher showing his portfolio at every opportunity. The gallery owners didn't encourage Topher. A few liked his work, but wouldn't commit to representing it.

"Start off with getting some pieces sold," offered a young woman who managed a gallery with paintings similar in style to his.

"But how can I sell if I don't have space in a gallery?"

"We have so many marketable artists here it's hard for us to give space to someone who might not produce sales."

Myra saw the circular argument Topher and the woman were having. She interrupted, "If you were Topher, what are the steps you would take to break into the art scene?"

The woman offered Myra a condescending smile. "It isn't that simple, dear."

Dear? She's younger than me, and the bitch calls me 'dear.' Topher's paintings are better than these.

"You have to establish yourself. You might try Taos or Albuquerque."

Topher shut his portfolio and thanked her.

Before closing the door behind them, Myra smiled at the woman and said, "Thanks for your time, dear." She took an exaggerated look around the empty gallery. "I can see how busy your marketable artists are keeping you."

Topher walked on, and Myra ran to catch up. "Maybe, this isn't the best place for us." He sat down on a low wall.

She rubbed his shoulders. "Let's drive down to Madrid. Betty said we needed to see it, and if it doesn't look like what we want, we'll get out the atlas and figure out our next stop."

"Sounds like a plan to me." Defeat muffled his voice. He patted her leg, stood, and headed for the vehicle.

Driving down State Route 14, they saw the signs for Madrid, but as they came into town, disappointment settled over them like desert dust. The old mining town held little more than a few shacks along dirt roads with signs announcing which of the ramshackle houses had something to sell. A tall, hairy biker stood next to his Harley-Davidson drinking a beer with one of the shack owners. As they drove by, he motioned for them to stop and come in. Topher sped up.

Near the center of town stood a large, weather-beaten wooden building with a sign saying it was the Old Coal Mine Museum and Restaurant. Topher parked in the gravel parking lot. The screen door slammed behind them as they entered. Everyone turned to look. A bar stretched the length of the room, ending at a small stage. Mismatched tables and chairs sat scattered across the rough plank floor where ragged, runny-nosed children chased each other. A few tables held customers, but most of the occupants sat on stools or stood at the bar. Myra went to a table near the stage, righted a chair, and sat down. Topher followed her.

"Just like the movies." She smiled.

Topher tentatively looked around. "Do you think we're safe here?"

"Sure, these are good people, just a little poor, but we grew up with that in Bristol. Besides, Betty said they were artists—a little dirty and dusty, but artists all the same."

A woman who looked to be in her fifties, but trying to look forty, came to their table with menus. Her blonde hair was held up on top of her head with a twist tie. She went straight to Topher and asked him, "What can I get for you, handsome?"

Myra took one of the menus out of her hand. "A couple of Miller Lites, please. We'll take a look at the menu."

She smiled at Myra, then looked at Topher's ring finger. "Single?"

Myra laughed and placed her left hand on his shoulder, her wedding ring shining. "He gets that all the time. I can't get him to wear his ring."

"Yeah, just gets in the way," Topher added, putting his arm around the back of Myra's chair.

"I'll be right back with those beers." She turned and left a trail of rose-tainted perfume in her wake.

"Okay, let's talk about our next adventure. Where to?" Myra smiled at the blush that hadn't left Topher's face. "Or do you want to settle here with your barmaid girlfriend?"

"Scary, isn't she? Can you believe a straight man could get excited enough to have sex with her?"

Myra laughed. "From the looks of the men, I'd say they'd be lucky to get her."

"Okay, enough trashing the locals," he said. "Where do you want to go?"

"We could try Phoenix or L.A."

He made a face. "Not L.A. How about San Francisco?"

Myra thanked the waitress as she delivered the beer and two plastic cups, and Topher gave her a few dollars. "California might not be bad. I could always get a job there." She thought about the banks headquartered in San Francisco.

"No, I don't think I'd get anywhere with my painting in California. Damn, we're running out of states." He took a swig from his bottle.

She thought for a while, pouring her beer into the plastic cup. "I don't know anyone out here. It would be nice to just stop for a few days and really plan something out."

"I've got it!" He slammed his beer down on the unsteady table. "Jennifer. Jennifer is in Arizona." He struggled with the town's name. "Sonoma? No..." He thought a while longer. "Sedona. That's it. She talked about it being surrounded by red rocks and new age stuff."

Myra didn't know anyone named Jennifer. "Who?"

"Oh, she's a friend from Charlotte. She moved out here about a year ago and loves it." His face became relaxed, and he smiled. "That's it. We have to go to Sedona."

Chapter Twenty

TOPHER REPACKED HIS suitcases as Myra brought back the last load of clothes from the hotel's laundry. They had spent a leisurely day and night in the Hyatt in downtown Albuquerque, enjoying the view of the desert bordered by mountains, lounging by the pool, reorganizing the back of the SUV, and cleaning clothes. "Should I call Tony before we leave?"

"That would be nice. You might give him Jennifer's address and phone number in case he needs anything." Myra folded shirts and jeans.

The phone rang several times then Tony's machine picked up.

"Hey Tony, this is Topher. We're in Albuquerque, and— "

"Hello? Hello?" Tony's strained voice interrupted.

"Hey, man, you okay? You didn't have to break your neck getting to the phone."

"Yeah...I'm okay. Where are you?"

"Albuquerque. We're on our way to see an old friend in Sedona."

"Where?"

Topher pulled out Jennifer's address and directions. "In Arizona, just south of Flagstaff. Get a pencil and I'll give you the address and phone number."

Tony repeated the information back.

"Santa Fe wasn't what we expected," Topher said.

"Toph— " Tony's voice stopped short, then continued. "I have to go. Bye." He hung up, leaving Topher with nothing but a dial tone.

Myra turned to look at him, "What happened?"

"I'm not sure." Topher hung up the phone. "I thought we had settled everything when we left, but he acted mad."

"Maybe he was having a bad day," Myra said. "Anyway, in a few hours, we'll be in Sedona. Let's get these bags back in the car."

PRICKLY PEAR CACTUS scattered the dusty ground that stretched out below the blue sky and blinding sun. Sweat rolled down Topher's face as he smoked a cigarette and paced back and forth, waiting for Myra to come out of the ladies' room at the rest area. He looked back to the east at the long line of interstate snaking back down and through the Acoma Indian Reservation and between the Zuni and San Mateo mountain ranges. They had just driven up and crossed the Continental Divide, and the cacti seemed to thin out a bit from the lower desert. Despite the heat, the air felt light and pure. The cigarette ruined the clean breeze, so he snuffed it out in a tin box ashtray bolted to a metal post. A sign caught his attention next to the sidewalk: scorpions and rattlesnakes, it warned, were plentiful just beyond the concrete. Topher stuck his Nike tennis shoe off the sidewalk and scratched a line in the dirt. He squinted, and said in his best Clint Eastwood voice, "Try and cross that, spiders and snakes, and you'll feel the hard rubber of this shoe on your friggin' head."

"Who you talking to?" Myra walked up to him with a Diet Coke in her hand.

"The scorpions and rattlesnakes."

"Where?" She jumped behind him, and peered over his shoulder at the windy desert.

"I'm looking for them. The sign says they should be attacking anything that leaves the sidewalk."

"I hate snakes, and Gil would freeze when he saw one, which was odd for an exterminator. He said he always made a lot of noise when he had to go under a house. Snakes, yuk." She made a pained expression. "Do you think there will be a lot in Sedona?"

"Don't worry about it. They won't hurt you if you don't hurt them. Just like in North Carolina, we had water moccasins and copperheads. It's no different here, except they have rattlesnakes and scorpions." He laughed as she checked each step of her route back to the car. Referring to the road atlas he opened across the steering wheel, he said, "Gallup isn't far, then we cross into Arizona. Look," he pointed at the map, "we'll go through the Painted Desert and the Petrified Forest. Should we stop?"

"Fine with me. As long as we don't stop at any roadside snake pits." Myra faked a shudder.

Billboards for Indian arts dotted the road as they passed through Gallup, and the railroad paralleled their route. They couldn't see much of the Painted Desert, except for the signs pointing the way, but they did see petrified logs scattered along the interstate as they neared the national park.

Myra said, "It's interesting, but do you really want to stop?"

"Not really. I'm too excited about getting to Sedona," Topher said. "Although Winslow is coming up. Shouldn't we get gas there and go stand on the corner?"

"What?"

"Come on, you know the Eagle's song?"

"A gas stop would be good, but the corner-standing is too cheesy." She turned and looked out the back window.

"No Gil sightings?"

"No." She squirmed back around. "No, just wide open spaces that I love. The sky is so massive. I love seeing the horizon all around. Wonder if we'll miss the green trees of the east?"

Topher was glad that thoughts of Gil didn't seem to dominate her mind like they had. The new environment and destination ushered in a change in their attitude. "I won't miss much of the east." He pointed toward the windshield. "Mountains to the west."

Myra consulted the atlas. "That's the San Francisco Peaks in Flagstaff. Not long now."

The drive climbed as they approached Flagstaff, and the trees grew larger and denser. They drove through a forest of ponderosa pines.

Hooking off I-40 to I-17, the pines soon gave way to the desert again. Arizona cypress, thick scrub brush, and clumps of prickly pear cactus and yucca took over the landscape. The road twisted as it wound down the Mogollon Rim. The open vistas evoked Topher's imagination of cowboys driving cattle. He thought about how difficult it would have been to take the route they'd covered from North Carolina a hundred years ago. At the Sedona exit, they followed a narrow two-lane road around curves and small hills.

Myra gasped. "Look," she pointed beyond the next hill. "It's beautiful."

He glanced up at a range of copper-colored ridges and buttes standing like huge, stone monuments, carved from the wind and rain of a million years, weathered into a dozen shades of red and preserved in the wilderness by the hand of God. With almost vertical slopes to the top of the buttes and spires, his first thought associated them with the skyscrapers of New York City, but these formations spread wide apart, as if placed for a purpose. The mountain range stopped and started without lining up with gaps of flat land between them—no deep, sharp valleys like the Appalachian mountain ranges. *Yes, this is arranged by God for a reason.* The view entranced him so much he had to force himself to watch the road.

"Wow," Myra said as she stared out the window. "This must be the place. No wonder Jennifer left Charlotte for this."

Road signs announced their arrival to the Village of Oak Creek and then Sedona a few miles beyond. They watched other cars pull off the road at trail heads to take pictures. The sun had lowered in the sky and cast red and orange light on the rocks, making them glow.

Continuing into Sedona, Topher maneuvered the SUV up and down hills and around curves that wound through the low juniper-forested landscape while Myra kept staring and pointing out the window. Traffic slowed. "Where did all these people come from?"

"Guess they're leaving husbands and old lives behind," she laughed. "Where are your directions to Jennifer's house?"

"She said we should go over Oak Creek, then to a Y-shaped

intersection, right into the uptown of Sedona, then turn onto Jordan Road. Look." He pointed as they rounded a bend and the town of Sedona spread out before them at the base of the blazing rocks. "I've never been much of a landscape artist, but painting this could be interesting."

Restaurants, stores, art galleries, and real estate offices lined the road, but the surrounding rock formations enchanted them. They crossed a small bridge and pulled into the right lane at the intersection. *This is it.* Topher exhaled forcefully. *I like. It feels right.* After finding the next turn, they pulled up to the building where Jennifer lived, a two-story series of townhouses. He saw Jennifer sweeping the front patio of her unit. Topher honked the horn. When she recognized him, she dropped her broom and ran toward Topher with her black mane of hair flowing in the wind. "Topher! I've missed you." She jumped up into his arms and wrapped her legs around his waist, hugging him with her whole body.

Myra cleared her throat. "Hi, I'm Myra." She held out her hand for a formal handshake.

Jennifer unwrapped her small frame from Topher, and shook Myra's hand. "Sorry. I'm so excited for you both to be here. I'm Jennifer. Let me help you with your bags."

The townhouse had two bedrooms upstairs and a couch that turned into a bed in the den. Topher took the couch because he said the den window had the best view.

After settling in, Jennifer fixed them a dinner of rice and grilled vegetables. The conversation centered on their drive across country and people Topher and Jennifer knew. Myra never mentioned leaving Gil or anything about her past.

"Tomorrow," Jennifer said, "I can show you around town. I think you'll love it here." She yawned. "I know, it's early, but I'm going to bed."

Topher checked his watch. "Nine o'clock?"

"I tend to wake up with the sun, and this time of year, that's about five in the morning, but you two stay up as long as you like."

They said their good-nights, and Jennifer left them in the den.

"You doing okay?" Topher asked Myra.

"Yes, glad to be out of the car, glad to be here—actually I'm excited to be here."

"Great, come outside to the patio. I want a cigarette."

They sat on a wooden bench in the dark watching the sky filled with thick clusters of stars. The tip of Topher's cigarette flared as he took a drag.

"I can't remember ever seeing so many stars," Myra said, her head leaning back for a direct view.

"Jennifer said there was an ordinance to cut light pollution, to preserve the view of the night sky."

"Nice," she said. "I like that the quality of things like the sky are important here. It certainly relaxes me." She leaned against Topher's shoulder. "So much relaxed that I'm heading to bed, too. Thanks for everything. I would never be here if it wasn't for you."

TOPHER WOKE LATE, tired from the drive and the exhaustion over the excitement of arriving and seeing Jennifer again. He didn't hear any sounds or smell any breakfast cooking and wondered if he was alone. He staggered into the downstairs bathroom. The sound of the stairs creaking overhead alerted him that Myra must be awake too.

When he emerged from the bathroom, he found Myra sitting at the kitchen table eating cereal and reading a two-day-old newspaper.

"Morning, sunshine," she said. "Jennifer had a couple of Reiki sessions this morning. Then she has one after lunch. We're on our own for a little while."

"That the local paper?"

"Yeah," she held it up, "only comes out Wednesdays and Fridays."

"What's the job listings look like?"

She laughed. "No corporate jobs here."

"Could be a good thing," he said, then turned to look out the window at a rounded hill Jennifer had identified as Steamboat Rock. "Let's walk up there after breakfast, to take a look at the town."

The short drive and difficult hike convinced them that they had too long a climb to reach the top, so they settled for a lower, open ledge with amazing views of the surrounding town and rock formations. The different textures in the lines of the limestone, shale, and sandstone drew Topher's attention. He ran his hand over the rough surface, envisioning how to show those different textures and rock patterns with acrylic and canvas. Myra sat on a smooth boulder facing the sun with her eyes closed; not a muscle moved. He watched her. It seemed he saw peace overtake her for the first time since he had found out about Gil's abusive behavior. The urge to say something to her, compliment her on her courage, subsided with the need to capture the moment in his mind and file it away for inspiration. He had found his muse in these mysterious, red rocks. She sat still as the warm wind picked up and released her hair with each soft gust.

She opened her eyes and smiled at him.

"So, how are you feeling?" He walked over to her.

She let out a long sigh. "Wonderful. It feels good being here. I could sit on this rock for days, doing nothing."

"I want to paint, capture this on canvas. I'll check with Jennifer on where I can get some supplies. Speaking of supplies, I noticed she didn't have any meat in the refrigerator. Let's go to the grocery store and get a few things for dinner tonight."

JENNIFER RETURNED HOME and took them on a quick tour of the area. She left the paved road and drove jeep trails right up to the bottom of some of the rocks, identifying them as they passed. They drove half way up the Airport Mesa, pulled off the road, and walked up to what looked like a saddle in the mountain. "The earth has a network of energy lines," Jennifer began. "Where those grid lines cross, power centers are created. Enormous energy, both magnetic and electric, flows from key spots around Sedona." She led them to a stone about the size of a car battery with smaller rocks encircling it.

Taking Myra's hand, she had her step over the circle and stand on the larger stone. "You are now standing on one of, if not the, most powerful places in North America."

Topher smiled at Jennifer's dramatic presentation, but he knew she believed every word.

"Should I feel anything?" Myra asked.

"Close your eyes and consider where you are in your life. This site is the crown chakra," Jennifer explained. "It's the open door to the Creator, where the physical life mingles with the spiritual life."

Topher watched Myra. Her face changed expression, as he knew she relived the past months. Tears began to flow down her face, and Jennifer stood back waiting, waiting, it seemed, for Myra to finish whatever she was experiencing. Finally, her eyes opened, fluttering at first, then staying wide open.

"What happened?" He said it before he knew it. Then he added, "If you want to talk about it."

She laughed. "Oh, I had a little talk with God. Really, it just feels like your mind is completely clear, uncluttered. Ideas and reasoning just click into place."

"It's the chakra system of the land," Jennifer said. "It aligns with your body's system and enhances it."

"Like good drugs?" Topher teased.

"The Sinagua Indians believed this area was sacred. They held rituals all over the valley and ridges. Many legends surround these rocks."

"Here?" he asked, looking around at the rocky slopes rising up on both sides of them.

Jennifer pointed toward the valley across the hill. "There are several sites in those buttes, and if you look back over your shoulder, several more line up in the opposite direction. This dip in the ridge leading up to the mesa is like a natural guide for several lines of energy to cross."

"So, there is a grid system across this area?" Myra asked.

"Yes and no. But that's the fun part of studying the energy vortexes. Lots of shapes appear, like looking at stars in the night sky. The Airport Mesa vortex falls in several patterns in the landscape. Two chakra systems, a hexagram, a pentagram, the throat of the Great

Bird that can be outlined using the Sedona landscape."

Myra came closer. "Bird?"

"Fitting, isn't it? This is where the airport was built." Jennifer pointed back into the valley. "Sacred animals are represented in the landscape. Besides this bird, over toward Chimney Rock and down past Coffee Pot Rock is the Serpent. These two animal formations are considered landscape temples."

Topher, intrigued, asked, "Can we go to one of those?"

"You're standing in the Great Bird now. In fact, all of Sedona lies within its wingspan. I can take you to see the Serpent, but we can't hike the length, the ridges are too steep in places."

Topher looked over at Myra. Her wide eyes told him she'd absorbed everything Jennifer said. *If she can find strength in this New Age stuff, great. Apparently, it works for some people.* Then his thoughts turned to more practical concerns, "Hey, Jennifer, where can a man find a beer in this swirling energy valley?"

"The Cowboy Club. It's a five-minute walk from my place. You ready for a few Oak Creek brews?"

TOPHER SCANNED THE clientele when they walked into the bar, an old habit he had developed years before to help gauge the gay-friendliness of a place. The first impression clouded his assessment. Dark-paneled walls supported cowboy hats, ropes, steer skulls, branding irons, and a large mural of a creek running through a canyon. *Decorated like a gay western bar, but the people...* Some obvious tourists crowded around a few of the tables with their shopping bags and cameras, while well-dressed locals looked like retirees with money. The younger crowd consisted of the waiters, waitresses, and bartenders. The hostess knew Jennifer and waved them on to the bar.

After Jennifer ordered Oak Creek beers for them. Topher turned to her. "So, is this your hangout?"

"Yeah, it's close, and they have great food. I've gotten friendly with most of the people who work here. A couple of the staff lives close by, but most commute from Cottonwood. Housing is very expensive for a waiter's salary."

Their tall, trim, blond bartender stopped and asked him how he liked the local beer. As he walked away, Topher leaned over to Jennifer. "Does he live here?"

"Cal? Yeah, but he's straight."

"Damn." He banged his fist on his forehead. "Any potentials for me in this town?"

"Topher," Myra piped in the conversation, "learn to be on your own. Remember? Get to know yourself."

"But— " He motioned toward the handsome bartender.

"Am I going to have to put you in a cold shower?"

"I'll be good. I just wanted to get a feeling for the place."

Jennifer shook her head and laughed. "It's not easy being single in this town. Most of the residents are retirees. There are a few single people under fifty, but not many. I had a date about a month ago. No chemistry, but we're friends now." She looked at Myra. "It's a close-knit group. Everyone knows everyone else's business. I don't know if I'll find anyone like Brenda here."

"How long were you two together?" Myra asked.

"Almost six years..."

Topher rubbed her shoulder and tried to lighten the mood. "Does this mean I'll be celibate as long as I'm in Sedona?"

"You'll be whatever you want to be. There are gay men here, not as many as there are lesbians."

He looked at Myra and smiled. "Maybe that's good. I do need some time without the pressures of dating."

Myra grinned. "It feels good to be away from constricting relationships."

"You left a bad one, too?" Jennifer asked Myra.

Topher butted in to explain Jennifer's ignorance. "I didn't tell her why you left. I thought I'd let you talk about it, if you wanted to."

"That's okay. I'm proud I had the courage to leave." Myra gave a brief summary of her relationship and escape from Gil, leaving out details of her alleged Gil sightings along the trip.

Jennifer got off the bar stool and hugged Myra. Tears rolled down both women's faces. "You are one strong woman, and you have my respect." She yelled down the bar, "Cal, more beer for my two good friends and new Sedona residents."

The crowd in the bar cheered.

"Now, hold on, Jennifer," Topher said, "we haven't decided anything yet. Jobs," he looked at Myra, and she nodded her head in agreement, "we need jobs that will support us."

"Yeah, yeah, yeah. And I need a woman." Jennifer waved off his concern. Myra almost spit out her mouthful for beer. "Sure, it's a tourist town with an elderly population, but we have each other. A gay man, a lesbian, and a battered woman, if we can't make it in Arizona, who can?"

Topher erupted in laughter. "Is that the New West?"

"Yes," she said with pride. "The New West is a place for survivors and adventurers."

Myra raised her glass. "I'll drink to that."

THAT NIGHT, MYRA went to bed early again. Jennifer and Topher sat on the folded-out bed in the den and caught up on mutual acquaintances in Charlotte. He felt he should add to Myra's version of her story, but hated to talk behind her back.

"I'm proud of Myra," he said. "It took a lot of courage. Gil threatened her to the point she thought he would poison her. In fact, since the time we left, she's convinced herself that he's following us. Several times, she said she saw him or his truck."

"Do you think it's true?"

Considering the possibility, he told her the truth that he had never said to Myra. "I think he has it in him. A few times, I believed she might have seen him, but we haven't spotted anything that could be associated with Gil since Dallas. Hopefully, if he was following us, we lost him. I called Tony from Albuquerque to see how he was, and to ask if he had noticed anyone fitting Gil's description around his house."

"Had he?"

"I didn't get the chance to ask. He wouldn't talk to me very long. He acted odd. I guess he's still a little pissed I didn't stay with him." The thought of Tony dying alone weighed down on him like the rust-orange rocks looming outside the window.

"Don't worry about Gil. I have a nice little pistol that will turn him from a bull to a steer with one shot." Jennifer pointed her index finger at Topher's crotch and dropped her thumb. "Bang!"

"Damn, woman," he laughed. "Have you turned into a militant, man-hating lesbian?"

"I love men, in their place." She gave him an devious look. "In the kitchen or in the laundry room. Oh, they can fix the plumbing, too. I hate that sort of thing."

"Is that what I need to do here to earn my keep?"

"No, baby. You know I love you." Her face sobered. "I'm not the only one. I've noticed how she looks at you."

"Myra?"

"Don't play dumb with me. You know it, too."

"Yeah, but it's just a good friendship. She knows better than anyone that I could never change who I am, no more than she could change to desire women."

"Straight people always believe—no matter how liberal they are—that the right person could change you. Cal, at the bar, offered to 'help me out' once. He meant well."

Topher smiled. "Maybe he'll give me the same offer."

"I honestly think that the penis runs a man's body."

"It steers most of the time," Topher said. "My mind struggles to gain control. Speaking of which, that boring old mind of mine just took over. Do you think we can find jobs here? Something where I could help establish myself as a painter?"

"I have contacts all over town. Don't worry. We'll come up with something." She started upstairs. "I have the morning off tomorrow. Let's go hiking. I want you both to fall in love with Sedona like I have."

"Where did you have in mind?"

"Devil's Bridge. It will change your life." She flipped off the light and faded into the darkness as she went upstairs.

Topher pulled back the sheets on the sofa bed, undressed, and climbed in. The full moon shone bright over the ridge outside the window, turning it crimson, like blood had poured down the sides of the rocks.

Chapter Twenty-One

WHEN MYRA CAME downstairs the next morning, she found Topher, still in his underwear, scrambling eggs and frying bacon, while Jennifer stood looking at the sizzling pans, shaking her head.

"How can you eat that greasy, fat-laced, chemical-injected strip of pig flesh?" Jennifer pulled the collar of her sweatshirt up over her nose.

"Ummm." He licked his lips and rubbed his stomach. "You make it sound so much better than what it is. Keep talking, veggie girl."

She slapped his shoulder and received a smack on her denim-clad butt as she left the kitchen. "Good morning, Myra. Try to get him to stop the animal sacrifices on my stove."

"Sorry, but I love bacon, too."

Jennifer shook her head again. "Must have something to do with having sex with men." She mumbled something else unintelligible as she left the room.

"Shouldn't you wear an apron when frying bacon nearly naked?" Myra asked.

He grabbed a potholder and stuffed it down the front of his briefs. "Okay, the important stuff is protected. Besides, I don't think vegetarians own aprons. Breakfast will be ready in about five minutes."

"Anything I can help you with?"

He looked around the kitchen for a moment. "Yeah, watch this while I pull on my jeans. Here, you can use this potholder." He whipped it out of his shorts and tossed it to her.

She caught it and held it by the corner with just her index finger and thumb. "I'll wash this before we get it near any of the food."

"Wait, I might use it again—down the front of my jeans. Hmmm, could be a nice conversation starter for me." He laughed, went to the den, and returned wearing his pants.

Myra handed the spatula back to him. "You know, for a woman, jeans are much sexier than underwear—more is left to the imagination."

"Dear, you forget, I don't want to look sexy for women." He lifted one eyebrow and smiled.

Shit, why do I say and do such stupid things around him? "So, are we going hiking today?"

Topher filled two plates and carried their breakfast to the table. "I'd love to do some hiking. Jennifer mentioned taking us to Devil's Bridge. I didn't know they had named a bridge after Gil." He laughed, but Myra managed only a faint smile.

I haven't seen anything that looked like him or his truck in over a week. Was it my imagination?

"Hey, Jennifer," Topher, with a mouthful of eggs, yelled into the den. "Come in here and tell us about Devil's Bridge."

She appeared in the doorway. "Are you sure that's where you want to go? We could go up Oak Creek Canyon. It's greener and has more trees."

"No. I want desert, dust, dirt, rocks." He waved his fork in the air. "Rugged, real men do manly things."

"Sorry," Jennifer said. "It's just the three of us. The Devil's Bridge trail is a moderate hike. It should make us all feel like manly men."

"How far is it?" Myra sipped her orange juice.

"We drive out to an old jeep trail, then walk from there." Jennifer looked directly at Myra. "It's a natural rock arch that looks like a bridge."

Myra smiled and nodded to acknowledge she already knew.

"Just wanted to make sure. Some people have asked why anyone would build a bridge way up in the mountain." Jennifer laughed. "Anyway, we can be at the top of the bridge in about two hours."

"Great. I'll put together a lunch for us." Myra finished her breakfast, put her dishes in the dishwasher, and started planning the picnic lunch.

THE JEEP RIDE to the beginning of the trail took them down Dry Creek Road. The cliffs of the rocks loomed ahead of them, and spires stood tall along the ridge, like sentries for their journey. Myra watched the houses thin out until only a few scattered driveways remained. Many of the driveways were gated, and a glimpse of a rambling house popped up from time to time as they sped down the road.

She tapped Jennifer on the shoulder. "Who lives in these houses? They're beautiful...and huge."

Jennifer looked in the rear view mirror to answer. "I hate to see them. Mostly retirees live out here. The developers are slowly overtaking the—hold on." She swerved onto an unmarked dirt road.

"What the hell was that about?" Topher almost bounced out of the front seat.

She slid to a stop and killed the engine. "I—" she turned to look behind them, "I thought I spotted a coyote, and I wanted you to see it." Standing on her seat, she looked over the low juniper and scrub pines back toward the road. "Okay, let's go. The turnoff is just a little way."

Myra noticed the confused look on Topher's face as he stared at Jennifer and how she didn't return his look. After another bumpy dirt road, they turned off at a small parking area with a trailhead marker. They pulled on their backpacks, and Myra retied her boots.

"The air is so still." Myra breathed in the quietness. "So, Jennifer, what is the significance of Devil's Bridge?"

"I told you about the landscape temples, and Devil's Bridge falls in the middle of the serpent. Since it is part of a twisting ridge, the views of near and far canyon walls are incredible. Also, there's beautiful red and white rock perched above the arch that's tied directly to the serpent, the Serpent's Heart. The thing is the size of a Cadillac and almost heart shaped."

The trail followed an old washed out road with deep gullies and large boulders they had to climb over. Myra wondered how many transmissions had been destroyed before it was closed to the jeeps. Topher wandered off into some bushes about chest high.

"Get back here," Myra yelled.

"Just yielding to the call of nature and the three cups of coffee I had this morning."

She heard him splashing the dry ground.

"Men," Jennifer huffed, and continued on.

"Look out for snakes," Myra called back as she followed Jennifer.

The urgent sound of a quick zip and the pounding footsteps of Topher brought him up with them. "Not funny, Myra."

"I didn't say I saw one, just to look out," she said.

"Okay, we start hiking up ahead. See if you can find a straight, strong branch to use as a walking stick." Jennifer had brought her own, and held it up for them as an example.

The trail narrowed into a thin path across rocks and between prickly ocotillo branches and the pointy leaves of century plants. As they ascended the hill, natural steps in the orange slate helped their climb. Topher grabbed a thin branch with tiny star-shaped flowers. "Jennifer, what's this? Smells like vanilla."

"A Creosote bush. Bees love them. Sniff that one. It's sagebrush. You can tell by its smell."

Myra, glad they stopped, caught up on her breathing. "This is getting steep."

"We're almost to a great lookout point. We can rest there for a while and have some water." Jennifer headed on.

Looking back at Myra, Topher smiled and yelled up to Jennifer, "Hey, Jenn, let's slow it down a little. We're not in a race to the top."

"Sorry, I just wanted to get to the lookout."

After another ten minutes of climbing, Myra heard Jennifer announce their arrival at the overlook point. She turned a corner in the trail and saw a sweeping view of the valley they had just climbed out of. A large, flat rock made a natural balcony for them to scan the valley and miles of country beyond it. Myra dropped her backpack at her feet and stared at the horizon of blue skies melting into the mustard and scarlet ridges and canyon walls. No one said a word. The light, even whistle of the wind, pierced with the occasional cry of a lone hawk, filled the air with sound. Myra watched the hawk circle, floating higher with each pass, then he made an adjustment, and the wind carried him over their heads toward the top of the canyon wall.

Topher spoke first. "Almost spiritual, isn't it? Like we're called to be here, to witness nature." He sighed and laughed. "Kinda makes you ramble on, doesn't it?"

"No, I understand." Myra walked over to him and stood on a rock to rest her chin on his shoulder so that they faced in the same direction. "Look." She pointed into the valley at two low round hills, almost identical, that looked like two large pitcher's mounds. Then a movement caught her eye. "There's another hiker. He shouldn't be out here alone. Maybe we should wait for him to catch up."

"No, no, we need to get moving." Jennifer grabbed her backpack and started back up the path.

Myra looked at Topher. "Is she always so," she chose her word carefully, "driven?"

"She's usually really laid-back. Guess she wants us to get to the top. It does look like rain on the horizon."

The trail twisted and turned up the side of the canyon. Topher helped by showing Myra the best way around washed out sections and loose rocks. Jennifer plodded ahead, looking back occasionally to keep an eye on them.

Sweat rolled down Myra's face as she and Topher caught up with Jennifer. She looked around to see that they had climbed over a ridge and now faced another valley. No sign of life could be seen in this valley, no houses, no roads, no people. *This is land before people came in to rearrange it for their own needs. This is the way it should be.* Out of the corner of her eye, Myra noticed a slight movement. "Oh, shit, a snake!" She ran to Topher.

Jennifer walked quietly over to see. "Stay back."

"Don't worry, we will," Topher said, backing up.

She took her walking stick and lifted a branch. The snake coiled up and hissed. Jennifer took a step back, but kept looking. "It's okay. That's a gopher snake—see his head? It's round, not triangular like a rattlesnake's. They imitate rattlers when they feel threatened. He's non-venomous. Just stay out of his way."

"You don't have to tell me twice," Myra said.

Leaving the snake where he lay, Jennifer turned and announced, "We're here: Devil's Bridge." She pointed toward the edge of the canyon. "See the top of the arch? Look down below it, and you'll see the opening."

A bridge formed out of the slate and sandstone arced from an outcropping about thirty feet from them to a lone pillar of rock. A couple of junipers grew in its cracks. Below the arch, an alcove sloped down and out over to the almost-vertical canyon wall.

"Can we walk out on it?" Topher headed in that direction.

"Hold on," Jennifer warned. "I'll go with you, but I need to backtrack. I think I dropped something a little ways back. Take Myra up that hill to the Serpent's Heart."

They looked up at a large, almost-round rock towering above the pinyon pines. The layering colors of sandy white and rose swirled around the perimeter, giving the illusion of motion. Jennifer pointed out the faint trail through the bushes. If she hadn't, they never would have seen it.

"Go on up, and I'll meet you there," Jennifer said. "The view is one of the best in Sedona. You can see several different canyons."

"Do you want some help?" Topher asked Jennifer.

"No, I'll just be a minute. See you up there." She turned and headed back down the path.

Myra took a few more steps away from the bush with the snake under it. "She's getting weird."

"Something's definitely bothering her. She didn't go back to look for something she lost. She's monitoring something." He looked around and found a rock to sit on. Pulling out his water bottle, he offered some to Myra.

"Thanks." She gulped down the cool water. "Should we go on up?"

"Let's wait here for a little bit. I'd like to walk out onto the arch."

"Not me, I like to have solid ground under my feet." She sat down next to him. The shade of a large pine offered relief from the bright sun. Puffy, white clouds floated slowly across the sky. Sapphire, turquoise, lilac, crystal blue, azure, she tried to think of different shades of blue that might be closest to the sky, then it hit her: *It's the color of Topher's eyes*. She chuckled a little.

He turned to look at her and asked, "What's so funny?"

"You know I love you..." She decided to bring her feelings out in the open.

"I love you, too," he said, too automatically for her.

"That's where my problem—" She stopped, horrified by what she saw.

At the end of the clearing, he stood with the gun in his right hand. Gil was scraped and dirty. Sweat mixed with dust streaked his face. He huffed trying to catch his breath from his climb.

With cold, dark eyes focused on Myra, he lifted the gun, and yelled, "Bitch, your ass is dead!"

She couldn't move her limbs. All she could do was look at him in disbelief.

Her body jerked and fell to the ground. Topher's arms had pulled her back behind the rock and tree.

A shot rang out, louder than she ever thought it would sound, like a quick sharp jab to her eardrums. Before her mind could process the images, sounds, and sensations that had happened in the past five seconds, Topher jumped over the rock and charged toward Gil.

He fell with a thud on the hard red dirt, with Topher pounding at his face.

The gun still lay in his hand, and as if he had just realized it, Gil brought the butt of the handle up fast and hard, smashing into Topher's temple.

Topher rolled off him with blood streaming from the wound.

Gil struggled to his feet, and Myra saw that he had his own blood flowing down the side of his face.

She grabbed a small rock and hurled it toward him, missing him by three feet.

He laughed a little, and took another step toward her.

Topher, up on his hands and knees, grabbed for Gil's foot and jerked it back, toppling him into the brush. He dove in after him.

Myra heard the gun crack its sharp, hard cry.

Both men rolled out of the brush, struggling, the gun still in Gil's hand.

Jennifer appeared from the trail and ran toward them with her walking stick raised. She slammed it across Gil's head, and the gun slipped from his hand. The steel-gray barrel sparkled in the noontime sun, available, free from the devil.

Myra sprinted to it, but she caught the black hatred in Gil's eyes and hesitated.

He snatched the gun from the ground as both Topher and Jennifer fought him. Gil swung wildly. An elbow to the nose took Topher down.

Gil turned to Jennifer. Her petite body held little challenge to his bulk. He cocked his right hand across his body, then, with full force, brought the back of his hand across her delicate face.

Myra knew the move well. An image flashed in her mind: Gil standing over her, threatening, poised for the blow, then the sting of his knuckles on her cheek. Numbness helped soften the next blow, and the one after that. The image faded, revealing Gil leveling the gun at her.

Topher, back on his feet, tackled him. Dust and dirt flew from their battle.

Jennifer hadn't recovered from the assault.

Myra's body, stiff with fear, stood watching while her mind screamed to run and hide.

A slur of words in Gil's voice rattled Myra's head.

He fired the gun.

Topher pushed her out of the way, then cried out in pain.

He lay on the ground, holding his shoulder, blood seeping into the red rocks and dirt, turning them rusty brown.

Jennifer howled. The terror in her voice filled the canyon. Her walking stick cracked across Gil's back.

He turned and backhanded her again.

She stumbled back, but remained standing.

His boot connected with her stomach.

She dropped, in a heap, holding her abdomen.

Gil took the opportunity. Methodically, like stalking prey, he moved toward her, then without any emotion, kicked her in the side. Jennifer's whole body jerked from the blow. He did it again and again.

The sight of Gil beating a woman, the sheer monstrosity of the scene, the shock of seeing her past played before her like some hideous movie, jolted Myra from paralyzing trauma. A jagged, thick piece of slate lay at her feet. Disgust and hatred boiled up in her. Topher lay bleeding next to her from Gil's bullet, and Jennifer groaned from Gil's beating, both meant for her, but now destroying her friends. She lifted the rock and ran for Gil, slamming it into the back of his head.

She heard a frightening crack.

Stumbling and then falling to his knees, Gil dropped the gun. Myra grabbed the pistol and pointed it at his bleeding head.

He looked at her with blood dripping from a gash in the back of his skull.

Tears filled her eyes. *This is the man I loved, another human being – I can't do it.* She flung the gun toward the canyon floor, but the sound of metal scraping rock caught her ears too close and too soon. The pistol lay on the edge of Devil's Bridge, at the very middle of the arch.

Myra turned back to Gil.

He had staggered back to his feet and had his fist pulled back for assault. The sting of his punch to her cheek surprised her, and she fell.

"You God-damned son-of-a-bitch." Jennifer stood over her emptied backpack holding a small pistol with both hands.

Myra heard the shot, lighter and quicker, than the one from Gil's gun.

Jennifer had missed.

Gil scrambled toward the arch, trying to retrieve his own gun.

Jennifer aimed again.

"No!" Myra yelled.

A look of disbelief filled Jennifer's face. She stuck the gun in her jeans and pulled Myra toward the tall brush for safety. A cell phone from Jennifer's backpack lay on the ground, and she tossed it to Myra. "Call 911." Then she went to Topher.

But as Jennifer began to pull Topher under cover, Myra saw Gil had made it to the edge of the bridge and had retrieved his gun. Myra dropped the phone and looked for Jennifer's pistol.

A branch moved next to her and something slithered. Before she could think, Myra had the gopher snake on the end of Jennifer's walking stick.

Gil aimed the gun at Jennifer's back as she pulled Topher along.

"Gil!" Myra yelled.

He turned to look at her, and she flung the snake right into his face. He screamed, stumbled back, and fell from the edge of Devil's Bridge.

Chapter Twenty-Two

TOPHER OPENED HIS eyes to find Jennifer and Myra waiting by his hospital bed. Both women had cuts and bruises, but nothing looked too serious. The antiseptic smell of the hospital made his nose tingle, and his blinding, white room caused him to squint.

"The doctor got the bullet out of your shoulder." Jennifer, her dark hair pulled into a loose ponytail, winced when she moved. "He said you should recover well. It didn't damage anything."

"The doctor," Topher etched out in a hoarse whisper as both women leaned in closer, "is he cute and single?" A sly smile inched across his face.

"Jerk." Myra, who had adopted Jennifer's loose hairstyle, sat back and crossed her arms in front of her like a disapproving mother. "I thought you needed help, on the edge of death."

Jennifer chuckled holding her side. "Don't make me laugh. I have two bruised ribs."

Bruised ribs? Shadows in his mind began to clear. "Where's Gil?"

Myra looked down at the floor letting her hair fall like a veil over her face.

"I called the police with my cell phone," Jennifer said, "and when they made it down to the canyon floor, Gil was dead."

He glanced over at Myra again. She wiped her eyes without looking up. A hazy image accompanied by the sound of Myra screaming crept into his mind. He had opened his eyes when he felt Jennifer pulling him along the ground, and just over her shoulder, he saw Gil's arms batting wildly and him falling back off the red rock arch.

"It was my fault. I killed him. I did it." Myra cried so hard her shoulders shook from her trying to catch her breath.

"No, you didn't," Jennifer said. "The police report stated he lost his footing, and that's what happened."

"He had his gun aimed right for your back...I just couldn't let him..." Myra sobbed.

Topher tried to remember exactly what happened. His struggle must have shown on his face because Jennifer shook her head slowly as if she could calm his mind by saying it wasn't important. "But, how did Gil," he looked from Myra to Jennifer, "find us?"

"On our way to the hike," Jennifer said, "I thought I saw a truck following us that looked like the one Myra described. When I left the two of you alone," she looked at Topher, turned her mouth down and furrowed her brow as if saying 'I told you so,' "and asked you to climb on up to the Serpent's Heart, I went back to see if that lone hiker could be Gil."

"You didn't know what he looked like. How could you be sure?" Myra wiped the tears from her eyes with the back of her hand.

Jennifer handed her a tissue from the bedside table. "I hid behind some bushes and saw a man struggling up the trail with a gun stuffed in the back of his pants. I didn't think he was a hunter. I stayed back so he wouldn't see me. I had hoped you two would be well hidden in the brush on your way up the trail." She sat down on the side of the bed and stroked Topher's hair. "I should have told you my suspicions, but I wasn't sure, and I didn't want to scare Myra."

"It doesn't matter now." Topher looked over at Myra. "You okay?"

"Yeah, but...Topher, I killed him. That snake? I took the walking stick and..."

"You did what you had to do to save us and yourself." Jennifer leaned back on the bed and propped her tiny boots up on the chair so that she faced Myra. "Sergeant Torres said they had been looking for Gil. The Dallas police department had a warrant out on him."

"Dallas?" Topher's thoughts went back to Tony.

"Right. That's how he knew where you were. Torres told me Gil was wanted for a home invasion, assault and battery."

His thoughts came out. "Tony?"

"Yes, I guess he lost your trail and stayed with Tony until you made contact again."

"No wonder Tony wouldn't talk to me when I called him from Albuquerque. But," Topher's mind struggled to think clearly, "Gil must have been holding Tony hostage for days. Is he okay? I need to call him."

"Sergeant Torres didn't mention Tony, but I'll call him. Rest, you need to get better."

The haze in his mind grew thicker, and he knew the drugs pulled him toward the comfort of sleep. "Myra, you freed yourself. He would have killed all of us. Thank you." He wanted to say more, but sleep overcame him.

THE DOOR TO the Cowboy Club opened, and Topher looked up from the pitcher of beer he was filling and watched Myra make her way to the end of the bar where he was standing.

"Did you get your test results?" She kept her voice low so that no one else could hear.

He leaned over the bar to reply. "Clean as a virgin. The bloodwork came back negative."

"Wonderful!" She kissed his cheek. "I have some good news, too." She straightened up and pulled her shoulders back. "I got it. I got the job." She was so excited, she almost bubbled.

"Congratulations, Ms. Loan Officer." He handed her a cold beer. "Now that I have an inside connection, can I have a loan?"

"I knew it. Now, everyone will think I can just hand out money. I taught bankers how to say no for years, and now I can do it for myself." She looked him straight in the eyes, smiled, and said, "No, you're a bartender."

"Oww, that hurt. At least I get good tips and have time to paint."

"I'm so glad you're painting again."

Cal walked up behind Topher and smiled. "Hello, Myra. You're looking beautiful again today."

"I got the job," she said with a grin.

"Great, let me take you out to celebrate." Cal winked at her.

Topher looked at Myra, then at Cal. "I'm going to deliver this pitcher. You two make your plans." From the other end of the bar, he watched as Myra laughed and Cal flirted. She wrote something on a piece of paper, and Cal slipped it in his pocket, then walked away.

Topher returned to Myra. "So? You slip him your phone number?"

"Yes," she said as she blushed. "We're going out on Saturday."

"Great! You go, girl."

"It's just a dinner date."

"Yeah, but he's cute and a lot of fun. You'll have a great time. Speaking of dinner, whose turn is it to cook tonight?"

"Well, let's see," Myra said. "I did it last night. Jennifer cooked the night before, and I cooked Sunday night. With my logical mind, seems like you're overdue."

"Damn, okay, I'll treat to dinner out." He smiled at how happy Myra appeared. The past weeks had allowed them to settle into Sedona and find jobs. The only basic need still missing, and he knew what it meant to Myra, was a home. Jennifer's apartment seemed to get more crowded by the day. "Is it time that we move out and find places of our own?"

The smile faded from her face. "I...I don't know. Did Jennifer say something?"

"No," he said, "I just thought you might like to have a home of your own. You know, spread out, settle down."

"I enjoy what we have now. But, if you and Jennifer need..."

"No, really, with the new job..." He tried to calm her fears. "I just want you to tell me when you're ready. I'm fine the way things are, and Jennifer told me the other night she's glad to have us around."

"I know we are three grown adults, very different adults, but I like it." Myra said. "You and Jennifer are like my family, the family I always wanted. Like she said, 'If a gay man, a lesbian, and a battered woman can't make it in Arizona, who can?' I know we can make it together."

Pride welled up in him. "You're right. I can't think of anywhere else I'd want to be, or anyone else I'd want to be with. We're a family."

THE END

Another Greg Lilly book you don't want to miss:

Fingering the Family Jewels

Derek Mason arrives in North Carolina for the funeral of his Aunt Walterene. He encounters the family who sent him away because he revealed he was gay. His mother and Uncle Vernon want him out of town because of Vernon's senate campaign. His sister and Aunt Ruby urge him to stay. His cousin Mark denies their past relationship. Derek uncovers mysteries in the death of a family gardner, possibly at the hands of a young Vernon. Secrets and lies unravel as Derek digs into the family history with the help of hunky reporter Daniel.

ISBN 1-932300-22-8
978-1-932300-22-2

A FORTHCOMING TITLE

published by
Regal Crest

Come This Way
by Victor Banis

This collection is unique in that it spans nearly a half century of the author's prodigious literary outpouring-nearly 150 published books and numerous shorter works.

Come This Way, a collection of nearly two dozen stories, edited by Lori Lake and with an introduction by eminent gay scholar, Drewey Wayne Gunn, is in a sense a retrospective of a unique career that has seen more than 140 novels and numerous shorter pieces in print.

What is even more astonishing, however, than the author's prodigious output, is the breadth, the sheer variety, of his writing. These stories look at life from myriad points of view.

The Story of God as History's First Trannie is a satirical look at pre-Christian goddess worship: "...only a little while earlier...men got together in the shade of the hawthorn fig tree...sacred to the Goddess, and ate the fruit of the tree...now, a bunch of Hebrew scribes were telling a story about this wicked, wicked woman who conned an innocent man (oh, right!) into eating this fruit off a tree and causing the good times to stop rolling..."

Jesus Days moves one hundred years into the future, to a U.S.A. ruled by fundamentalist fanatics.

Jackie Returns offers a glimpse into the life of the super-rich. The characters in Neighbors live in a trailer park.

Queer Titles pokes fun at the fine art of jacket copy. Tell them Katy-Did is chilling, An Apple a Day whimsical. Spiro Does a Day's Work captures the innocent eroticism of puppy love, while in If Love Were All, two damaged souls struggle to make a connection.

Indeed, love-getting, losing, the defining of it-is a common thread through most of these stories, and the author's love for the people of whom he writes shines through in all of them.

And in The Emerald Mountain, which begins, "We are all hearts in exile, stumbling alone in the dark...the author has perhaps created a new literary genre all his own: the erotic metaphysical mystery story.

There are surely few writers more prolific, and it is difficult to imagine any more versatile, or who could spin a yarn any better.

Available May 2007

Other Regal Crest titles to look for:

Reiko's Garden
by Brenda Adcock

Hatred...like love...knows no boundaries.

How much impact can one person have on a life?

When sixty-five-old Callie Owen returns to her rural childhood home in Eastern Tennessee to attend the funeral of a woman she hasn't seen in twenty years, she's forced to face the fears, heartache, and turbulent events that scarred both her body and her mind. Drawing strength from Jean, her partner of thirty years, and from their two grown children, Callie stays in the valley longer than she had anticipated and relives the years that changed her life forever.

In 1949, Japanese war bride Reiko Sanders came to Frost Valley, Tennessee with her soldier husband and infant son. Callie Owen was an inquisitive ten year old whose curiosity about the stranger drove her to disobey her father for just one peek at the woman who had become the subject of so much speculation. Despite Callie's fears, she soon finds that the exotic looking woman is kind and caring, and the two forge a tentative, but secret friendship.

When Callie and her five brothers and sisters were left orphaned, Reiko provided emotional support to Callie. The bond between them continued to grow stronger until Callie left Frost Valley as a teenager, emotionally and physically scarred, vowing never to return and never to forgive.

It is not until Callie goes "home" that she allows herself to remember how Reiko influenced her life. Once and for all, can she face the terrible events of her past? Or will they come back to destroy all that she loves?

ISBN 1-932300-77-5
978-1-932300-77-2

Snow Moon Rising
by Lori L. Lake

Mischka Gallo, a proud Roma woman, knows horses, dancing, and travel. Every day since her birth, she and her extended family have been on the road in their *vardo* wagons meandering mostly through Poland and eastern Germany. She learned early to ignore the taunts and insults of all those who call her people "Gypsies" and do not understand their close-knit society and way of life.

Pauline "Pippi" Stanek has lived a settled life in a small German town along the eastern border of Poland and Germany. In her mid-teens, she meets Mischka and her family through her brother, Emil Stanek, a World War I soldier who went AWOL and was adopted by Mischka's troupe. Mischka and Pippi become fast friends, and they keep in touch over the years. But then the Second World War heats up, and all of Europe is in turmoil. Men are conscripted into the Axis or the Allied armies, "undesirables" are turned over to slave labor camps, and with every day that passes, the danger for Mischka, Emil, and their families increases. The Nazi forces will not stop until they've rounded up and destroyed every Gypsy, Jew, dissident, and homosexual.

On the run and separated from her family, Mischka can hardly comprehend the obstacles that face her. When she is captured, she must use all her wits just to stay alive. Can Mischka survive through the hell of the war in Europe and find her family?

In a world beset by war, two women on either side of the conflagration breach the divide—and save one another. *Snow Moon Rising* is a stunning novel of two women's enduring love and friendship across family, clan, and cultural barriers. It's a novel of desperation and honor, hope and fear at a time when the world was split into a million pieces.

ISBN: 1-932300-50-3
978-1-932300-50-5

Available at booksellers everywhere.

OTHER REGAL CREST PUBLICATIONS

Brenda Adcock	Reiko's Garden	978-1-932300-77-2
Lori L. Lake	Different Dress	978-1-932300-08-6
Lori L. Lake	Snow Moon Rising	978-1-932300-50-5
Lori L. Lake	Stepping Out: Short Stories	978-1-932300-16-1
Lori L. Lake	The Milk of Human Kindness	978-1-932300-28-4
Greg Lilly	Devil's Bridge	978-1-932300-78-9
Greg Lilly	Fingering the Family Jewels	978-1-932300-22-2
Cate Swannell	Heart's Passage	978-1-932300-09-3
Jane Vollbrecht	Heart Trouble	978-1-932300-58-1
Jane Vollbrecht	In Broad Daylight	978-1-932300-76-5

About the Author:

Growing up in Bristol, Virginia, and then living in Charlotte, North Carolina, the rich storytelling tradition of the South pulled Greg Lilly into writing.

He first turned to writing short stories after plot lines and characters emerged from the technical manuals he wrote for a large family-owned corporation. With the assistance of a hearty critique group of writers in Charlotte, he has published several short stories, numerous articles, and completed three novels.

After writing *Devil's Bridge*, the plot bloomed in his life and he decided to break free of the corporate world and simplify his life.

Today, Greg lives in Sedona, Arizona with his partner Brad and Great Dane Koda. He is working on his next novel.

Please visit his website at www.GregLilly.com.

Printed in the United States
85855LV00004B/203/A